BEYOND THE BRIDGE

Also by Tom MacDonald

The Charlestown Connection
The Revenge of Liam McGrew
Murder in the Charlestown Bricks

BEYOND THE BRIDGE

A Novel

TOM MACDONALD

OCEANVIEW PUBLISHING

SARASOTA, FLORIDA

ISBN: 978-1-60809-449-3

Published in the United States of America by Oceanview Publishing,
Sarasota, Florida
www.oceanviewpub.com

2 4 6 8 10 9 7 5 3

PRINTED IN THE UNITED STATES OF AMERICA

This book is dedicated to Joe Boyce, a man I loved and respected, a man who lived his life by an unwavering code of honor; and to Jack McCarthy, poet and teacher, an inspiration in my life. Jack lived by a set of principles, and he practiced these principles in all his affairs, one day at a time.

Both men represented the best of humanity. I will miss them.

ACKNOWLEDGMENTS

To my wife, Maribeth McKenzie MacDonald. Maribeth saw the value in this manuscript and resurrected it from the bottom drawer. It starts and ends with Maribeth.

Oceanview Publishing: Bob and Pat Gussin, Frank Troncale, David Ivester, and editor Susan Hayes. Their support and good judgment proved invaluable in this project.

Editing team: Dick Murphy, whose Charlestown sensibilities added grit and realism to the scenes and dialogue. Chris Hobin, whose ideas on plotting and pacing sharpened the story arc. John Malkowski, whose language proficiency smoothed the rough edges and brought out the finish with a lapidary's knack. Patricia Mac-Donald, my mother and the proofreader, whose blue pencil was worn dull by the time she finished reviewing the text. I am most grateful to this group.

Forensics: Sharon Hanson, Chief of Staff, Boston Police Department. Amy Brodeur, Assistant Director of Biomedical Forensics, Boston University School of Medicine. Sharon and Amy shared their expertise on evidence analysis and chain-of-custody handling. Although the story is not a police procedural, Sharon's and Amy's recommendations permeate the story, adding authenticity to a subject I know little about.

The Stonehill College connection: Tom MacDonald Sr., '53 and Olly Beaulieu, '53 provided excellent advice on the story as a whole and one scene in particular.

Also: Brendan and Missy McKenzie, Rick "Spike" Brophey, Sister Margaret Ann McSweeney, Judy Burton, Mary Walsh, John Dillon, and Peter Pappas.

He was a self-made man who owed
his lack of success to nobody.
—Joseph Heller, *Catch-22*

No matter. Try again. Fail again. Fail better.
—Samuel Beckett, Irish playwright

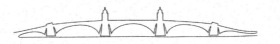

BEYOND THE BRIDGE

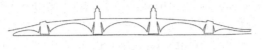

CHAPTER 1

I was sitting in my office at Saint Jude Thaddeus Parish in Charlestown browsing a tattered paperback written by the late George V. Higgins when my mind drifted to a story about my father. It was a story that one of his Marine Corps pals from Vietnam told me when I was young. Some of it I knew, some of it I didn't, all of it fascinated me.

The leatherneck vet said that my father's favorite actor was Robert Mitchum, and that my father's favorite Robert Mitchum movie was *The Friends of Eddie Coyle*, filmed here in Boston in the early seventies, years before I was born. My father, Chief Sparhawk, was a Micmac Indian from Antigonish, a small fishing village turned college town in the northeast corner of Nova Scotia, thirty miles west of Cape Breton Island.

He came to Boston to find work. Two tours of Vietnam later, with a head full of shrapnel and a chestful of medals, he found work. Dangerous work. Indians expect this. He scraped bridges and welded high-rises, but mostly he was a man in search of his next job. During the filming of *Eddie Coyle*, Chief worked for the Teamsters alongside mob boss Howie Winter, head of Somerville's Winter Hill Gang. Howie ran the Teamsters, though his name never appeared on the masthead, and Paramount Pictures begged for his mercy throughout the shoot. Howie bestowed his blessings on Paramount the way popes of old bestowed indulgences on prosperous sinners: for cash up front.

The Teamsters had everything nailed down. You couldn't take a shit on set unless the union approved the outhouse. They organized all transportation, and my father landed a job as a driver. Driving big shots in limos was easy for Chief, especially compared to washing windows on the Hancock Tower. A dry steering wheel beats a wet squeegee every time. My father's philosophy was a simple one, taken from *The Friends of Eddie Coyle*, and it went like this: "Life is tough, but it's tougher if you're stupid." The Coyle quip didn't prove true for Chief. Nobody was smarter than my old man. Nobody had a tougher life.

I was thinking about all this when a rap on the door disrupted my reverie. I bookmarked the paperback and answered it. A woman bustled in smelling of mothballs and cigarettes. Vaporous steam churned from her mouth. It was early January yet she wore no coat, but that didn't stop her. She plowed ahead as the metal door slammed behind her.

"Friggin' door's dangerous." She shivered and blew on her hands. "You oughta fix it before someone gets killed."

"The hydraulic gizmo is out of whack," I explained.

She looked up at me. "Jaysus, you're a big bastard." Her washed-out blue eyes matched her washed-out complexion. On top of her head, clumps of bleached hair sprouted like the straws of Saint Bridget's Cross. "Friggin' cold out there. Ain't much warmer in here, not that I'm complaining."

"The heat's out of whack, too. How can I help you?"

"I need something to eat, Father. My check don't come for two weeks."

"I'm not a priest, I just work here." She didn't look familiar. Most of the people in the projects looked familiar. "Let's go to the pantry and see what we can scare up."

"Thanks, Father." She huffed on her knuckles. Her fingernails were bitten to milky crescents. "Mind if I warm up first? My son swiped my jacket. Drugs."

"Have a seat," I said, and walked to the kitchenette. "I'll pour us some coffee. What's your name?"

"Gladys Foley. I just moved into Carney Court, been waiting eight months for a place. I lived in Southie for a while, over there in Old Colony. Then my son got pinched. Drugs again."

"It's epidemic."

"Housing is strict on drugs, 'specially if you're white. Me and my kid ended up homeless. Lived in shelters for a while, lived under the expressway, we met some nice people under the expressway. Then we got lucky, got this place in Charlestown. I was scared we'd end up in Roxbury or Dorchester. A white woman shouldn't live in Roxbury or Dorchester, not by Franklin Park anyways."

"Cream and sugar?"

"Yeah, cream and sugar." She flexed her hands, good as new. "Meant to ask you, what do you think of them priests getting crucified? Can't blame you for not wearing a collar."

"I'm not a—"

"You gotta be scared shit about them killings."

"Gladys, I'm not a priest. I just work here. My name is Dermot Sparhawk."

I usually give up telling women I'm not a priest after a couple of tries, unless they're good looking. Gladys sipped her coffee. My hand trembled as I raised mine to my mouth.

"Rough night there, padre?" She leaned in for a swallow and something plopped into the cup. "Cripes, my plate fell out. That dentist of mine can't get nothin' straight."

"Fit them back in."

"Nah." She shoved the dripping teeth in her pocket. "It ain't really the dentist's fault. I ran out of that gooey shit to glue 'em in with."

The paperback called to me. The bookmark stuck out like a tongue, teasing me to come back to it. Distractions are important when you work in the projects. Without them you're forced to look directly at the truth, and the truth can be damaging. It's best to view hardship indirectly, the way a schoolboy views an eclipse through a pinhole projector. Otherwise you'll go blind.

"I'm starving and you're staring at a book?" She chewed her thumb like a teething child. "Just kidding."

We finished the coffee and walked to the pantry. Gladys loaded a bag with dry goods and milk and meat, and her hands shook as she was doing this. Life had beaten Gladys Foley senseless, yet she refused to give up. She fit my definition of a winner.

"Got any work for me?" she asked. "I like volunteering, you know, doing favors for people."

She probably needed community service hours to offset the rent. Boston Housing would require it if Gladys didn't have a job. I asked her if she had a driver's license; she said yes. I told her I might have volunteer hours, running errands for the food pantry. She said that would be "mirific."

"Hey, since I'm gonna be doing you favors down the road, maybe you can do me a favor right now and front me a finnif till Mother's Day."

Mother's Day, the first of the month when the welfare checks go out. I handed her five dollars.

"Thanks." She put the money in her pocket next to the teeth. "I'm going home, gonna sit in my chair and rest my feet on the hassock."

CHAPTER 2

As I headed back to the office, a lean man with dark hair and dark features fell in stride next to me. I knew him from the pantry, but I couldn't recall his name. He smiled at me with straight, white teeth. This was unusual for a food pantry client—both the smile and the teeth. The man followed me into the office and sat across from my desk. He didn't bat an eye when the metal door slammed behind him.

"Can I help you?" I asked.

He took a pen from the desktop and wrote, *My name is Blackie Barboza. I'm deaf. I can't speak.* He wrote stenographer fast. *I read lips.*

The name Barboza got my attention.

"Help with what?"

He shook the pen and wrote, *My brother was Father Netto Barboza.*

"The slain priest?"

He nodded.

The killing of Father Netto Barboza dominated yesterday's news cycle, spurred by the shock that he was the second Boston priest within a week to be crucified. The first victim, Father Axholm, had been found nailed to a concrete highway buttress in Dorchester. Joyfully for the press but sadly for the Archdiocese, Father Axholm was an accused pedophile. The press hinted at revenge as a possible motive—a brilliant deduction. Father Axholm had been awaiting trial at the time of his murder.

Yesterday, Father Barboza got it. He too was an accused pedophile priest, and he too was crucified, nailed to a wharf on the

Boston side of the Charles River Basin. Monday morning Red Line commuters gawked at the wharf-turned-cross that jutted from below the Longfellow Bridge.

"I'm sorry for your loss." I wasn't sure what to say. I've dealt with trauma before. It happens all the time in the projects. "I can recommend a good grief therapist."

He wrote, *I don't want that kind of help.*

I leaned forward and rested my elbows on the desk.

"What kind of help do you want?" I found myself annunciating each syllable. "Do you want to talk to a priest? Father Dominic will be glad to help you."

I don't want a priest. I want you to find my brother's killer.

"What?"

He wrote again, *Find my brother's killer.*

"Sure, no problem," I said. "I'll find him on my lunch break. Anything else while I'm at it?"

Yes. He wrote. *Prove my brother is innocent. He is not a pe- dophile.*

Apparently, lip-readers don't translate sarcasm.

"You can't be serious." I waited, but Blackie didn't respond. "You're pulling my leg, right?"

He scribbled, *I am serious. Find my brother's killer.*

I could tell by his expression that he was in fact serious. Was he also wacky?

"You're asking the wrong guy, Blackie. You should talk to the police."

I don't trust the police.

"Don't trust the police? What does trust have to do with it? I don't trust my bookie, but he's the guy I go to when I place a bet. The cops will find the killer. They're all over it."

He tore off the top sheet. On a fresh page, he wrote, *Maybe the cops will find him. Maybe they won't. Maybe some rich guy will pay them to look the other way. It happens.*

"You watch too much TV."

I trust you. I know you. You won't stop until you find the truth.
"You think I'm a guy who won't stop?"
I know you are.
Blackie unfolded the morning tabloid, which showed Father Netto Barboza's image plastered on the front page. He pointed to it and wrote *Help me* under the photo.
"This is crazy," I said.
You help people.
"I run a food pantry. I don't track down killers."
I sat back and looked to the harbor. Arching above the projects like a rusting rainbow was the green hulk of the Tobin Bridge. An inbound semi humped across the upper deck and shook the building we sat in. It intruded further, blowing its air horn.
He scrawled, *You are smart. You went to college. You played football.*
"Sure, I played football. Big deal."
He pointed at the newspaper again. *My brother is innocent. He was holy! He never hurt a child. Never! Those kids are lying. Fuck them!*
Kids? Them? As in plural? More than one kid accused Father Barboza? What were the chances he didn't do it?
"Listen to me, Blackie. I can't prove your brother is innocent of those charges, and I don't find killers. It's not part of my job. Besides, it is way out of my league. I wouldn't know where to begin."
Just try. You will find the truth if you just try. He pointed at me, writing, *You're supposed to help us.*
"Oh, man."
He kept at it. *I have faith in you. We all have faith in you back here. You are one of us. You are special.*
"I'm not special, and your faith is misplaced."
He dropped the ballpoint and grabbed a Sharpie. In thick red letters he printed, *Our faith is NOT misplaced. You are one of us.*
The Sharpie fumes intensified the thumping in my head. Maybe

the toxic inhalant was part of Blackie's ploy to get me to give in, and if it was, it was working.

"Cap that thing, will you?"

I tried to ignore him, but he wouldn't leave the office. He kept pointing to the newspaper and retracing the words *Help me* under his brother's photo. He showed me another photo; this one of Father Barboza distributing Communion at Mass. Blackie then took a twenty from his wallet and slid it across the desk to me.

My last twenty. Take it. I'll get you more.

"No." I pushed the bill back to him. "No money."

Maybe it was the way his eyes said it, the way his eyes believed in me when nobody else believed in me anymore. Blackie stared at me the way teammates once stared at me in the huddle, knowing I'd make the play. A faint memory of enthusiasm pinged in my soul, a ping I hadn't felt in years. I toyed with the idea of finding Father Barboza's killer, dismissed it out of hand, and toyed with it more.

I had to admit that the idea of looking for Father Barboza's killer excited me, but the excitement arose from self-interest and not moral duty. Looking for the killer offered an escape from the mundane, a diversion from eyeballing expiration dates on soup cans and rotating boxes of breakfast cereal. An escape, that's what excited me. And, besides, this guy wasn't going to let me say no.

"Let me think about it." I held up my hands. "No promises."

Blackie fumbled for the pen and wrote, *Thank you.* He hopped to his feet and shook my hand.

"I said I'll think about it."

The rest of the day crawled by like traffic on the Tobin, and, no matter how hard I tried, I couldn't shake Blackie Barboza's eyes from my mind. At five o'clock I locked up the office and walked to Packy's Liquor Store in Hayes Square. My knee throbbed with each step, indicating a low front was underway. A hell of a way to tell the weather.

Across the square in the Harvard-Kent playground, two boys

passed the pigskin back and forth, enjoying the greatest game in its purest form. On a vacant lot behind Packy's, the city had broken ground on a new police station, and next to it, a new men's recovery house. At one time Charlestown had more bars in more places than AT&T wireless. Now we're building a recovery house to handle the fallout from those bars.

Inside the liquor store I grabbed a six-pack of Narragansett and a pint of Old Thompson and placed them on the counter.

"That all, Dermot?"

"That's all, Packy."

And I handed over my money.

CHAPTER 3

Daybreak was tough, but I've had tougher. I washed down five aspirins with two Gatorades and began to feel human again. Some people might call this the waste of a day off. I call it morning. And now to fulfill an agreement I had made to a deaf and dumb project man to find the person who murdered his brother. Although I hadn't made an explicit promise to Blackie, I had implied a promise, and when a Townie implies a promise, he had better deliver on it. Why had I said yes to Blackie Barboza? Why did I get his hopes up? There was no way possible I could find the killer. An entire police force was already at work on it. What could I add to that?

I dragged my ass out of the house and hitched through the projects to the church office, where I planned to use the computer. I logged onto the Internet and searched for Father Netto Barboza. The search yielded hundreds of hits. I read some of the stories, looked at the pictures, and learned nothing new. Then I read an article about the first murder victim, Father Axholm.

Father Axholm had been found crucified on a concrete expressway stanchion at Neponset Circle. The article went on to say that a newspaper hawker discovered the body the morning after the killing when he was setting up his stand for work. I decided to visit the hawker and ask him about the dead body he saw. If I learned nothing new, I'd have an excuse to tell Blackie Barboza that I was done, that his request was over my head.

I locked up the office, walked to Community College, and rode the Orange Line to Downtown Crossing, where I picked up the Red Line for Ashmont. At Fields Corner, I boarded the 202 bus and stayed on it the length of Neponset Avenue and got off near the expressway.

Across the way, I saw a man standing beneath the highway overpass, selling newspapers to commuters as they stopped at the traffic light. I hoped it was the same newspaper hawker that found Father Axholm's body. Even the fact that I hoped it was the same guy surprised me. After all, I was looking for an excuse to drop the whole thing. With my knee now loose, I dodged three lanes of a Dorchester speedway called Gallivan Boulevard and made it to his makeshift milk-crate stand in one piece.

"Any *Globes*?" I shouted as I caught my breath.

"Don't sell *Globes*, just *Heralds*."

I asked for a *Herald* and gave it a token browse. The hawker eyed me as if I were a curiosity. Pedestrians never bought newspapers here, only drivers, and they were always in a rush. I waited for a truck to pass overhead, and then I asked him the question I came here to ask him.

"Are you the man who found the priest's body?"

The traffic light turned green, giving the hawker a moment to talk. He was a small man, and he was wearing a brimmed camouflage hat embossed with the Marine Corps emblem. A Sinn Fein pin decorated one side of the crown, a shamrock sticky the other.

"You a cop?" he asked.

"I'm not a cop, but I can use a little help." I paused while a motorcycle roared by. "I'm investigating the priest's murder."

"Why do you care about that? The son of a bitch got what he deserved. The world's a better place, him dead."

"No argument from me on Father Axholm, but I'm looking into the murder of the priest, Father Netto Barboza. The Barboza family thinks he was innocent of any wrongdoing. They asked me to clear his name and find his killer."

"That's a tall order, pal."

"I know it is, but I told them I'd try. The Barboza clan wants to know what happened, that's all. They want closure," I said. "You can understand that, can't you?"

"Sure I can understand it, but you came to the wrong place. See, I don't know nothin' about Father Barboza. Axholm I know about, but not Barboza. You gotta understand something, pal. It was Father Axholm that got killed here."

"I know." An ambulance sped up Gallivan Boulevard toward Carney Hospital. The traffic pulled to the side and let it pass. When the siren was out of earshot, I pushed ahead. "Would you be kind enough to tell me what you saw the morning of the murder?"

"Be glad to tell you. I saw a priest nailed to that footing over there. Big masonry nails through his hands and feet." He pointed with a thin finger toward the buttress. "Not much else to tell."

"Did you see anything odd?"

"Odd? You mean odder than a priest nailed to a slab?" He looked at me with suspicion. "Are you all right, pal?"

"It depends who you ask."

"You might be big, but I don't gotta to talk to you."

"I know you don't."

"You got no authority over me."

"I agree with you."

"As long as we got that cleared up."

He nodded to himself as if he'd straightened something out, and then he seemed to relax a bit. I wasn't sure how to handle him. I sensed he wanted to talk to me, but only on his terms. I pointed to his hat.

"Were you in the military?"

"Yeah, long time ago, Nam, sixty-eight."

"My father served in Vietnam, two tours with the Marines." I gave the hawker a chance to think about what I said. "He got shot to shit over there."

"Poor bastard." He looked up from under the hat brim. "Is he doing okay now?"

"He's dead."

"Shit, sorry to hear that. I served with the infantry and got out clean. Lucky, I guess." He touched the brim. "My son's hat, he's in Afghanistan now, was in Iraq before that." He cleared his throat. "Are you for or against the war?"

"Never gave it much thought."

"Well, as long as he comes home in one piece, that's all I care about. And that includes the mental stuff. PTSD is worse than getting a leg blowed off." He picked up a few *Herald*s and counted them with his thumb. "I did see something kinda odd that morning."

The light turned red. The hawker sidestepped slowing cars and waved newspapers in the air for drivers to consider. He sold one and came back.

"About the dead priest, the odd thing you saw?" I asked.

"He had a red hood on his head."

A red hood?

"Was it a sweatshirt or a—"

"No, no, it was tied around his head like a whatcha call it, detachable hood."

"Father Axholm had a red hood on his head, anything else?"

"Nothing you didn't read in the papers." He hesitated as an eighteen-wheeler rumbled above. How the hell does he stand the noise? "Wait a minute, there was something else, something I didn't think to tell the cops. It didn't seem like much at the time." He halted. "I talk too much."

I didn't say anything in response. He walked to his stand and restacked the tabloids. High above a pigeon landed on an overpass underpinning, pecked its feathers and flew for greener pastures. The hawker sold a *Herald* to a man in a pickup truck and came back to the stand. I approached him again.

"What's your name?"

"Teddy Neenan," he said. "Been selling newspapers here for more'n twenty years. What's yours?"

"Dermot Sparhawk." I faced Neponset Avenue. "My grandmother lived on Popes Hill, name of O'Hanlon."

The light turned red, but Teddy stayed put.

"The O'Hanlons on Train Street?" His brow relaxed. "That's my neighborhood."

"She lived at the corner of Train and Westglow."

"Yeah, right, I remember now. One of the daughters married a crazy Indian." He cleared his throat. "Sorry, Native American. The O'Hanlons were damn fine people, came here in the seventies from Belfast, I think."

I glanced at his Sinn Fein pin.

"My grandmother said it was inhumane in the North."

"Inhumane? That ain't the half of it, pal."

"I heard about it growing up."

"Yep, I recollect the O'Hanlons, straight outta Belfast. They did okay by me." He pointed with his chin toward a bait shop on the other side of Gallivan Boulevard. "That morning, the morning of the murder, I saw a man walking fast as a bastard, like he wanted to get out of here. Kept his head down low, he did. Wore a baseball cap that covered his face, like he didn't want no one to see him. He was cautious. Can't tell you much more, except he wasn't no kid." The light turned red and Teddy waded into the braking traffic. He turned and said, "Yep, the O'Hanlons were damn good folks."

CHAPTER 4

The next morning, I walked from Charlestown to Massachusetts General Hospital and then to the oxidizing edifice of the MGH T stop, the approximate site of Father Netto Barboza's wharf crucifixion. I scaled the stairs of the elevated station and waited for the next inbound train to arrive from Cambridge. A few minutes later, it pulled in and squealed to a stop. The exiting riders spurted through the turnstiles fast enough to generate electricity. I approached some of them as they stampeded by, but they had no time for me. I was getting frustrated when someone slapped me on the back.

"Dermot," he said.

He wore a charcoal-gray suit, a pressed white shirt, and a crimson necktie with a paisley swirl of gold. His haircut probably cost more than my weekly food allowance. I finally recognized him and wondered if he'd been sick. Phil Broderick had lost weight since I'd seen him last, and it showed in his face and shoulders.

"Phil," I said.

"Great to see you, Dermot. How are you surviving these hardscrabble days?"

He enunciated his Rs as if he were a Beacon Hill Brahmin, not the son of a Charlestown bus driver. The neighborhood naiveté had vacated Phil's eyes, replaced by a calculating gaze. Was he going to sell me something?

"Surviving just fine," I said, "and it's good to see you, too."

"Let's grab a coffee. I have a few minutes before work."

We stepped into a franchise café on Charles Street that served a pricy brew. I only had a few dollars in my pocket and ordered a small coffee. Phil ordered a grande latte with cinnamon stick and spice. When I reached for my pocket, he held my arm.

"Expense account, I haven't reached my monthly limit yet."

We sat on high stools that overlooked the street and watched the goings-on. I felt more akin with the bums begging for change than the suits ignoring them.

"I heard you're a lawyer, Phil."

"I sure am. I matriculated into Harvard Law School after I graduated from Tufts, and I now litigate for Wanzer and Jaynes, the most important law firm in the city. How is life treating you?"

Matriculate? Litigate?—how about nauseate.

"No complaints, Phil. I work in Charlestown at Saint Jude Thaddeus. There's plenty to keep us busy. Father Dominic got me the job."

"Father Dominic, from the projects?"

"Yes," I said. Phil and I knew each other from Charlestown, but we hadn't kept in touch over the years. Women keep in touch, men don't. "I was landscaping for a buddy of mine when Father Dominic saw me. We had lunch and the next thing I knew I had a job in the parish. They give me health insurance."

"Health insurance, hey that's great to hear." He tasted his grande latte. "Where do you live?"

"In Charlestown with my great aunt," I said. "She owns a two family."

"With your aunt, huh? Hey, great. I must invite you down to my summer place in Hyannis Port for a barbeque some weekend. We'll toss horseshoes."

Horseshoes?

The closest I ever got to tossing horseshoes was tossing down beers at the Horseshoe Tavern. We continued to drink our coffees. Phil pretended not to look at his watch, and I pretended not to notice. The seconds limped along.

"I have to be getting to the office." Phil tightened the knot of his tie. "You look pretty good considering the, um, you know, how that knee injury derailed you."

"Derailed me?" I put down my cup. "What's that supposed to mean?"

My hands clenched to fists. Phil's face went white.

"Take it easy, Dermot. I didn't mean anything." His cockiness vanished, his lawyerly poise barely remained. "It's just too bad. You were so great, and I mean real great. I loved watching you play football, we all did. We were proud of you, everyone in Charlestown was proud of you."

"Yeah, sure."

I looked through the plate-glass window. Out on the street success passed me by. Executives barked into cell phones, businessmen jumped out of cabs, women strutted in high heels. They were important people with important lives, just like Phil.

"Dermot," Phil said, interrupting my funk. "I shouldn't have said that. I acted like an asshole and I'm sorry. It really *is* good to see you. I mean it."

"Things haven't gone my way." I looked at him. "It's my own fault. If it wasn't for Father Dominic, I wouldn't even have insurance. And if it wasn't for my aunt, I wouldn't have a nice place to live. I'd still be in the bricks."

"Forget all that. We're both Townies and here I am acting important." He drank the last of his cup. "Because of this foolish façade I have to portray, I sometimes forget where I came from."

"Don't worry about it, Phil." A thought came to me. "Maybe you can help me out on something. I'm looking into Father Barboza's murder."

"Why?"

"His brother asked me for help. He wants me to find the killer."

"You do P.I. work? I ask because we hire investigators at our firm, not as employees but as consultants. The pay is excellent. I'd be glad to recommend you." He seemed genuinely excited. "You always had a nose for the streets."

"I'm not a private investigator, not by a long shot. I'm just helping out a project guy who asked me for help." I relaxed on the stool. "Did you see Father Barboza's body on the wharf the other morning?"

"I did, on my ride into work, but I didn't see much." He pushed the cup aside. "By the time the train went by, the police had already covered the body with one of those tarpaulin things."

"Was his head covered, too?"

"Yes, his head was covered. His whole body was covered, head to toe."

"What time did you see it?"

"It was early. I was on the first train. Every morning I take the first Kendall train, and it was the same thing that morning. The police were there when the train went by. Does that help?"

"Sure it helps," I said, even though it didn't. "Thanks."

Phil stood to leave. We shook hands and smiled at each other and promised to get together, but we knew it would never happen. Phil and I lived in two different worlds now. Horseshoes in Hyannis Port and whiskey in the bricks just don't mix. Phil matriculated for his litigator's job in the most important law firm in the city. I finished my small coffee and watched him slouch through the door, a little more grateful for my place in life.

I looked outside. A beat cop strolled on the sidewalk and smiled at the pretty girls as they walked by him. No heavy lifting on Charles Street, that's for sure. And that's when it hit me. My cousin Cameron O'Hanlon is a Boston cop.

CHAPTER 5

Cameron worked in Government Center, the Area A-1 precinct, a short walk from Charles Street. I hiked up Cambridge Street, past the hideous Hurley Building at the corner of Staniford Street, past Cardinal Cushing Park at Bowdoin Station, and on to the station house. I went inside and asked the desk sergeant if I could speak to Officer Cameron O'Hanlon. He nodded me to a seat and told me to wait. Fifteen minutes went by before Cameron came out.

"Dermot," Cameron said, as he walked out of the back room. "It's been too long." He turned to the desk sergeant. "Sarge, meet my cousin, Dermot Sparhawk."

"I remember Dermot." Sarge shook my hand. "You were a hell of a football player."

"Thanks, Sarge." I put my arm around Cameron's shoulders and turned him away from the front desk. "I need a favor."

"Sure." He patted his coat pocket and looked outside. "Let's take a walk."

We left the station and crossed New Sudbury Street to City Hall Plaza. The weather was mild and the breeze was negligible, which was a good thing, because Government Center channeled the worst wind tunnel in the city. We traversed the concrete wasteland of City Hall Plaza and walked down Court Street, stopping in front of the State Street MBTA stop.

"What do you need?" Cameron's peach-fuzz face turned pink in the cool outdoors. "I'm listening."

"I need information privy to the police. I'm looking into the murder of Father Netto Barboza."

"I don't understand." Cam undid his top button. "Why do you care about that?"

"Father Barboza's brother is in my food pantry. He asked me to find his brother's killer and to prove he was no pervert."

"You're shitting me."

"I'm serious. I need an answer to one detail on the murder. That's all."

"That's all?" Cameron's expression changed from a cousin's face to a cop's face. He took a cigar from his coat pocket and lit it. "Even if I wanted to talk to you about the Barboza case, I couldn't tell you much. I don't work Homicide."

He offered me a cigar.

"Macanudo," I said. "I can't take your good—"

"Shut up and smoke it." He lit a match for me. "Anything else?"

"I know this Boston cop, a guy I played football with at BC." I got the cigar going. "He works in Homicide."

"So?"

"So I was wondering if you'd ask him a question for me." The cigar was smoother than the ropes I smoked. "It would be better coming from another cop."

"What is this?" He took the cigar from his mouth, inspected it, and stuck it back in. "I can't do that."

"Why not?"

"Because I'm a cop, that's why. And if I keep my nose clean and my mouth shut, someday I'll be a retired cop with a pension. What you're asking is simply not done."

"It's just one question." I stepped closer. "I need to know if Father Barboza was wearing a red hood when they found him."

"What difference does it make? And why do you care?"

"I care because Father Barboza's brother asked me for help. The guy is a deaf mute, and I couldn't say no to him. He swears that Father Barboza was framed on the pedophile charges."

"So what if he was framed? He's dead, Dermot. It's over," he said. "What is this really about?"

Cam had asked a good question. Why was I so eager to investigate the murder? My zeal couldn't be fully explained by a deaf man's plea. There had to be more to it. And why did I expect Cam to help? He wasn't obligated to help me on anything, and yet I was asking him to meddle into a police matter that could jeopardize his career. If I was going to investigate this murder, if I was going to ask Cam for help, I'd better be damn sure it wasn't on a whim. I'd better be certain my motivation was grounded.

"I began to look into the Barboza murder," I said. "The whole thing started as a favor to his brother, and, to be frank about it, I was looking for an excuse to stop. But then some things happened. Pieces of information came to me, and my insides caught fire. The next thing I knew my juices were flowing. The next thing after that, I felt alive again. It's the first time I've felt alive since I got hurt."

"Come on, Dermot, that was years ago."

"I'm doing something that excites me, something I can get after." I gnawed the cigar. "You know what I do for work? I stack cans of peas on a shelf, neat little rows of Jolly Green Giant peas. Ten across, six deep, two high and it is boring as hell."

"Every job gets boring." He kicked a pebble with his buffed black boot. "Even being a cop."

"I'm not complaining about the job, but this is different. This is for me. I can use my brains a little bit."

"Dermot—"

"You're the only guy who can help me on this thing. Only a cop can get this information, and you know that." I pushed it. "I'm godfather to Cameron Junior."

"Don't con me."

"I'm not conning you."

"The hell you aren't." He looked at me. "I can't do it, understand?"

We stayed silent for an inch of cigar. A city bus squeaked to a stop in front of us and let out passengers. I sucked another puff.

"How are Kerry and the kids?"

"Good, everyone's good." He no longer looked at me when he

spoke. "You know Kerry, Mass every morning, novenas every night."

"Cam, this is important to me. I can't explain why, but I need to chase this thing. I goddamn need it."

"Jesus, Dermot."

"Don't make me beg."

"Dermot Sparhawk beg?" He sighed. "You are an enormous pain in my ass, you know that?"

"I'll get on my knees if I have to."

"You act as if it's your salvation." He launched the cigar airborne. "Hell, if it's that important to you. The Homicide detective, what's his name?"

"Thanks, Cam. His name is Adam Jenner."

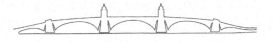

CHAPTER 6

Early the following morning, a police car sped into the projects with its siren blaring and woke me from a deep sleep. I dressed in sweats, drank a cup of instant coffee, and walked to the basement for a daybreak workout. After warm-ups and stretches, I performed rafter pull-ups, handstand push-ups, and cinder block curls. I stretched again and then trained twenty minutes with Indian clubs.

Back upstairs in the kitchen, I drank another coffee. I showered and shaved and walked to the pastor's office for our weekly status meeting. The receptionist told me that Father Dominic was expecting me and to go right in.

Father Dominic motioned me to a chair and then rolled his eyes as he continued to talk on the phone. His curly, gray hair was cut short and brushed straight back. His rimless bifocals rested low on his strong Roman nose. An unlit pipe protruded from his mouth.

"It's always something," he said, as he hung up. "How are things in the bricks, bright and cheery?"

"Cheery as ever, Father. The food pantry is busy. The women's support group is developing, but slowly. The women are afraid they'll get smacked around if their husbands find out. The youth program is teeming."

"How about the AA meetings?"

"AA is overflowing."

"Does the hall have sufficient seating?" he asked. "Is there enough room to accommodate newcomers?"

"There's plenty of room."

"Good, because you never know when a man might realize he's got a booze problem." He leaned back. "What else is going on?"

I started to say something and then stopped. Father Dominic picked up on my hesitation.

"What is it, Dermot?" His teeth clicked on the pipe stem. "Talk to me."

"It has to do with Father Barboza."

"Netto Barboza?" He raised his chin. "What's going on?"

"His brother came to see me."

"Netto's brother came to see you?" He rose up in the chair. "Why did he come to see you?"

"He wanted to talk to me about Father Barboza."

I told Father Dominic about Blackie's visit to my office. I told him that Blackie wanted me to find Father Barboza's killer and to prove that Father wasn't a pedophile.

"I didn't realize that, oh, never mind. What have you learned so far?" He twisted the pipe stem a full rotation. "I would like to know."

"I'm still gathering information, so the whole thing is still sketchy to me. I suppose you could say I'm making progress, or at least it feels like progress." I thought about the red hood. "I might be onto something."

Father Dominic didn't respond. He remained seated in his chair, rocking back and forth. His eyes gazed as he swayed. The absence of talk threw me.

I said, "Are you okay with this, Father? Are you okay with my working on Father Barboza's killing?"

He rested the pipe in a clean glass ashtray. Father Dominic never smoked the pipe, but he was never without it, either. He stopped rocking and his eyes focused on me.

"Is your office covered?"

"The office is covered. Victor Cepeda is retired now and likes to stay busy. He handles the desk when I'm out on runs." I kept talking. "I suppose it sounds strange that I'm investigating a murder."

"Agreed, it sounds strange."

"I know it does." I stood from my chair and collected my thoughts. "I like it, Father. I like finding connections and piecing together clues."

"I'm glad you like it, Dermot. But I'm concerned it might be dangerous."

"I'll back off if I think I'm in danger."

He started to say something and then stopped.

"What is it, Father?" I removed his pipe from the ashtray and examined it. "Is there anything you want to tell me?"

"Netto Barboza and I were classmates in the seminary. We were quite close back then." He swiveled his chair and looked out the office window. "We roomed together for a year. I can tell you straight-out that Netto Barboza was not a child molester. There is no way possible he'd harm a child."

"You two were roommates?"

"The allegations against him," he paused, "if anything, I thought Netto might struggle with the ladies, not kids." He chuckled to himself. "We used to sneak out of the seminary on weekends, let our hair down, so to speak. Sometimes we'd have dates waiting for us. It was all innocent stuff. One of the girls became a nun."

"Do you think Father Barboza was falsely charged?"

"I absolutely do." He spun his chair to face me. "Keep working on it, Dermot. See what you find out. And, for the love of God, stay safe."

From Father Dominic's office I walked to the AA hall to make sure the heat was up. When I got there, a longtime Townie with reddish gray hair stepped forward and stuck out his hand. I remembered him, but I hadn't seen him in years. As I recall, he was a contemporary of my father.

"Mickey Pappas," he said. "I remember you from McNulty Court. You were just a tike back then. I remember your old man too, the Chief, God rest his soul. Tragic, what happened to him. He never got involved with the other Vietnam vets, but he was a good guy all the same."

"Thanks for saying that."

"It's the truth." We talked about McNulty Court and the proj-ects. Mickey told me he lived in Everett now, but he was still a Townie through and through. When I turned to leave, he said, "We have room for one more, Dermot."

"Excuse me?"

"We have an extra seat if you want it. I see that you hit the liquor store most nights, not that I'm keeping track." He smiled. "It doesn't have to be that way."

"What are you saying?"

"We're here if you need us. That's all."

I left the hall and thought about what Mickey Pappas said to me. Sure I drink a little, but I don't get drunk every time I drink, not like my father. My father woke up to Narragansett every morn-ing and he passed out with an Old Thompson every night. I've never been much of a morning drinker. All right, I swig the occa-sional eye opener, but not every morning, not like my father.

Victor Cepeda was on his feet when I got back to the office.

"Dermot, your cousin Cameron just called. He said to call him right away. It's important."

"Thanks." I dialed Cameron O'Hanlon's cell phone number. When he answered, I asked, "Cam, what's up?"

"Are you at your office?"

"I'm on the office phone now."

"I'll be right over."

Twenty minutes later a Boston Police cruiser drove into the church parking lot. The AA guys watched as the car rolled to a stop. They seemed relieved when Cameron came toward me.

"Let's walk to the basketball court," he said. "We need some privacy."

We walked to Kane Cage next to the church parking lot. Cameron scanned the area, turned to me, and said, "Detective Adam Jenner said that Father Netto Barboza was wearing a red hood when they found him."

"I knew it." The priest killings were connected. "Cam, I don't know how to thank you. I put you on the spot, and you—"

"No sweat," he said, waving his hand for me to stop. "Adam Jenner made an amateur mistake, never saw anything like it in my years on the force."

"What happened?"

"When I first approached him he stonewalled me, which is exactly what I expected him to do. Then I mentioned your name. I told him we were cousins, and Jenner got all excited. And that's when he let it slip about the red hood. He caught himself after he said it and told me not to say anything. But I couldn't believe he let it slip."

Adam Jenner was never the brightest of men.

"I didn't mean to be so pushy earlier, Cam."

"Forget it." He turned toward the cruiser. "I have to run. Be smart and use your head. You're swinging in the big leagues now."

I was on the right track. I went back to the office and said to Victor, "Let's lock up and get a drink at the Horseshoe."

"Some other time, Dermot. Gotta get home to my señorita."

CHAPTER 7

I blew off the Horseshoe and grabbed a pint at Packy's instead. I drank at home, but couldn't relax. After supper I bought another pint and drained it, and then I tapered on Ballantine Ale, a forty-ouncer. The thrill of Father Barboza's red hood had flushed my adrenaline and triggered my thirst. Even with a flood of booze dulling my nerves, I knew I'd never sleep. I walked to my office and logged on to the computer. For the first time since my college gridiron days, I felt a purpose in life. Investigating the killing of Father Barboza roiled my competitive spirit, a spirit that had lay dormant for too long.

I thought about the evidence.

Father Axholm and Father Barboza both wore red hoods. But there had to be more to it, something else they had in common. What was Father Axholm's story? And how was he connected to Father Barboza? I reread the newspaper accounts online. Axholm was sixty years old, ten years older than Barboza. Both were accused pedophiles. Both had attended the same seminary. What else tied them together? I clicked on a few more articles and learned nothing new.

My hands fidgeted for liquor. I uncapped a jug of Old Thompson I kept in the file cabinet, poured three fingers' worth into a glass, and swallowed it. A can of Narragansett from behind the bookcase found its way into my other hand. I popped it open and swigged it down. I didn't want the whiskey to feel alone in my belly. My hands rested. But in a preventative measure, I poured more whiskey and cracked another beer. I drank for an hour or two, unrolled a sleeping bag from the closet, and slept on the floor.

• • •

Police sirens pierced my ears in the morning. A patrol car sped up Bunker Hill Street. Another came from Sullivan Square. I sat up, but my big head drove me back to the floor. I needed aspirin. I needed a Coke. I had neither.

Atop the file cabinet sat the whiskey bottle with two inches of hooch darkening the bottom. I drank a mouthful. Most of it stayed down. I took another drink and felt better. After finishing the whiskey, I swilled the bitters from the beer cans and burped. Then somebody pounded on the office door. It was Victor Cepeda.

"Dermot, I thought you were here. I saw the lights on last night. Something's going on at the monument." He stepped back. "You don't look so good."

"I'm fine." The booze kicked in and my stomach stopped churning. "What's up?"

"Don't know. Police cars everywhere."

We walked up Lexington Street to the Bunker Hill Monument. My head began to clear, but I couldn't tell if it was the booze or the fresh air that was clearing it. We reached the top of the hill and saw a cadre of cops in Monument Square. They had cordoned off the area with yellow tape and blocked the streets with squad cars. Uniformed cops patrolled the perimeter, making sure no one crossed the line. Detectives, wearing gold shields and smoking cigarettes, exchanged murmurs. Victor and I looked at each other.

"Something big is going on," I said.

"Mucho big," he replied. "I know that cop over there. Let me talk to him, see what he says."

Victor walked over to a Hispanic cop, exchanged some words with him, and came back to me.

"Another priest got crucified," he said.

"What?"

"The Puerto Rican cop told me it was a priest named Father Del Rio. He couldn't say much, 'cause the big, black detective over there don't like him."

Victor and I stood outside the yellow tape and watched the

police milling about. None of them seemed rushed. None of them showed emotion. They talked to each other in pairs, the way a catcher talks to pitcher on the mound, heads down, hands screening their mouths.

The promising start with Neponset Circle's newspaper hawker Teddy Neenan had generated good results, and I wanted to keep the momentum going. The big, black detective walked to the perimeter and muttered a few words to a uniformed cop. They were ten feet away from us. Whether by whiskey or stupidity, I asked, "Was Father Del Rio wearing a red hood?"

The black detective glared at my face. He pointed at me and then at the cop he'd been speaking to, and said, "Take this clown to the interrogation room at headquarters. If he gives you any trouble, arrest him for public drunkenness."

"Yes, sir." The cop seemed confused. "Should I handcuff him, Captain?"

"Cuff him, stuff him in the squad car, and get him out of my sight."

The cop walked me to the rear door of a cruiser, handcuffed. As I was getting in, two SUVs with tinted windows sped up Monument Avenue and stopped at the police-car blockade. Six agents hopped out wearing dark-blue jackets, matching baseball caps, and plenty of Dacron. The letters FBI were stenciled on their backs in bright yellow.

The black detective bellowed, "What the hell is this?"

CHAPTER 8

They locked me in a windowless room lit by fluorescent lights. Half the tubes were burnt out and the ones that weren't flickered. A gunmetal table centered the worn linoleum floor. Smells of disinfectants and sweaty socks added grit to the atmosphere, smells that reminded me of a locker room after a muddy football game. My head ached for aspirin. My mouth hankered for a drink, even tap water. I sat alone for an hour and waited, and then two detectives came into the room.

The first one was Adam Jenner, still massive and still moving mechanically, as if muscle-bound by steroids. The second one was the black cop from the monument. They looked down at me in the chair. Jenner seemed bigger than he had been in college, when we practically lived in the weight room. Was he juicing? It wouldn't matter if he was, because Jenner was never tough; but huge and harmless, like Greenland. The black cop wasn't much smaller, but he was more natural in his build and more fluid in his movements.

Both of them wore dark suits that matched like uniforms. They positioned themselves across the table like offensive linemen ready to double-team me. Then they took their seats. Adam Jenner opened a manila folder and clicked a gold pen and wrote the date on the top of the page.

"Long time, Dermot," he said. "Dermot and I played football at BC, Captain. Dermot, this is Captain Pruitt."

"A college boy." Pruitt's voice grumbled from somewhere down low—not a guy to screw around with. He interlocked his fingers and thumbs like a strangler, and then he spoke. "At the

monument you mentioned Father Del Rio by name. That information wasn't released at the time. How did you know his name?"

"I overheard a cop saying it."

"Bullshit," Pruitt said.

"Okay, Captain, I'll come clean. Father Del Rio told me his
name as I was nailing him to the monument."

"Still the same Dermot," Adam Jenner snorted.

"A wise guy." Captain Pruitt unlocked his hands and pressed
his fingers on the tabletop. "You also said something about a red
hood."

"I did."

"Nobody knows about the red hoods, nobody but the police
and the serial killer," Pruitt said. "You're not a cop, so you must
be the killer. Did you kill those priests, Sparhawk?"

"No," I said.

"Good answer," Pruitt said. "A one-word answer shows certi-
tude. No elaboration, no emotion, just plain no." The chair creaked
under his mass. "If you aren't the killer, then who told you about
the red hoods?"

"Nobody," I said.

"Nobody? Another one-word wonder." He rolled his shoulders
like a fighter between rounds. "Are you a psychic or something?
How the hell did you—"

"I saw Father Barboza's body from the train," I said. "The red
hood was sticking out from under the tarp."

"Tarp?"

"The tarpaulin that was covering him."

"The tarpaulin?" Pruitt slapped his thighs with both hands and
laughed. "That's good, Sparhawk. Hell, that's better than good,
that's great. You're a damn good liar. Cool under pressure, never
blinked an eye. Most people can't come up with a lie that fast, and
a plausible one at that."

"That's what I saw."

"Sure it is, sure it is. What do you say, Jenner? I'm satisfied, aren't you? Let's kick him loose." Pruitt leaned across the table, his nose mere inches from mine. "Who told you about the red hood?"

"I saw it from the train."

"You're lying, Sparhawk."

"Captain," Jenner jumped in, "let me talk to Dermot for a few minutes."

"Sure, Detective, go ahead and talk to your old pal. Make him feel nice and comfy. Let's give him the old good-cop-bad-cop routine," Pruitt said to Jenner. "Get Sparhawk's whereabouts on the nights of the murders." He walked to the door and turned to face me. "I'm not through with you yet."

Captain Pruitt exited the room like an exorcised spirit. My pores opened and discharged a distillery stench. The room wobbled, or maybe it was my brain. I grabbed for the table to stabilize myself.

"He's not as bad as he seems," Adam Jenner said. "He really isn't."

"Huh?"

"Pruitt, he's not a bad guy. He's under pressure. All of us in Homicide are under pressure. The District Attorney is strong-arming us. He's recruiting the State Police to help close our cases, our fuckin' cases. Pisses me off, the whole damn thing."

"Can't blame you," I said, just to say something.

"Ever hear of CPAC?"

"Six-pack?"

"Criminal Protection and Control, they operate under the State Police. A trooper named Lieutenant Staples heads it up in Suffolk County." He relaxed his fists. "Staples is tight with the DA, and because of that, CPAC is nosing around the priest killings. Captain Pruitt doesn't like CPAC barging into our territory, and neither do I."

"What about the FBI?"

"The Bunker Hill Monument is federal property. The National

Park Service has jurisdiction. We've been told that the park rangers called the FBI." Jenner thought for a moment. "We caught the 911 call and got there first, so we're in charge of the case for now. Plus it's part of an ongoing investigation."

"Boston Homicide is in charge, but you're dealing with CPAC and the FBI?"

"The problem is CPAC and Lieutenant Staples. We're refusing to work with Staples and he's pissed off." Jenner's large frame dwarfed the gunmetal table. His wispy hair and flushed face belied his physical power. My shoulders unknotted, but only for a second. Adam switched topics, catching me flatfooted. "Cameron O'Hanlon told you about the red hood."

"Excuse me?"

"He's your cousin," Adam said. "Cameron O'Hanlon is your cousin."

"What are you talking about?"

"O'Hanlon came to see me. I dropped my guard and told him about Father Barboza's red hood." Adam sighed. "Cameron O'Hanlon, that's how you knew about the hood. It had to be O'Hanlon."

"I don't know what you're talking about, Adam."

"Then how did you find out about the hood? And don't give me that crap about seeing it from the train. You didn't see it from the train. I was at the scene that morning. Barboza's body was in the bus before the trains started. The tarp you claimed to see was covering physical evidence, so don't tell me about the hood sticking out from the tarp."

My mind raced for a way to protect my cousin Cameron. An angle came to me, a way to wiggle off the hook.

"I talked to a Neponset newspaper hawker named Teddy Neenan, the guy who found Father Axholm nailed to the Expressway buttress. Teddy told me about the red hood on Axholm's head."

"Teddy from Neponset Circle? He wasn't supposed to say a word about that. Did he tell you anything else?"

"No." I thought about the man Teddy saw leaving the scene that morning. "That's all he told me."

"I don't get it, Dermot. What's your interest in the priest killings?"

"I'm helping a friend."

"What friend?"

I told Adam Jenner about my job at Saint Jude Thaddeus. I told him that Blackie Barboza, one of my food pantry clients, asked me to find his brother's killer. I told Adam that Blackie's request had prompted my trip to Neponset Circle. Adam Jenner's mouth slackened.

"A deaf guy from the projects asked you for help, and you start poking your nose into a multiple homicide?" He drummed his pen on the table. "You're kidding me. This is a joke, right? Please tell me that a bishop asked you to look into the killing, not a dumbass project rat."

"It was Blackie Barboza."

"A project rat." Jenner stood up and kicked his chair. He circled the table and rubbed his ample forehead. He grabbed the chair and sat down again. "I guess it's pretty simple. I'll tell Captain Pruitt that you got the info on the red hood from Teddy Neenan at Neponset Circle."

"That's how I found out, Adam." I got out of my chair and stretched my arms. Every part of my body cracked. "I didn't want to involve Teddy Neenan unless I had to."

"I suppose I can understand that."

"The monument killing," I said. "I know the victim was Father Del Rio."

"Yeah, so?"

"Was he wearing a red hood?"

Adam Jenner said nothing.

"Father Del Rio didn't serve in a Charlestown parish," I said. "So what was he doing in Charlestown?"

Still no response.

"Why was Father Del Rio in Charlestown, Adam?"

"That's police business."

"Where was Father Del Rio's home parish?"

"Look it up in the Catholic Directory," he said. "It's time for you to leave now, Dermot. And stay the hell out of our investigation."

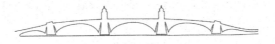

CHAPTER 9

The next morning, I sat in a lawn chair on the flat, rubber roof of my office, enjoying an unexpected January thaw as I smoked a Parodi cigar. The murder of Father Del Rio headlined all the Boston newspapers. One article said that the killer had crucified Father Del Rio on the south wall of the Bunker Hill Monument. The same article went on to say that the killing replicated those of Father Axholm and Father Barboza in most ways, nails through the hands and feet, a wound in the side, a crudely made crown around the head. I was surprised that the police had divulged so many details. The story made no mention of a red hood.

Unlike Fathers Axholm and Barboza, Father Del Rio was not an accused pedophile priest, which seemed to me a significant point. The city's broadsheet printed a profile of Father Del Rio, complete with yearbook pictures, wedding photos, and ordination shots. He had taken his holy vows just eight months before, at the age of sixty.

Del Rio had been married with six kids. Three years after his wife's death, he entered the seminary. I had just finished the piece when Father Dominic joined me topside. He looked east to the harbor and then looked at me. Something was on his mind. I crushed out the cigar in a barbell weight that anchored the table against the wind and stood up from the lawn chair.

"What's with the barbell plate?" he said, and then waved his hand. "Never mind, let's go to my office. We need to talk."

I followed him to the office and sat across from his desk. His eyes danced, but I couldn't read the tune they were dancing to. He leaned back in his chair, appeared to gather his thoughts, and rocked forward.

"I talked to Bishop Downey earlier today," he said. "I told him what you've been working on."

"You talked to him about the priest murders?"

"Yes, I did."

Uh-oh. "Do I still have my job?"

"Don't be ridiculous. Of course you have your job." His dancing eyes stopped. "Bishop Downey wants a favor. He wants you to work full time on the priest murders."

Full time on the priest's murders? Yes!

"I'm not really qualified."

"Oh, for the love of Pete. False humility doesn't become you, Dermot. You're a smart guy, despite the self-effacing cracks. And besides, your so-called lack of qualifications hasn't stopped you thus far. You have been nothing short of a bulldog on this investigation—that's what I've been told." Father Dominic looked right at me. "Do you want to pursue this case or not?"

"I want it."

"Good, because it is my belief, and I shared this belief with Bishop Downey, that your zeal will overcome your lack of experience. I also believe that this fact-finding mission you've started is a mission you were born for. And *that's* the reason I called the bishop." Father Dominic picked up his pipe. "As you can imagine, Bishop Downey's clerics are horrified beyond belief, especially after Father Del Rio's killing."

"What's so special about Del Rio?"

"He wasn't an accused pedophile, yet he was murdered anyway. Bishop Downey assumed the killer was stalking accused priests. Frankly, we all assumed it."

"And now that's changed."

"With the murder of Father Del Rio, it seems anybody wearing a Roman collar is a potential target."

We remained silent for a moment, and in the silence an increasing uncertainty crept into my consciousness. I loved investigating the murders, true, but I had no training or competence in the field. All I had were my instincts.

"I'm not sure what more I can do, Father. I have no authority. And the stuff I dug up so far I got with luck."

"Relax, Dermot. Don't listen to that negative voice inside your head. Nobody expects you to find the killer. Heck, the police can't even find the killer. All we want is your support." He bit the pipe stem and blew air into it. "The Lord provides, but He provides a little more to those who work at their craft, and that's what you do."

I nodded my head. Father Dominic smiled and nodded back.

I said, "I'll need help to do it right."

"Be more specific."

"If you can arrange for it, I'd like to see the files of the murdered priests."

"Hmm, an interesting request." Father Dominic tapped his empty pipe in the clean ashtray. He sniffed the bowl and said, "The files are confidential, but the priests are dead, so I'm pretty sure I can get you access to them. Anything else?"

"If you can get Boston Homicide off my back—that would help. And if you can pay Victor Cepeda to handle the office while I'm working on the case—that would help, too."

"Victor is covered, no problem," he said. "As for the police, that's another matter. Let me see what I can do about the police. What else do you need?"

"That's all for now," I said. "Thanks, Father."

CHAPTER 10

Four days later, after the autopsy and release of Father Del Rio's body, I rode the Red Line to Harvard Square, where I picked up the 72 Huron bus. The trackless trolley hummed out of the tunnel and cruised along Waterhouse Street as quietly as a golf cart. At Cambridge Common the bus merged onto Concord Avenue and at the top of Concord Ave. it turned left onto Huron Avenue. The corner was sharp, but the driver was up to the task, and the poles remained attached to the electrified lines above. I got off at the next stop and walked back to Saint Peter's for Father Del Rio's funeral Mass, arriving in time for the eulogy.

I settled into the last pew. Father Del Rio's family occupied the front pews. The presiding priest recited the prayers of commendation and incensed the coffin. An aroma of perfumed smoke permeated the church. Six dour pallbearers rolled the coffin down the center aisle, and the mourners processed out behind it. One of the mourners was Father Dominic. He saw me and came my way.

"Dermot, it's good to see you here."

"I'm surprised you didn't celebrate the Mass," I said.

"I was covering another Mass for one of the concelebrants. I got here just now," he said. "Did you drive?"

"I took the train."

"Ride with me to the cemetery."

We drove to Mount Auburn Cemetery and joined the grievers around the graveside. Strong winds made the freezing temperatures seem colder. The priest finished the observance, closed his prayer book, and walked away. The undertaker, while breathing on his hands, said there would be a funeral reception at Frazier's Restaurant. He handed out directions to the Concord Avenue locale. We all went back to our cars to warm up. Father Dominic shifted into gear and drove out of the cemetery.

He negotiated two rotaries en route to the restaurant and pulled into the parking lot as if he'd been there before. When we entered Frazier's dining room, Father Dominic left me and sat with fellow priests at a round table. Like a seagull at a Dumpster, I hovered over the hors d'oeuvres table and nibbled finger food. After I wiped out half a platter of chicken salad sandwiches, an older gentleman joined me. I wondered if he thought I was crashing the party.

"Thank you for attending my brother's funeral," he said. His white hair was short and his tinted glasses were thick. "You look familiar, but I don't believe we've met. I'm Pete Del Rio."

We shook hands. I told him I was sorry for his loss.

"My name is Dermot Sparhawk," I said. "I work for Father Dominic at Saint Jude Thaddeus. I run the parish food pantry there."

"That's why you look familiar, the food pantry," he said. "So, you accompanied Father Dominic today."

"No, sir, I didn't accompany him. I ran into him at the funeral Mass." I paused and said, "I had another reason to be there."

"You don't say?" His face seemed to flush. Maybe it was the lighting. "What reason is that?"

"I'm investigating the priest killings."

"Excuse me?" Pete Del Rio stepped back from me. "Why are you investigating the priest killings?"

"The archdiocese asked me for help on the matter."

"Is that so?" His eyelashes fluttered. "The archdiocese asked you for help?"

"I didn't mean to throw you off, Pete." I should have been more mindful of the circumstances. "This is a heartbreaking day for you. I apologize for being insensitive."

He listened and appeared to be processing my words.

"No need to apologize, young man. You meant no harm. It's

just so hard for me to accept that he is gone. The murder is surreal to me. My brother was a good man. And to have his life taken in such a brutal way," his eyes filled up, "it's not right."

"I know it's not right."

Pete dabbed his cheeks with a handkerchief.

"So, you are investigating my brother's murder."

"Yes, sir. I am."

"In that case, I need to tell you something that might be of relevance. Father and I had dinner together on the night of his murder." He pocketed the hankie. "That's why he was in Charlestown. I live in Charlestown, and we dined at my house that evening. And because of that, I feel responsible for his death."

"It's not your fault, Pete. There's a serial killer on the loose."

"Still, I feel culpable." He took a deep breath and exhaled like a weight lifter. "Please find my brother's killer, Dermot. If I can help you in any way, let me know."

Pete Del Rio shook my hand and walked away. I returned to the hors d'oeuvres and sampled the stuffed mushrooms and hotdogs in a blanket. I abstained from the open bar, not wanting to get hammered in front of Father Dominic. I sat on a couch and my eyes glazed over.

Then something got my attention on the other side of the room. An attractive woman with frosted hair was crying. It got so she couldn't contain herself. Several attendees attempted to console her, but their efforts went unheeded. An older priest retrieved her coat and escorted her from the restaurant.

The gathering ended. Father Dominic offered me a ride back to Charlestown. I said yes and we walked out to the parking lot. We chatted in the car as he maneuvered along Storrow Drive, the Grand Prix motorway of Boston.

"The woman with frosted hair looked pretty upset," I said.

"Very upset," he said, without expounding.

We passed Beacon Yards and Boston University and Nickerson Field, formerly Braves Field, home of Warren Spahn and Johnny Sain.

"She was almost despondent," I said. "Who is she?"

"Her name is Helen Lally. She is the receptionist at Saint Peter's. Helen and Father Del Rio were extremely close."

"That much was obvious."

Father Dominic drove past Back Bay and Beacon Hill and Teddy Ebersol Field and veered toward the Museum of Science. He crossed Prison Point Bridge and drove along Austin Street into Charlestown. He stopped on Bunker Hill Street in front of my house.

"Father, I need to ask you another favor."

"I'm listening, Dermot."

"Will you contact Helen Lally for me?"

"I can do that," he said. "For what purpose?"

"I'd like to talk to her about Father Del Rio."

He shifted into park.

"I'll call Helen, but let's give it some time first. As you said yourself, she was despondent."

CHAPTER 11

It took Helen Lally three workdays to return to work at the parish, five if you count the weekend. Father Dominic called her on my behalf, as he said he would, and Helen told Father Dominic that she was willing to talk to me about Father Del Rio. She also told him that she had time to see me that afternoon.

I drove to Saint Peter's in Victor Cepeda's rotting Plymouth Acclaim, which blended in nicely with the rusting guardrails that fringed Storrow Drive. I crossed the Charles River into Cambridge and pulled into Saint Peter's parking lot. I walked into the parish office and found Helen Lally sitting at the reception desk. She looked up, and when she did, a forced smile cracked her sullen face.

"My name is Dermot Sparhawk," I said. "Thanks for seeing me today."

"I've been expecting you." She got up from the desk and walked to a small kitchen area off the office. Speaking louder from inside the galley, she said, "I'm making tea for myself. Would you like a cup of instant coffee?"

"I would love a cup, cream and sugar please."

The kettle whistled. Helen made tea and coffee and returned to her desk, carrying a mug in each hand. She set them on stone coasters. I sipped from the mug and singed my lips, forgetting that instant is hotter than brewed.

"I'm sorry for your loss," I said.

"Father Del Rio's passing is a big loss for everyone in the parish, for everyone in Cambridge, actually." She removed her glasses and wiped the steam from her tea with a Kleenex. "Father

Dominic said you wanted to ask me about Father Del Rio. Well, I'm ready for your questions. Fire away, Mr. Sparhawk."

"Thank you," I said. "Did you notice anything unusual in the week leading up to Father Del Rio's death?"

She put her glasses back on.

"No, Mr. Sparhawk, nothing unusual happened, nothing eventful. It was a typical week in the parish. Funerals, weddings, baptisms, and the like."

"I can relate." Working in a parish myself, I know the typical week. "How often did Father Del Rio meet with his brother Pete?"

"I didn't realize you knew Pete."

"I met him at Frazier's."

"My goodness, Frazier's. What an awful show I put on there." Her face darkened, which made her look younger. "Father and Pete went to dinner every two or three weeks. Most times they went out to restaurants."

"But the night of the murder they dined in Charlestown at Pete's house."

"Yes, they did."

"Why didn't they go out to a restaurant?" I asked. "What prompted the change?"

"It really wasn't much of a change. They occasionally dined in."

Helen seemed to be getting into the question-answer mode, a good sign, and I kept going.

"What happened on the afternoon that Father and Pete met for dinner?" I said. "Can you give me a rough timeline of events?"

"I can certainly try to if you think it might help."

"I'd appreciate it."

"Let's see. I went home at the usual time, around five o'clock. I always walk home from the office. You see, I live on Larch Road, not too far from here." She sat back and tapped a pencil on the desk. "Father Del Rio had already left for Pete's by the time I left for the day."

"Walk me through what happened when you left," I said. "Did you lock doors, turn off lights?"

"Yes, I locked the doors and turned out the lights. I shut down my computer and clicked off the screen." She hesitated. "And then I usually call the answering service."

"Did you forget to call that night?"

"No, I called."

I waited a few seconds.

"Did something happen when you called them? Did someone leave a strange message or—"

"Not a message, no." She tapped the pencil again. Her cheeks reddened. "Just before I called the answering service, I took an incoming call. It was, um—"

She stopped cold in mid-sentence. Her eyes opened wide. I waited for her to start talking again, but she didn't.

"Helen," I said, "the incoming phone call?"

"Oh, yes, the phone call. It was a man. He asked to speak to Father Del Rio, and I told him that Father had gone for the day."

"Did he give you his name?"

"No," she said. "He never gave his name."

"Did he say anything else?"

"He said he was supposed to meet up with Father after work. And I said, 'For dinner at his brother's house in Charlestown?'"

"And what did he say?"

"He said yes." Her speech pattern slowed. "And then he said he'd catch up with Father Del Rio there, in Charlestown."

The caller knew that Father Del Rio would be in Charlestown.

"Thanks, Helen," I said as I stood. "You've been a big help."

"I have to ask you something before you go." Her face was pale. "Did that phone call have anything to do with Father Del Rio's murder?"

"No, of course not," I said, trying to sound convincing. "But the man who called might be able to help me. Does your office phone have caller ID?"

"No, it doesn't."

I put on my coat.

"Thanks for your time, Helen."

She was still pale when I left.

From Saint Peter's I drove back to Charlestown and went into Finbar's Saloon, where I saw Spike Shanahan sitting in the last booth. A newspaper was spread on the table in front of him. His glasses rested low on his nose as he filled in the crossword puzzle. I ordered a couple of draught beers from the barman, Tall Ed, and carried them to Spike's corner. I placed a mug in front of him and joined him in the booth.

"Thanks, pal." Spike resembled NBC news anchorman Brian Williams, with a dash of street salt. As a retired vice president of a major Northeast phone company, Spike was plugged in. He could get information fast, and he was glad to do so if he liked you. "What are we talkin', Dermot?"

"I need a favor."

"That's a shocker." He removed his glasses and drank a gulp. "In my experience, a favor follows a gratis beer. You could call it a chaser. What do you need?"

"I need a phone call traced."

"And the quid pro quo for a gratis beer is a pro bono favor." He chuckled. Spike had encountered no difficulty whatsoever transitioning from corporate stress to retirement bliss. "No problem on the trace."

"I need it fast, Spike."

"I'll probably get it faster if you buy me another cold one. Make it a Molson Canadian. I think better on imported stuff. And give me the phone number you want traced, the time parameters, too."

"I wish I had some e pluribus unum for you."

"I prefer the barter system, Dermot. Somehow it feels more honest. Besides, I'd only spend it on beer anyway."

CHAPTER 12

The following day, I sat in my office nursing a Narragansett lager from a Friendly's Fribble cup. To the casual observer, the foamy head passed for a vanilla shake. I had just refilled the cup from a forty-ounce bottle when the phone rang. On the fourth ring, I picked up the receiver. It felt like a dumbbell.

"Yeah?"

"That's a hell of a way to answer the phone," the man on the line said. "This is Francis Ennis, Suffolk County district attorney. I'd like to speak to Dermot Sparhawk."

"Is this a crank?"

"Crank?" he said. "I received a call from the Archdiocese of Boston. At their directive, I phoned you to set up a meeting today."

"The archdiocese called you?"

I leaned back and the chair tipped over. Stars flashed when my head bounced off the floor. The Narragansett lager soaked my face and shirt. I rolled onto my knees and grabbed the phone.

"What's going on, Sparhawk? Did you fall or something?"

"I dropped the phone." I set the chair upright and sat in it. "Thank you for calling. I didn't expect this."

"Neither did I, but such is the life of a Boston politician." He cleared his throat. It sounded like a snow blower starting. "Stop by my office this afternoon, say five o'clock?"

"Five is fine."

"Better make it six," he said. "I don't want an audience to see you come in."

"Six. See you then."

It was eleven o'clock. I had seven hours to get ready for DA Francis Ennis. An afternoon nap sounded like a good idea, so I locked up the office and went home.

The alarm woke me at five. I showered, dressed, and called a cab, which picked me up at my front door and dropped me off downtown at the Suffolk County Courthouse. I went into the lobby and scanned the directory, found the floor, and waited for an elevator. I rode it express to the DA's level and located his corner office at the end of a carpeted corridor. District Attorney Francis Ennis greeted me in the empty reception area when I came in and led me to his office, closing the door behind us.

I had never seen Ennis in person before, only on TV, and I found the disparity striking. His face showed a mosaic of maroon blotches. Splintering blood vessels bridged his nose and pooled in his cheeks. Patriotic eyes—red and white and blue—ballooned behind thick glasses. His shiny black hair was plastered against his head and parted down the middle. The only white showing above his neck was the scalp line.

We shook hands and Ennis started in.

"This meeting never took place, Sparhawk. Is that understood?" He came closer to me. "It never happened."

"If you say so."

"Everything we discuss here is confidential, as in hush-hush." Ennis walked to a window and looked out on his city. "That said, I'm not sure how much I can help you on the priest murders. I can talk about the case, the evidence, if you will. I can get you access to law enforcement personnel, cops and the like. And I suppose I can clear the way for you to interview witnesses, off the record, of course."

Something didn't make sense.

"Why are you even seeing me at all?" I asked. "You're one of the busiest men in the city."

He turned from the window.

"I'm seeing you because Bishop Downey asked me to," Ennis said with gravel in his voice. "He told me about your role, the archdiocese's liaison on the priest murders."

"Bishop Downey set this up?"

"We're quite close, the bishop and I." Ennis shifted topics. "I was a big fan of yours back in the day."

"You don't say."

"I'm a Triple Eagle, Sparhawk. BC High, BC, BC Law, I graduated top of my class from all three. Plus I'm a BC season ticket holder, football and hockey. Bishop Downey and I watched you play most every Saturday. You were a local legend."

"More like an urban myth." A clean ashtray sat on the corner of his desk. "Okay if I smoke?"

He nodded. I lit a Muriel Magnum and handed one to him. He stripped off the cellophane and fired it up with a desktop lighter. We blew smoke in the air like high school teens in the boys' room.

"What can you tell me about the murders?" I said. "I already know about the red hoods."

"Indeed." He cleared his throat. "We in the DA's office are quite impressed with your investigative acumen, the way you learned about the red hoods." He puffed. "I mean it, nice job."

"Thanks." *I'll hang the bunting when I get home, Francis.* "Beginner's luck."

"Bullshit. I've been hearing things about you," he said. "For an ex-jock, you're fairly urbane."

"Well, I grew up in the city."

"Huh? Ah, yes, indeed." Ennis flicked dead cinders into the ashtray. I inhaled a lungful and blew it to the ceiling. Ennis watched the smoke rise. "The killer immobilized the victims with a Taser gun. They died from the crucifixion wounds, but they were immobilized with a Taser. You now know what we know, which is dick. One thing's for sure, the same killer murdered all three victims. We have us a serial killer."

Because of the unique evidence—the red hood, the Taser, and the crucifixion—it made sense that there was a single killer. I then thought about the grilling I took from Captain Pruitt and Detective Jenner.

"What's Captain Pruitt's story?"

"Ah, Pruitt." He sat behind his desk and invited me to sit with an open hand. "Pruitt is a good cop. Tough and nasty, not what you'd call a people person, but the man is honest. I'm not saying he doesn't take the occasional free cup of coffee, but he's not for sale. Pruitt possesses that rarest of qualities known as integrity." Ennis puffed. "He's a pain in the ass about CPAC. I'm trying to get Boston Homicide to work with the State Police. Oil and water, it has turned into a tug of war and Pruitt is the anchorman." Another puff. "Sometimes I wonder about him."

"Wonder about what?"

"Captain Pruitt is so driven that I wonder if his zeal gets the better of his judgment. We tried a high-profile homicide case a few years ago, gang related, and Pruitt headed the investigative team. He was a sergeant detective back then."

"What happened?"

"The evidence lined up perfectly," Ennis said. "So perfectly I questioned its veracity."

"What do you mean the evidence lined up perfectly?"

"If I had to draw an analogy, I'd compare it to a poker player drawing four cards and ending up with a royal flush. It can happen, but it's not likely."

"I'm not good with analogies. You'd better spell it out."

"Okay, I'll spell it out. I thought the fix was in. But it was a murder case and I knew the son of a bitch was as guilty as Judas, so I let it go. I suppose the evidence could have been legitimate, but it fit together a little too neatly for my liking. Maybe I'm wrong. Maybe Captain Pruitt is simply a brilliant cop."

"And Adam Jenner?"

"Detective Jenner is Pruitt's footman, nothing more," Ennis said. "Let me ask you the same question. You played football with Jenner in college. What was he like?"

"Plenty of ambition, limited ability, but he worked pretty

hard." I twirled the cigar in the ashtray, knocking off the gray. "He just didn't, um, never mind, it's not important."

"Didn't what?"

"It's old stuff, Francis, college stuff. You'd be bored by it."

"Not at all. Tell me."

"I don't know." I leaned back and stared at the ceiling. Things were looking up. The chair didn't tip over this time. "Jenner loved the glory of football. You know, the letter jackets, the publicity shots, the awards banquets. He loved football for its status, not its beauty." Something about Jenner had always bothered me. "He wasn't on the up and up. Jenner maneuvered to get a starting position, but once he got it, he didn't do anything with it, as if getting the job was all that mattered. And, um, I don't know."

"This is interesting. Please continue."

"Jenner was all show, didn't like to mix it up. He growled in the weight room, but whimpered on the field. I'm not saying he was a complete pussy, but he didn't like the physical stuff, the violence."

"And yet he won a starting job."

"It depends how you define win," I said. "The starting tackle got hurt."

"And Jenner was the backup, correct?"

"Correct."

"And he filled in when the starter got hurt and won the job. That fits the definition of winning the job. Look at Lou Gehrig after Wally Pipp went down. Hell, look at me after my predecessor went to Washington."

I wondered how much to say to Ennis. I decided to tell him Jenner's story.

"It was a rainy week in October when the starting offensive tackle got hurt. Adam was a reserve. We were playing Florida State the next Saturday in Tallahassee, a big game for us. Adam Jenner told the player he was competing against that practice had been moved back an hour because of thunder and lightning. The kid showed up late to practice. Jenner got—not won—the starting job."

"Son of a bitch."

"Some of the guys I played with, they didn't care if ten fans were in the stands."

"Which was probably a good thing if you played at BC."

"They just wanted to punch someone in the mouth. Jenner wasn't one of those guys." I was getting angry. "He paraded around campus like Knute Rockne. The real guys, the guys who loved the game, they hung their letter jackets in the closet or gave them to homeless guys. Did you ever notice how many homeless guys wear BC jackets?"

"I assumed they were alumni."

We both laughed. The cigars were still burning. The skies outside had turned dark.

"Tell me about Bishop Downey," I said.

"Bishop Downey is the shrewdest man I have ever met. I say that with admiration, and he is smarter than smart, too. If Downey ran against me, he'd kick my ass." Ennis waited. "He possesses a polished quality, a sophistication, an elegance of sorts, he is—"

"Fairly urbane for a bishop?"

"Urbane, yes." He looked at me more closely. "Touché, Mr. Sparhawk."

"Before we go and canonize him, is there anything else I should know about Bishop Downey?"

Ennis was still looking at me.

"He's ambitious, which is a prerequisite to be bishop. He works with popish fervor to carry out the Church's marching orders. He is a holy man." Ennis deflated into his chair. "You probably don't know this about me, but I wanted to be a priest at one time. Bishop Downey and I were in the same seminary class, the same class as Father Axholm."

"You were in the seminary?"

"Yes, I was."

"Why did you leave?"

"I hated Latin." His head rested on the back of the seat. "Just kidding, I studied Latin for six years and loved it. No, it wasn't

Latin. I saw the future and didn't want it. I wouldn't have made a good priest anyway."

"Why not?"

"The vow of obedience wasn't for me." His eyes stared ahead. "Have you ever noticed the shape of a hierarchy? It narrows as it ascends."

"It's over my head."

"You're not much for talking religion," Ennis said. "I like Bishop Downey, I respect him too, but I wouldn't want to be in his shoes. The man is saddled with huge responsibilities and there's no letup. He carries the yoke of perpetual duty, and the yoke weighs like a millstone." He paused. "Heavy is the head that wears the miter."

"You make it sound horrible."

"Responsibility for others is horrible. I should know, being district attorney. Bishop Downey and I got what we deserved in life, not what we wanted."

If I majored in psychology, I'd probably know what he was talking about.

We relaxed a few minutes. The cigars petered out in the ashtray. The office grew silent. Francis Ennis and Bishop Downey were in the same seminary class as Father Axholm. Interesting.

"I better get going." I stood up and put on my coat. "It's getting late."

"Before you go, there's something I didn't mention. It has to do with the murder of Father Del Rio."

"You said the same killer murdered all three priests."

"I said that and I stand by that, but Father Del Rio was different. Del Rio wasn't a pedophile. Of the three murdered priests, only Del Rio had a clean record."

"How is that a factor?"

"Our investigation had focused on the families of pedophile victims, presumably with an ax to grind. The list was foreboding."

"And now?"

"The list went from foreboding to endless." He sighed. "The

killer could be anybody. Father Del Rio's killing shot our investigation to pieces."

"Copycat?"

"No way possible. The red hoods. The Taser. We held that information back from the public."

"Any tips for me?" I asked. "Is there someone I can talk to about the case?"

"There is someone I had in mind for you. Her name is Kiera McKenzie. Kiera works in the crime lab at Boston Police Headquarters. She is the criminalist processing the physical evidence in the case, rather cases. Very smart, very diligent, very pretty, very Irish. I'll contact Kiera and tell her to expect your call."

"Appreciate it."

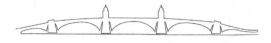

CHAPTER 13

I was resting on the parlor couch the next morning when the phone rang. Spike Shanahan was on the line. He had the information I'd asked for, and he told me to meet him at Finbar's Saloon at three o'clock. I asked if he could tell me over the phone, but he said it had to be in person. It made sense that it had to be in person. How do you buy a man a beer over the phone?

At three o'clock, I walked to Finbar's and found Spike in the same booth as the last time we'd met. I ordered two large Molson Canadians for Spike and a Narragansett draught for me and walked to the booth. Tall Ed delivered the beers on a tray.

"Ice cold Molson Canadian," Spike said. "One mug would have been plenty, Dermot."

"I'm a big spender." I drank a third of the Narragansett and placed the glass on a Haffenreffer coaster. "What are we talkin', Spike?"

"I traced the call." He drank a swig. "It came from a pay phone inside a liquor store on Concord Ave. in Cambridge, a place called Cantabrigian Wine and Liquor, proprietor Hank Bonnet. It's across the street from Saint Peter's."

"Anything unusual about the call?"

"Nothing that I could see. The call lasted two minutes and thirty-three seconds. That's about all I can tell you." He held the mug an inch off the table and swirled the beer inside it. "Pay phones are becoming a thing of the past."

"Thanks for the help, Spike."

"My pleasure. It gave me something to do besides the crossword and Sudoku."

I drank the remains of the 'Gansett and exited the bar.

• • •

I took Storrow Drive to Soldiers Field Road and crossed the Eliot
Bridge into Cambridge, a route I'd been taking a lot lately. I stayed
on Fresh Pond Parkway to Huron Avenue and followed the trackless trolley lines above the street. At Fresh Pond Market, I stopped
for a coffee and a newspaper. At Concord Avenue I turned right,
swung around, and parked in front of Cantabrigian Wine and
Liquor, which sat directly across the street from Saint Peter's
Church.

I walked into the store and saw a man with sparse, white hair
behind the counter ringing the register. His eyes bulged and his face
glowed like a man who drank the profits. A velour Alpine hat with
a feather in the band hung on the coatrack next to him. A surveillance camera screwed to the ceiling pointed at the cash register, but
it almost certainly took in the phone booth, too. I extended my
hand to the man, and he reluctantly shook it.

"I'd like to speak to the owner."

"Are you a salesman?" he asked. "Yeah, sure, you must be a
salesman. Leave your brochure, and I'll look at it later."

"I'm not a salesman, Hank. I'm a guy who needs information."

"How did you know my name was Hank? Are you with the
state commission? Look, I do everything to code around here."

"I'm not with the state commission, whatever that is. My name
is Dermot Sparhawk. I work for the Archdiocese of Boston, and
I'm looking into the murder of Father Del Rio. I was hoping you
might help me out on something."

"You're not with the state?"

"No, sir."

He seemed to relax, but not completely.

"I knew Father Del Rio. He always treated me right. Saint
Peter's buys their communion wine from us."

"I attended Father Del Rio's funeral Mass," I said. "When the
hearse left the church, I saw you on the sidewalk in front of your
store. You were holding your hat over your heart."

"Like I said, Father treated me right."

"He was a good man." I moved ahead. "I'd like to ask you a question, if that's okay with you."

"What question?"

"On the night Father Del Rio was killed, a man called Saint Peter's from that pay phone over there." I pointed to the booth in the corner. "The parish receptionist, a woman named Helen Lally, answered it."

"So?"

"I'd like to find out who made that call."

"What's the difference who made the call? Why do you care?"

"I care because I think the killer made it."

"Are you for real?" Hank marched out from behind the counter. "How can you possibly know that? And how do you know the call was made from my pay phone?"

"I traced it."

"That's illegal."

"I know it's illegal. But I'm not a lawyer and I'm not a cop, so I don't care about legal and illegal. I only care about finding Father's killer."

"Believe me, I hope you find him. But that doesn't mean he used my phone. You can't be certain the killer called from here."

"I'm not certain about anything. I'm looking into a murder, and when you look into a murder, you never know which piece of information might bust the case open," I said. "The call to Saint Peter's came from your pay phone. If I can find out who made the call, it might help me find the killer."

He put his hands on his hips.

"You'd better move along." He went back behind the counter. "No offense, but you ought to leave."

"I didn't mean to insult you." I walked to the door and pushed it open. "You'll be dealing with the State Police from now on."

"What's that supposed to mean?" Hank stared at me. "Is that a threat?"

"It's not a threat. I am simply telling you what will happen. If I leave here with no answers, I will forward what I know to CPAC, the State Police Criminal Protection and Control unit. CPAC is investigating the priest killings, and CPAC will take over. A trooper named Lieutenant Staples will be contacting you."

I stepped outside the door.

"Hold on a second. What's your rush?" He motioned me back in. "I run an honest business here, but that doesn't mean I want the State Police swarming into my store. They might scare away customers. What do you want?"

I looked up at the camera.

"I want to see the surveillance tape."

"That's all?"

"That's all." I gave Hank the date and the time range. "I want to see who made that phone call to Saint Peter's. And there's one more thing."

"What's that?"

"I didn't mean to back you into a corner."

"Nobody backs me into a corner no matter how big he is. I'm helping you because I like Helen Lally. She buys her Cracker Barrel cheese here, and she's a nice lady."

"Pretty, too."

Hank's pinkness brightened.

"Just keep the State Police out of my store, okay?" He told an employee to handle the register and thumbed me to the backroom. After closing the door, he said, "All my security equipment is in here. Alarms, surveillance apparatus, computers, hell, even the thermostat. Everything is automated."

Hank queued up the video and rolled the footage. He found 4:47 p.m. on the night of the murder, the approximate time of the phone call. The video continued and then it happened. A nondescript white man wearing a long-billed fisherman's cap walked into the store, the visor concealing his face.

"Looks like the cap Humphrey Bogart wore in *The African Queen*," Hank said.

"I can't see a thing under the visor." I looked closer. "Not a damn thing."

The man stepped into the phone booth and closed the folding door. The interior light went on, but his face remained concealed. At 4:49 p.m., according to the time stamp on the monitor, the man lifted the receiver and dropped in some coins. Two minutes later he hung up the phone and came out of the booth. At 4:53 p.m., he purchased an item and left the store.

"I wonder what he bought," I said. "Is there a way to find out?"

"Are you kidding, in this day and age?" Hank logged onto another computer and scrolled a few pages. "Here's the transaction, 4:53 p.m. He paid cash for a roll of butter rum Life Savers."

"Too bad he didn't use a credit card."

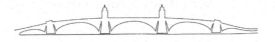

CHAPTER 14

I phoned Boston Police Criminalist Kiera McKenzie, and she told me that Suffolk County DA Francis Ennis had warned her I'd be calling.

"I didn't realize I merited a warning," I said.

"And I didn't realize the Archdiocese of Boston had a crime liaison."

"They do now." I thanked her for taking my call. "I'd like to learn more about the priest murders."

"That makes two of us," she said.

I was sitting in my office at the parish, waiting for Victor Cepeda to come by to relieve me. Outside the windows the skies were blue, but the clouds were building. An AM radio weatherman said something about snow coming in.

"Can you talk to me about them?" I asked. "Are you okay with that?"

"Francis Ennis gave me the okay, so I'd be glad to talk to you, but I'd rather talk to you face-to-face."

My lucky day.

"That's fine with me. Should I drive over to headquarters?"

"No, not here, the walls have ears. Let me think for a second. I know where we can meet." She told me to meet her at Doyle's Cafe in Jamaica Plain. She said that Doyle's would be better than headquarters, even though half the patrons were cops. "I get out of work at six," Kiera said. "I'll see you at Doyle's at seven."

"I'll see you then."

I rode the Orange Line to the Green Street stop in Jamaica Plain and walked to Doyle's from there. I entered the raucous taproom, an Irishman's El Dorado. The place was packed with merry red faces. A cheery hostess with a Galway Bay smile asked me if I wanted a table. I told her I was waiting for someone and made my way to the bar.

I had just finished my third mug of Sam Adams when a tall woman came through the door carrying a briefcase. Long strawberry-blonde hair flowed around her face, a face centered with a straight nose that was sprinkled with plenty of freckles. She scanned the crowd, which was growing louder by the drink. I waved to her, and she came my way. Her trim body and Irish face moved across the room with grace, Our Lady of Knockout.

"Dermot Sparhawk?"

"Thanks for meeting me, Kiera." I got off the stool. "Table?"

"A table sounds good."

I got the attention of the hostess, who escorted us to the middle dining room and seated us in a booth that had a picture of Mayor John B. Hynes overlooking it. Kiera and I talked for a few minutes about the upcoming storm, about the Celtics and Bruins, and then she sat up straighter, ready for action.

"Tell me, Dermot, what is your interest in the priest killings?" She had an alert manner and intelligent eyes, which crinkled at the corners when she smiled. "You work for the Church, so I guess that explains your interest in the dead priests."

She had a blunt way of putting things, which I found appealing.

"Working for the archdiocese is part of it." I then told her about Blackie Barboza's visit to my office. "Blackie convinced me to look into his brother's murder. That's how I first got involved. The archdiocese heard what I was doing and assigned me as their liaison to the killings."

"Interesting," Kiera said.

"I started looking into the murder of Father Netto Barboza and loved it. I don't know why exactly, but investigating the Barboza killing felt good."

"You don't have to convince me it felt good. I'm a forensic scientist."

A waitress came to the booth. We ordered a couple of beers and a pizza. After she left, Kiera took a folder from her briefcase and opened it on the table.

"I have the notes on all the murdered priests. Tell me what you want to know."

Right to the point.

"Was Father Del Rio wearing a red hood?"

She didn't need to refer to the material.

"Yes, Father Del Rio was wearing a red hood. All three priests were wearing red hoods."

"Were all three priests killed in the same way?"

"Yes, they were. The cause of death for all three was a stab wound to the heart. The killer shoved a metal rod up through the ribs and into their hearts. With Axholm and Barboza, the killer used rebar. With Del Rio, he used a tire iron."

"Del Rio's murder was a little different."

"The killer disabled the priests with a Taser blast to the groin. After disabling them, he killed them with a rod." She flipped a page. "The killer nailed their hands and feet with masonry nails, postmortem. The nails were made of brass and spiral fluted."

"The nails matched precisely?"

"Yes, they matched precisely. The killer wrapped a metal wreath around each of their heads, similar to a crown of thorns. With Axholm and Barboza, the killer used barbed wire. With Del Rio, a bicycle chain."

"Again, Del Rio is slightly different."

"Here's another difference, Father Del Rio was crucified upside down," she said. "The killer pulled a Saint Peter on him."

"That's a big difference."

"I agree."

"Could there be two killers? Could it be that a second man crucified Father Del Rio?"

"Despite the minor differences, I don't think so. The Taser jolt to the groin, the rod to the heart, the crucifixion wounds, the masonry nails. All the physical evidence lines up perfectly. I'll grant you that the tire iron and bicycle chain aren't exact matches, but the wounds are." She closed the folder. "I'm not a person who believes in conspiracies, Dermot, but if I were such a person, there is one piece of evidence that convinces me beyond all doubt that the same killer murdered all three victims."

"What evidence is that?"

"The red hoods," she said. "The red hoods are identical. All of them were manufactured by Resnick Clothiers."

"Never heard of them."

"Resnick Clothiers was a small, family company in the South End, well before gentrification. They went out of business in the seventies when Ed Resnick retired. In my opinion, the hoods could not have been duplicated. They were stamped with a distinct diamond pattern. They were sewn of Assam silk. The company tags were made of twilled cotton and had a unique logo dyed into them. And the tie strings are no longer available."

"But it's possible that someone duplicated them."

"I argue no to that premise," she said, as hair fell into her eyes. She pushed the strawberry strands back behind her ear. "The ritualistic mark, the killer's calling card, if you will, is the red hood. And the red hoods are identical."

"A clothing expert might be able to copy them."

"Theoretically, yes—if the clothing expert had access to a hood to use as a model, which he didn't. And if he could age the Assam silk thirty years to match the fading, and if he could replicate the stamping pattern and the twilled tags and the company logo and the tie strings," she said. "Dermot, the same killer murdered all three priests."

"You must be right."

The food and drinks arrived on the same tray. We ate and drank and the conversation turned to more casual topics. Kiera, in no doubt a preemptive measure, mentioned that she had a serious boyfriend. I, in a feeble attempt at humor, told her to congratulate him for me. Kiera laughed. We continued to talk, and the time flew by. She excused herself to go to the ladies' room.

While she was gone, the busboy came to clear the table. Kiera's mug had a few swallows left on the bottom. I chugged it empty before the busboy dropped it in the bucket. Kiera returned to a clean table, but didn't sit. She put on her coat instead.

"If you have any more questions, call me." She handed me her card: Kiera McKenzie, Boston Police Department, Senior Criminalist. "Or e-mail me. I'll be glad to help with whatever you need."

"Thanks."

"Is there anything else you'd like to ask before I leave?"

Yeah. Do you have a twin sister?

"How about I walk you to your car," I said.

We walked out of Doyle's Cafe, and the well-oiled necks of the well-oiled patrons swiveled to glimpse Kiera striding by. It was nice to pretend I was with her. We were standing in the parking lot now. As she was opening the car door, something came to me.

"Is it unusual for a Homicide captain to be on the street?"

"I don't understand your question."

"Captain Pruitt is hands-on in the investigation," I said. "Is it customary for a police captain to be hands-on in a case?"

She tossed the briefcase onto the passenger seat and turned back to me.

"Homicide teams are comprised of three detectives, with a sergeant detective leading the team." She paused a moment. "A police captain in any department, including Homicide, is mostly an administrative job. He oversees the entire squad."

"And yet Pruitt is actively investigating." I smelled her faint perfume and almost blanked on my next point. "Captain Pruitt is hip deep in the details of the case."

"So I've heard." She got into her car. "Maybe he's involved because it's such a high-profile case. In big cases, it's all hands on deck."

"That must be it."

"Or maybe it's something else," she said. "I'll see what I can find out."

● ● ●

I went to the office the next day and thought about the murders. Blackie Barboza had hired me to find his brother's killer, and now I needed to talk to him. I was about to do just that when someone knocked on the metal door. Gladys Foley stumbled in, sniffling on her coat sleeve. She had a bruised eye and a scraped nose. She jumped when the door slammed behind her.

"Friggin' clanging," she said, "reminds me of MCI Framingham."

MCI Framingham, the Massachusetts Correctional Institution for women. This news surprised me. Gladys had passed a criminal background check.

"Framingham must have been difficult for you."

"Huh? Oh, it wasn't me. It was my sister. Short time, she only had to do a six-month bit." Gladys rubbed her eyes. "I got a confidential matter. You alone?"

"We're alone."

"I'm a wreck on account of it. I hadda double up on my nervous pills."

"Tell me what's going on, Gladys."

"You know the van, the one Packy lets us use for errands?"

"Of course." I had "hired" Gladys to run small deliveries in Packy's van. "Do you need gas money?"

"I drove through a red light, missed the brake, and hit the exhilarator."

"Exhilarator?"

"I slammed into a parked car."

"You hit a car?"

"I lost my glasses last week. I'm saying hi to people I don't even like." She fished out a Chesterfield. "Don't worry, no witnesses."

"It was an accident. Don't worry about witnesses, and I'll talk to Packy about the van."

"Thanks." A siren chirped in the projects, and Gladys dropped the cigarette. "I almost forgot to tell you. The car I hit—it was a police cruiser." She peeked out the window. "After I hit it, I screwed down Monument Street. Nobody saw nothin'."

"You hit a police car?" I didn't want to unnerve her. "Is that how you bruised your eye?"

"Nah, I tripped. I lost my um, my um . . ."

"Balance?"

"No, equilibrium."

It sounded like a scene from *Get Smart*.

"Was the van damaged?"

"Thing's a tank, just a small dent. Well, pretty small. But the police cruiser, that's another matter. The cruiser got crushed." She sucked her teeth back in. "The stack is decked against me, Dermot. I can't do nothin' right."

"Don't worry about the van, Gladys. I'll take care of it."

"You're the only friend I got on this lousy planet."

"People like you."

"Right, they call me all the time. I can't barely keep up with all my friends." She dropped the Chesterfield again. "Wanna know something? You inspirate me."

Inspirate? "Thanks, Gladys."

"One other thing, do I still get paid for today?"

I walked to Blackie Barboza's apartment and knocked on his door. Then it hit me, Blackie can't hear. I tried his neighbor's apartment. She cracked the door open an inch and looked at me. Her cleavage cracked opened an inch, too—like an ATM deposit slot.

"Ah, Padre, Padre. *Dar la bienvenida a Padre*. Welcome, welcome."

We recognized each other from the food pantry. She unlatched the chain and let me in. I tried to explain that I wanted to talk to Blackie. I kept pointing to his apartment. She kept bumping me with her breasts. I was beginning to like it, but I could feel a lawsuit coming against the parish, so I said adios and left.

When I stepped into the hall, Blackie Barboza was standing there and he gave me the thumbs-up. We went into his apartment. He picked up a pencil and wrote on a shopping bag, *Bonita is pissa. How much did she charge you?*

"What are you talking about?"

Blackie wrote, *For sex.*

"I didn't have sex with her." Why was I explaining myself? "I came here to see you, not her. I need to talk to you about Father Barboza."

Blackie wrote, *His name was Netto.*

"Fine, Netto." I thought back to my conversations with Suffolk County DA Francis Ennis and BPD criminalist Kiera McKenzie. "A serial killer crucified your brother. The same man who killed Father Axholm and Father Del Rio also killed Netto. Netto is somehow connected to Axholm and Del Rio."

Blackie scratched, *Maybe they were randomly picked.*

"Not when you look at the physical evidence. The evidence links the three dead priests to the same killer." Francis Ennis had talked about the Del Rio murder, saying it undercut the DA's motivation theory. The theory being that a relative or friend of a pedophile victim was taking revenge. "The DA believes that the dead priests are not connected by the sex scandal."

He scrawled, *If they aren't connected by the sex scandal, maybe a different killer crucified Netto.*

"The DA insists on one killer, a serial killer." Kiera insisted on a serial killer, too. "The evidence is conclusive, Blackie. There's a single killer."

He wrote, *Are you making progress finding him?*

"A little," I said. A couple of kids ran across the flat roof and landed on the fire escape. I'd almost forgotten the sound. "I need some history on Netto. Parishes, friends, hobbies, habits, anything you can think of."

Blackie filled half a page. The last thing he wrote was *Netto's favorite parish was Saint Stephen's in Billerica.*

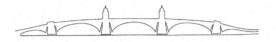

CHAPTER 15

I borrowed Packy's dented van, drove north to Billerica, and found Saint Stephen's Church and school in a quiet neighborhood enclave. It must have been recess, because the kids were tearing around the playground. The girls wore plaid skirts. The boys wore navy pants and white shirts. They looked like *Happy Days* gone Catholic.

The parish offices sat behind the rectory. I parked in a spot marked for visitors and went in. A receptionist with coiffed gray hair greeted me with a crooked smile. I told her my name and why I was there.

She said, "Could you please say that again?"

"I'm hoping to find Father Barboza's killer and to restore Father's good name. I am working on behalf of his family."

"You think he was innocent?" She folded her hands on a green desk blotter. "Finally, someone is sticking up for Father Barboza. The accusations against him are completely false, of that I am certain. My husband and I entertained Father in our home on many occasions. We have four children, you know."

"Thanks for taking the time, Ms. — "

"Annie Mannion," she said. "I'm originally from Dorchester, Saint Gregory's Parish."

"Lower Mills," I said. People love their Dorchester roots. "My grandmother was an O'Hanlon from Pope's Hill, but I grew up in Charlestown."

"The moment I saw you I said to myself, he's a Townie. You have that Charlestown look." She leaned forward. "Did you play hockey?"

"I didn't play hockey and I don't rob banks." We both laughed. "The charges against Father Barboza, what exactly happened?" I asked.

"No one is quite sure. You know how it works, the archdiocese sealed the agreement." Annie slid a glass paperweight onto the green blotter. "Mothers have a sense for danger when it comes to their children."

"And?"

"I never sensed danger with Father Barboza. He was a wholesome man. Father Barboza was fifty years old when he was accused. He had no criminal history. By fifty, usually there's a file on those creeps. I don't know how better to put it. He didn't seem the type."

"They never do."

Nobody who knew Father Netto Barboza thought he was the type. Blackie didn't think so, Father Dominic didn't think so, and now Annie Mannion didn't think so. I needed to find someone who knew him more intimately, someone who knew his secrets.

"Did Father Barboza have a confidant?"

"A confidant?" She touched the paperweight again and kept her fingers on it. "I'm not sure whether to tell you privileged information."

"I understand your caution, but I'm trying to catch Father Barboza's killer. The more I know, the faster I'll get to the truth. I'm on Father's side, Annie."

"I believe you are." Annie set aside the paperweight and thumbed through her Rolodex. She removed a card and handed it to me. "Father's confidant, her name is Sister Cynthia Doherty. She works at Saint Anthony Shrine in Boston. Father Barboza met with her weekly."

"Thank you, Annie."

I went back to my car and called the shrine and asked for Sister Cynthia.

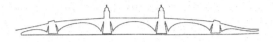

CHAPTER 16

I parked on Otis Street behind Saint Anthony Shrine and went in through the side chapel, lit a votive candle for Our Lady of Guadalupe, and rode the elevator to the fourth floor. Sister Cynthia opened her office door when I knocked. She wore a pleated, brown skirt and a pressed white shirt. Her hair was curly and brown. A wooden Franciscan cross hung around her neck. She had a warm smile.

"Dermot Sparhawk?" she asked.

"Yes, Sister." I followed her into the office. "Thank you for seeing me on such short notice."

"You are most welcome. Please sit."

We sat in upholstered armchairs that faced each other. The room had a cozy feel to it, with carpeting and draperies. Sprays of autumn strawflower and flickering wax candles added to the serene atmosphere. Sister Cynthia spoke first.

"I gathered from our phone conversation that you want to talk about Father Netto Barboza."

"I'm looking into his death, yes. I work for a parish in Charlestown, but I've been assigned a temporary task by the archdiocese. They asked me to look into the priest murders, and right now I'm looking into the murder of Father Barboza."

"And you are doing this task at the behest of Bishop Downey?"

"Yes, Sister."

"That speaks well of you, Dermot. It affords you a certain gravitas. Bishop Downey is a man of good judgment." She kneaded a string of worn rosary beads. "It is my custom to begin each meeting with centering prayer. Is that agreeable to you?"

I told her it was fine with me.

"I'm glad to hear it." She opened a Bible. "Luke eleven-nine: Ask and you shall receive. Seek and you shall find. Knock and it will be opened. It's a beautiful passage, isn't it? Contemplate these words."

She closed her eyes and drew a breath. I wasn't sure what to do, so I did the same. We remained this way for a while, eyes closed, breathing deep. During this time of contemplative prayer, I focused on one plea. I beg of you, Lord, don't let me fall asleep.

"Open your eyes now, Dermot." She placed the Bible in the bookcase. "How do you feel?"

"Good." I looked around the room. "I liked it."

"Whenever two or more are gathered in His name," she said. "Centering prayer is powerful. I teach it to all my clients. It helps them deal with the stresses of daily life."

"I can understand why," I said, and then changed topics before the conversation took us to Vespers. "I'd like to ask you about Father Barboza."

"I'm listening, Dermot."

I told her about Blackie Barboza's visit to my office. I told that Blackie insisted his brother Netto had been falsely accused.

"I need to know more about Father Barboza," I said.

Sister Cynthia walked to the window and adjusted the drapes. She shook loose the wrinkles from her brown skirt and sat again.

"Netto's affairs are Netto's affairs," she said. "Our meetings were confidential."

"I respect that, but he's dead, and I want to know why he's dead. I don't want to hurt him. I want to help him."

She picked up the beads again.

"I want to believe you."

"What harm can it do to talk about him at this point? His reputation is ruined and his family is reeling." I leaned in closer. "I now believe that Father Barboza was falsely accused. And if he was falsely accused, I will work to restore his standing. But I can't do it alone, Sister, will you help me?"

She kissed the cross.

"You're a persuasive man, Dermot Sparhawk. I am not easily swayed."

"Then you'll help me?"

"Yes, I will help you," she said, and put the beads in her pocket. "I'd been seeing Netto for a little more than a year. We initially met to discuss spiritual matters. I was serving as his spiritual advisor. Then our meetings shifted direction."

"Which direction was that?"

"Netto was struggling to square his feelings with his convictions." She bowed her head. "We all wrestle with this, of course, aligning our behaviors with our beliefs—but for Netto the incongruity nearly broke him." She raised her face. "Netto fell in love with a woman he was counseling, one of his parishioners. Strangely enough, he was counseling the woman to save her marriage."

"Which parish was she from?"

"He never mentioned the parish. During our time together, Netto was transferred from Saint Stephen's in Billerica to Saint Andrew's in Braintree," she said. "I sensed the woman lived in Billerica. He never said so explicitly, but that's what I sensed."

"Makes you wonder about celibacy, doesn't it?" As soon as I said it I regretted it. "Sorry, Sister."

"Not at all," she said. "I struggle with celibacy from time to time. Sex is of God, which means sex is sacred. A healthy sexuality is central to every sensible person, including celibate nuns."

I never heard a nun say *sex* before. "Did Netto mention the woman's name?"

"He referred to her only as 'my client.' He never humanized her with a name," she said. "She was having an extramarital affair."

"And Father Barboza fell in love with her while he was guiding her away from infidelity." I looked at my watch. Sister said she'd give me an hour. "Would Father Barboza help himself along the way?"

"Sexually, you mean?"

"Yes, sexually."

"The relationship between them had more to do with love than sex, and the love was mutual. The woman loved Netto, too. The affair was highly charged."

"Highly charged, but platonic?"

"Platonic is too sterile a word. Love precludes platonic." She folded her hands on her lap. "Netto verged on a breakdown toward the end of our sessions. He couldn't reconcile his love for the woman with his love for the priesthood."

"Was he transferred because of the love affair, even though it wasn't sexual?"

"I don't think so," she said. "Nobody knew about the affair except the two of them. And me, of course."

"Yet he was assigned to another parish," I said. "Maybe Father Barboza initiated the transfer. Maybe he thought a transfer would break the woman's spell on him. Why are you laughing?"

"You said break the woman's spell. It's always the woman's fault, isn't it? Starting with Adam and Eve, Eve was the baddie." She continued to laugh. "Adam didn't help himself to the goodies. Eve tempted a hapless man."

"Sorry, Sister."

"You didn't offend me."

"Father Barboza falls in love, and then he gets tagged a pedophile."

"The accusations destroyed him." Her smile was gone. "Netto was reeling, to use your word."

"He must have been," I said. "When you said Netto verged on a breakdown, you meant a nervous breakdown."

"Yes, that's what I meant."

"Is there anything else you can think of that might help?" I asked.

She said there was nothing more she could think of, except that she was certain beyond doubt that Father Barboza never touched a child. She told me to keep that in mind when things got tough, that Father Netto Barboza was an innocent man.

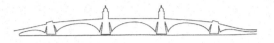

CHAPTER 17

Packy stood behind the cash register, flinging a scratch ticket into the trash. He flipped a coin on the countertop and rubbed his head.

"Lucky penny, my ass. I haven't hit a winner all week."

I placed a bag of potato chips and a bottle of Coke on the counter, took a pencil from Packy's shirt pocket, and filled out a lottery ticket for Mega Millions. He printed the ticket and handed it to me.

"Two hundred million," he said. "Good luck."

"Thanks." I slid the ticket into my pocket. "You must have seen the van."

"Yeah, I saw the van. Don't worry about it." Packy massaged his eyes. "The van gets banged around in the projects. I don't plan on fixing it."

"There's a little more to it," I said. "The dent resulted from a collision, and the collision involved a parked car."

"A parked car?" He started to reach for another scratch ticket, then balked. "I wish you had told me this earlier. That'll increase my premium. Maybe not, it wasn't a moving violation, not really. But there's the deductible, I have a five-hundred-dollar deductible."

"There won't be a deductible. The accident wasn't reported." I walked to the snack stand and grabbed a bag of beer nuts. "It was a hit-and-run. The driver works for me. She panicked and took off."

"She took off? Why did she take off if it was an accident?"

"She hit a police car."

"A police car?" He placed both palms on his head. "She hit a police car and took off?"

"She hit the accelerator instead of the brake." I opened the beer nuts and dumped the contents into my mouth. "The cop wasn't in the cruiser. She drove off and hid in the church parking lot. No witnesses."

"Jesus in heaven." Packy glanced around the store. "This isn't good, Dermot."

"Did the cops talk to you?"

"Not yet, but they must know it was my van."

"Maybe not, maybe we got away with it."

"We?" He tore off a scratch ticket and retrieved his unlucky coin. "Was it that lunatic Gladys Foley? She runs around the projects like she's the mayor or something."

"I say let sleeping dogs lie. The cops don't seem to care," I said. "It's the projects, Packy. Stuff like this happens."

"Not reporting an accident isn't exactly honest," he said, "and you work for the church. What does Father Dominic think?"

"I didn't tell him."

"It had to be Gladys Foley."

"An incident like this could send her over the edge." I tossed the empty beer nuts bag into the trash can and put a twenty on the counter. "It could, you know."

"I don't know what to do." Packy scratched another number and blew away the residue, shook his head, and scratched again. "I guess nobody got hurt. And nobody had to pay money out of his own pocket. I suppose we could let sleeping dogs lie. But from now on nobody but you drives the van. Keep that whacko Gladys Foley away from it."

"Thanks, Packy."

CHAPTER 18

I took a cab to the chancery where the archdiocese housed their personnel files. Bishop Downey had alerted the receptionist that I'd be coming, and she escorted me to an empty office when I got there. A few minutes later, she returned with two manila folders that overflowed with yellowing pages of handwritten notes, dot-matrix printouts, and certified documents, all topped with a layer of dust.

"Nice filing system," I said.

"Will you need anything else?"

"Got Pledge?"

I waited for her roar of laughter. She didn't even smile.

I started with Father Axholm's folder. Axholm had been molesting children for twenty years with the archdiocese's tacit consent. Whatever Bishop Downey's intentions, his strategy of reassigning Axholm to unsuspecting parishes resulted in the same horror each time. Bishop Downey handled each of Father Axholm's crimes in the same manner. He never reported the abuse to the police, he paid money to the victims for damages, and he transferred Father Axholm to fresh hunting grounds.

When Bishop Downey finally ordered him to treatment, he provided the therapist with sketchy details of Axholm's actions. When the therapist discovered he'd been duped, he lashed out, saying the bishop's misleading statements resulted in the wrong treatment, thus sending a sexual predator back into society, back to priestly duties.

My stomach roiled with each document I read. I kept telling myself, you're here to find a killer, not to judge a child molester, not to judge a bishop's cover-up. But as I read the victims' pleas, my objectivity vanished. I finished Axholm's folder and wanted more than ever to catch his killer, so I could shake his hand. Father Barboza's folder was next, but I couldn't read any more. On the way out of the building, I thanked the receptionist.

"Can I help you with anything else today?" she said.

"Is Downey in?"

"Bishop Downey?" Her throat muscles tightened. "Bishop Downey won't be in until later."

"Tell him I need to speak to him."

The frigid air slapped my face with the kind of cold that usually cleared my head, but today it added oxygen to my rage. I crossed Commonwealth Avenue to Boston College and went inside Saint Mary's Chapel, where I prayed for peace of mind. The prayers went unanswered.

Down on the lower campus the Alumni Stadium gates were opened. I walked onto the football field. No chills went up my spine. Nobody cheered when I came out of the tunnel. No referees awaited me at midfield for the coin toss. Not a single coach signaled in a defensive play. The top façade of the stadium had my retired uniform number painted on it. The number still glimmered. Next to the number was a rendering of the Butkus Trophy, for the nation's top collegiate linebacker.

I exited the field and found myself on Beacon Street. I walked east toward Cleveland Circle, walking alongside a beautiful reservoir where beautiful coeds jogged without sweating or smelling or tearing up knees. They jogged with fluidity, not hostility. They probably never fantasized of hitting a man so hard that his mouth guard flew out with his teeth still in it. At Chestnut Hill Avenue I came to a watering hole on a side street. I entered the room and ordered a drink.

CHAPTER 19

I awoke on a cot with no mattress, next to a toilet with no seat. Vertical gray bars told me all I needed to know. A court officer came into the holding area and told me I had a visitor.

"Wanna see him, tough guy?" he asked.

I said yes. The officer handed me a plastic bag with my belongings in it and took me to the visitor's area where Father Dominic was waiting. He forced a smile when he saw me come in. I sat across the table from him.

"What did I do?" I asked.

"You don't remember?"

"Not a thing."

"You verbally attacked Bishop Downey at the chancery." Father Dominic frowned. "You stormed past the receptionist and flung open his door."

"I don't remember any of this."

"Bishop Downey is fine, thank God." Father Dominic drew a breath. "The police arrested you. Bishop Downey didn't call the police. The receptionist did. The bishop is refusing to press charges. He doesn't want the publicity. The police detained you in protective custody."

"Bishop Downey botched Father Axholm's case," I said. "I don't understand it. Why did he let Father Axholm get away with molesting all those kids?"

"Take it easy, Dermot."

"You don't understand, Father. I read the victims' letters. I read the victims' pain." The pounding in my head intensified. "Bishop

Downey should have stopped Axholm. He knew Axholm. They went to the seminary in the same class."

"Listen to me closely." Father Dominic slid closer. "Attacking a bishop is bad business, especially if you're employed by the Catholic Church—a job I retained for you by the way."

"I appreciate it, Father. I really do—"

"Quiet, Dermot." He squeezed my arm. "You were in a blackout, so I suppose you could make the case that you didn't mean the bishop any harm. But what if you attacked him physically instead of verbally? What if you had injured him? Blackout or not, you'd be going to prison, and you'd be dogged with a criminal record for the rest of your life."

"I guess you're right," I said.

"Do you hear what I'm saying? Are you listening to me? What happened yesterday had nothing to do with Bishop Downey or Father Axholm or cover-ups or reassignments. It had to do with your drinking." He let go of my arm. "You look like hell. Let's get out of here."

"What about bail?"

"Protective custody," he said. "No bail was tendered."

We drove back to Charlestown and got there in time to hear the bells ring out the midday Angelus. AA called it the curfew bell, signaling the start of the noon meeting, even though half the members came in late. Father Dominic shifted into park.

"Let's go to the meeting," he said.

"You're not a drunk."

"I know I'm not."

After the meeting Father Dominic dropped me at home. I thought about visiting Aunt Agnes upstairs and then thought better of it, since I was still half smashed. I'd talk to her later when I felt better. I rested my head. The softness of the parlor couch embraced me, and I went off to sleep.

My eyes jolted open. A young black man was standing over me, and he was shaking my shoulder. I jumped to my feet, but when I saw that he was wearing a paramedic's uniform, I calmed down.

"What's wrong?" I said. "How'd you get in here?"

"The missus upstairs called 911."

"Aunt Agnes? Is she okay?"

"No, sir, she's not okay. The poor lady had a heart attack."

"Aunt Agnes had a heart attack?"

"Yes, sir. I'm sorry, she didn't make it." He stared at the wall behind me. "We used the defibrillator on her, but couldn't restore her heartbeat."

"She's dead?" I couldn't believe it. "When did she call?"

"Let's see." He checked his clipboard. "She called at four eighteen. We got here, let's see, we got here at four thirty. Twelve minutes."

"Jesus." The light blinked on the answering machine. Had I missed her call for help? If I wasn't sick with a hangover, I could have saved her life. "She's gone?"

"She's gone." He tucked the clipboard under his arm. "Nothing you could've done, sir."

Two days later Aunt Agnes was waked three blocks from the house. I dry-cleaned my suit, laundered my dress shirt, buffed my wingtips, and listened to the radio playing Tommy James and the Shondells' "Mony, Mony," a song my father loved when he returned from Vietnam.

I walked up to the funeral parlor, my knee stiff, and got ready for the visitors. A long line of Townies came to pay their respects. They left spiritual bouquets and sympathy cards. Father Dominic entered the parlor and knelt at the casket and blessed himself. He rose from the kneeler, hugged me, and offered his condolences. Then he took me to the side of the room, away from the crowd.

"Bishop Downey still wants you on board," he said.

"Are you sure about that? I thought he'd fire me after the stunt I pulled. He still wants me on the case?"

"*Want* is the wrong word, Dermot. *Need* is more appropriate.

Bishop Downey is scared witless." Father Dominic then whispered, "He took to wearing a bulletproof vest."

"He should be wearing a hockey cup."

"What was that?"

"Nothing." I walked Father Dominic to the door. "I'll call you soon."

"Do that," he said. "And think about getting to more AA meetings. I'm praying for you, Dermot. We've lost too many young people in this town to addiction. I don't want to lose you, too."

I sat for the first time all evening. The undertaker steered the lingerers toward the exit. He had nearly cleared the room when a tall straggler with a gray ponytail strolled into the parlor. He wore a navy-blue suit, a white shirt, and a string tie. The tie was fastened at the neck with a silver and turquoise clasp. His cowboy boots were worn but polished. He stopped at the casket and blessed himself, but he didn't kneel. Then he walked toward me. The roll of his stride, the sway of his shoulders, there was something familiar in it. He stood in front of me.

"My name is Glooscap." He talked like a ventriloquist, barely moving his lips. His twisted ponytail served as a natural facelift, pulling his bronzed skin tight. He cleared his throat, hesitated, and then cleared it again. "I realize that this is a strange time to introduce myself. I am your uncle."

"My uncle?"

"Your father was a Sagamaw, a chief," he said. "I am his half-brother."

Did he say my father's brother? I must have heard him wrong.

"What did you say?"

"I apologize for dropping this bombshell on you at Agnes's wake." He waited a second and said, "I am Chief's half-brother."

I did hear him right.

"I never knew he had a brother." The funeral parlor closed in on me. "And I thought Chief was just a nickname."

"He was a tribal chief. Your father's mother was my mother, too. We had different fathers, but we treated each other as full-blooded brothers." He reached inside his jacket pocket and removed a picture. "Our mother, your grandmother."

"My father never told me about my grandmother." I studied the cracked photograph. "He never told me anything Indian."

"Your father and I are Micmac Indians."

"I knew he was a Micmac."

"We came to Boston over forty years ago from Antigonish, Nova Scotia. You can keep the picture." He handed me a piece of paper. "My phone number. Call me if you want to, and I will introduce you to my son, your cousin." He pulled out a small chain with a shriveled piece of rubber attached to it and gave it to me. "Your father's key chain. He would want you to have it."

"What's the rubber thing?"

"A Vietcong's ear."

"An ear?" I pinched the chain with my fingertips and let the severed lobe dangle low. "Thanks, I think."

"Chief fought in the Battle of Hill eight hundred eighty-one, proudly attached to the Twenty-sixth Marines. They awarded him the Silver Star."

"I heard he was a war hero. He never talked about it. I think my mother told me, or maybe my Irish grandmother."

I sucked it up and held the ear in my hand. Most fathers give their sons a rabbit's foot. I get a human's ear. Where did the undertaker keep the hand sanitizer?

"How'd you know about me?" I said. "Tonight, I mean."

"I scan the death notices daily." Glooscap paused. "You were listed as family in the obituary. The name Sparhawk flew off the page at me. But I knew Agnes, and she was a fine lady. I am sorry for your loss."

We talked a while longer. The whole conversation seemed dreamlike to me. And just like that, Glooscap said goodbye and left.

A Micmac uncle, petrified ear, Silver Star, tribal chief. On the way home I stopped at Packy's and played the daily number: 881.

CHAPTER 20

Three dead priests, all wearing red hoods, all jolted in the groin with a Taser. Fathers Axholm, Barboza, Del Rio, I wondered who'd get it next. The common thread of pedophilia got sacked with the murder of Father Del Rio, who had been a priest for only six months. Before that he worked as a tenured professor at the Harvard Divinity School. He had been married with six kids. His wife died of natural causes, if cancer is a natural cause. Nothing in his personal life spurred suspicion of any kind. Father Del Rio loved his church and yearned to serve it. He didn't fit the pedophile profile.

Father Netto Barboza had no history of sexual abuse until recently, but those who knew him questioned the charges. Father Dominic thought Barboza might struggle with women, not kids. Father Dominic should know. He was Barboza's roommate in the seminary. Annie Mannion, the receptionist at Saint Stephen's, claimed that Father Barboza wasn't the type to touch children. Sister Cynthia Doherty at Saint Anthony Shrine talked about Father Barboza's love affair with a married woman, insisting the affair wasn't sexual. She also insisted that Father Barboza wasn't a pederast.

But Father Axholm's pathology surprised no one. Everyone knew he was a sick bastard. Bishop Downey knew it better than most. He reassigned Father Axholm each time he got caught. Father Axholm's therapist figured it out too, despite Bishop Downey's smokescreen.

Father Del Rio changed everything. The killer as avenging angel for pedophile victims got torpedoed with the murder of Father Del Rio. It wasn't about child molesters. There had to be another connection. Alphabetical order was out. Scores of priests between Barboza and Del Rio were skipped. I needed another look at the personnel files. I needed to finish the job at the chancery, a job I had left half done.

I rode the Green Line to BC and crossed Commonwealth Avenue to the chancery. The same receptionist that had greeted me on my first visit, greeted me again, but this time the smile was gone.

"Bishop Downey said you'd be back," she said, "which shows his merciful nature."

I muttered, "He's quite a guy."

"Excuse me?"

"I'll need those files again."

"Bishop Downey already informed me of that. You may use the same office as before, and I shall deliver the files momentarily."

"Ma'am," I said. "I'm sorry about the other day."

"I'll meet you in the office."

She delivered the folders without a word and left the room without a goodbye, and I didn't blame her. I focused on Father Barboza's file this time, beginning with the top sheet and sifting through the stack. I noted the names and addresses of the alleged pedophile victims, both of whom lived in Billerica and attended Saint Stephen's School. The parish receptionist Annie Mannion should have known the victims lived in the parish. Maybe not, it's hard to be sure.

I flipped to the next page.

Father Barboza had been a priest for more than twenty years and maintained a spotless record until six months ago, when two boys leveled accusations against him. The archdiocese transferred Father Barboza to a parish in Braintree, but the transfer took place before the accusations came to light. Father Barboza had served in Braintree for only a month when the Billerica problem surfaced, at which point he got benched.

This didn't match the archdiocese's handling of Father Axholm.

In Axholm's case, he was reassigned to new parishes after he was accused, not before like Father Barboza.

I finished writing my notes, restacked the papers in the folder, and placed them on the corner of the desk.

The next day I drove to Billerica to visit the families of the pedophile victims. I found the O'Dell home first and parked on the street in front. Bill O'Dell Jr., age seven, had accused Father Netto Barboza of doing inappropriate things to him, things of a sexual nature. How do you talk to a kid or his parents about this stuff?

I rang the doorbell, but nobody answered. I knocked, still no answer. No car in the driveway. I looked through the garage window. No car in garage. My shoulders unknotted. A woman yelled out from a neighboring house.

"Are you looking for the O'Dells?"

"I am." I walked down the driveway toward her. "I was hoping to—"

"Oh, hello Officer." She stepped onto the porch wearing only a housecoat. "The O'Dells just left for Disney World."

I didn't correct her assumption. "For how long?"

"A week would be my guess, school vacation week," she said. "He works hard, that Bill. It's good he got away. Should I tell him you came by?"

"No need, I'll call him later."

She went back inside. Strike one.

I located the Bordeaux home, the second family that Father Barboza allegedly victimized, and knocked. The inside door opened and a woman about thirty looked at me through the storm door, which framed her like a centerfold page.

"Yes?" she asked. "What do you want?"

I want to stare at you for a few minutes. She blinked her big eyes, waiting for an answer. "I'd like to ask you a few questions." I zipped my coat tighter against the cold. "About Father Barboza."

"Barboza?" She crossed her arms across her chest. "Who are you?"

"My name is Dermot Sparhawk. I'm looking into Father Barboza's murder. I'd like to ask you—"

"The archdiocese promised that our deal was confidential. How did you find out about my Michael?" She stepped nearer to the storm door. "He's been through enough already, hasn't he?"

"I'm looking into Father Barboza's murder, not the ah—"

"If you find the killer, tell him congratulations." Her eyes enlarged. "Father Barboza deserved what he got."

"I didn't mean to upset you."

"I'm raising Michael on my own. Do you know what that's like? Do you have any idea what it's like to raise a boy alone?"

"No, I don't. I'm sorry. I didn't know—"

"Of course you didn't know," she said. "My husband died and left me with nothing. No insurance, no savings, nothing. Then that monster preyed on my Michael." She opened the storm door an inch. A cold breeze swept across her blouse and goose pimpled her skin. She noticed my stare.

"Can I help you in any way?" I said like an idiot.

"You can." She pushed back her ash-blonde hair. "You can leave us alone. Michael is away anyway, in Disney World."

"With the O'Dells?"

"What did you say?" Her eyes blinked. "How did you know that?"

"I just came from the O'Dell house. I wanted to talk to Bill Jr. and his parents about Father Barboza." I shoved my hands into my coat pockets. "O'Dell's neighbor told me they went to Disney World."

"That Nosey Parker, Mrs. Smithfield, no doubt."

"No doubt," I said, trying to get on her side. "All I've done is upset you." I stuffed my hands deeper. "I'm looking for a serial killer. I'm not looking to hurt you or your son in any way."

She opened the storm door and stared at me. The two of us

knew about her son, we knew about the murdered priest who supposedly molested her son, and we knew about my hungry gaze when the wind brushed against her blouse.

"Tell me your name again."

"Dermot Sparhawk."

"Astrid Bordeaux." She opened the door all the way. "Come in."

I stepped inside after wiping my feet. The carpeting was thick and the house was quiet. The drawn shades blocked the outside light and provided a privacy you don't find in the city. A dog wandered into the room, an older golden retriever named Fluffy. Astrid and I talked for a few minutes, but we didn't say much of significance, and then for some reason she said, "Would you like a drink?"

She mixed two drinks, gin or vodka or something clear, and placed them on coasters atop the coffee table. We sat on her sofa and sipped carefully. No words, just sips. Fifteen minutes later she mixed two more drinks, and this time we drank not so carefully. Sips gave way to gulps. Astrid's freckled throat grew blotchy and her eyes glistened in watery orbs. I placed my empty glass on the coaster.

"Did you suspect anything before the allegations came to light?" I asked.

"What do you mean?"

"Did Michael's behavior change at all?"

She crossed her thin legs and drank more.

"His behavior changed subtly, I suppose. At first I thought he was reacting to his father's death."

"That makes sense." I leaned back on the cushion. "When did you learn about Father Barboza?"

"Not until Bill O'Dell talked to me." Her body slackened into the shape of the couch. "He came to my house with Bill Jr. one evening." She took another sip and her jaw loosened. "That's when I learned about Father Barboza." Astrid got up and went to the sideboard and mixed two more drinks, handing me one as she brushed past me on her way back to the sofa. "Before Bill's visit, I had no idea."

"Who told you the story? Was it Bill O'Dell, Bill Jr.? Michael? Who actually told you what happened?"

"Bill Sr. mostly, but the boys backed him up. Father Barboza started molesting Michael shortly after my husband died. Then he started in on young Bill. The boys attended Saint Stephen's together."

We sat for a time, not saying anything, content to swig gin. We examined our cocktail glasses as if they held answers, as if the gin and lime and ice turned them into crystal balls.

"Did Michael confide in you directly?" I tried again. "After the O'Dells left your house that night, did Michael talk to you about Father Barboza?" I walked to the sideboard to reload my glass. Astrid held up hers. I filled them both, sans the ice. "I was wondering if Michael confided in you."

"No, not really. Michael became agitated whenever I brought it up." I handed her the drink and we touched glasses. "So I decided to drop it."

"Probably best."

Time flew by, the conversation was easy, dusk surrendered to darkness, and moonlight trimmed the shades in silver.

"You don't strike me as a drinker," I said.

"I don't get out much these days, and I never spend time with men." She rested her neck on the sofa back. "My husband died two years ago."

"I'm sorry."

"I haven't had sex since his passing." She swallowed more gin. "Oh my God, I can't believe I said that."

I leaned in.

"Please don't," she said. "I don't think I'm ready."

"Sorry," I said, and sniffed her neck. She smelled of soap and shampoo and springtime lilacs. She arched up, and I kissed her throat. "Are you okay with this?"

"I'm not sure," she said. "Are you trying to persuade me or seduce me?"

"Which do you prefer?" I unfastened her top two buttons. "Just don't say neither."

"We shouldn't." Her eyes burst into enormous goblets, big as channel markers guiding me into port. "What do you think?"

"I think it's up to you," I said.

"I'm a little drunk."

"Me too."

I tossed aside her blouse and admired her toned shoulders. Her breasts remained game after I commandeered the bra. She reached her arms high and stretched her torso accordion long, expanding every rib, each delineated by a diagonal shadow. And together we went absent from the world.

We were in her bedroom now, under the sheets, with the smell of sex wafting about us. Sighs of pleasure hovered in our throats and delightful music chirped in our ears. She leaned over and kissed me and then worked her way south.

"My God, I've never seen such a thing."

"I'm half Micmac Indian. We're known for our—"

"Those horrible scars on your knee, they look like railroad tracks." Astrid ran her fingers along the maroon lines that criss-crossed my kneecap from thigh to shin. "It looks so painful."

"The other half's Irish."

"Excuse me?"

"It's a football injury from college."

"My God." She pulled back the sheet for a full view. "My husband had knee surgery. He hurt it playing squash."

Squash?

"All athletes get injured," I said.

"My husband's incision was so small, not like yours. Does it still hurt?"

"Only on the inside."

Astrid nuzzled closer to me and rested her face on my chest. I could feel her heartbeat and hear her breathe. She looked up at me.

"That was nice." She hooked her arm into mine. "I needed

that, Dermot. I don't sound like a tramp, do I? You're the first since my husband died."

"I don't make a habit of it either, you know."

"That's what I thought. You seem like a nice guy."

"Thanks." I still had my arm around her. "Would you like to see me again?"

"Yes, very much." She kissed me. "And next time without the liquor."

CHAPTER 21

Victor Cepeda was in the office when I called the next day. He told me that everything was cool. I went to my bedroom and fell asleep on the covers and didn't wake up until seven that evening. After taking a hot shower and dressing in clean clothes, I cooked franks and beans in an iron skillet, ate, and walked to my office. In Hayes Square, a gale wind blew in from the Navy Yard, kicking up sand and grit from the streets and gutters. My eyes were still blinking when two men stepped in front of me. I didn't pay much attention to them, but when I tried to step around them, they blocked my path. I looked more closely. They acted tough, but they weren't from the projects.

"What's this?" I asked, "Laurel and Hardy?"

The men were white but not Irish. Laurel stood tall, almost my height. Hardy was short and built like a weight lifter. We were about twenty yards from my office.

I said, "If you're here to sign up for the food pantry, you'll have to come back tomorrow."

"A wiseass," Hardy said, flexing his chest. "A Townie wiseass."

"I don't like people blocking me," I said.

"Too bad," Laurel piped in. "We need to talk to you."

"Call me on the phone." I tried to go around them again, but they stayed in my way. "I'm about to get angry with you two."

"Angry with us?" Hardy said, bulling his corded neck. "You got it backward, asshole. We need to talk to you about Father Barboza, as in forget about him. Ya understand? Let Barboza go 'fore you get yourself hurt."

"Step aside, stout fellow," I said.

"You're forcing us to get tough," Laurel said, and then he reached inside his coat and pulled a gun.

I shuffled forward and launched a left hook at his jaw. The punch landed solid, like good wood on a baseball on a cold spring day. Laurel's eyes rolled up into his head, and he hit the pavement before the gun did.

Hardy unleashed a pistol. I shoved him off balance and dodged away. Darkness was my ally. I zigzagged toward my office like a broken-field runner. A gunshot rang out; a bullet ricocheted at my feet. I fumbled for the keys, turned the corner of the building, and sprinted for the entranceway. The brick edging provided cover. I unlocked the deadbolt and dove inside. The metal door slammed behind me.

I raced to the rooftop, two steps at a time. Hardy yanked on the handle. Topside on the roof, I grabbed the forty-five-pound weight from the table, carried it to the edge, and looked below, trusting I wouldn't get my head blown off. Hardy fired another round into the lock and jerked the handle. One more shot and he'd be in. From two stories above, I released the weight. Gravity did the rest. The steel cylinder struck Hardy's head like a steam-hammer peen. He fell off the stoop and landed on the blacktop. The flat round weight wobbled on the tar next to him like a manhole cover after a gas explosion.

Boston Homicide Detective Adam Jenner stood over Hardy's dead body. The crime-scene personnel snapped pictures, chalked the pavement, and collected evidence. Kiera McKenzie wasn't part of the crew, and my heart sank a beat. Detective Jenner told me to stand next to him, inside the circle of yellow tape, and instructed me not to corrupt the area—whatever that meant. He pointed at Hardy.

"So this guy pulled a gun on you for no apparent reason. He simply aimed and fired because he didn't like your face."

"That's what happened, Adam. I was walking from my house to use the office computer when two guys attacked me." I nodded toward Hardy. "They both had guns."

"Where's the other guy?"

"Don't know, I punched him and he went down." I looked to where Laurel had landed. "No blood, I caught him high on the jaw." I could still see Laurel's eyes spinning in his head. I could still hear his gun skittering on the tar.

"I don't see a second gun," Jenner said. "What did they want?"

"They wanted to talk to me." Something told me to keep my mouth shut about Father Barboza. "I refuse to talk to anybody under those conditions."

"I see." Jenner wrote something in his spiral notebook. He looked up at the roof, then down at the body. He wrote something else and turned up his collar. "You went up to the roof and dropped a weight on the victim's head."

"I thought I was the victim here."

"How'd you get the weight to the roof?"

"It was already up there, holding down a table."

"What?"

"The weight anchored a table. The wind blows it over without it." I lit a cigar and took a puff. "I go up there to smoke."

It went on like this for a while: Jenner's dumb questions, my dumb answers. I felt like a *Jeopardy!* contestant stuck on the hundred-dollar row. A young Asian man wearing thick glasses signaled Jenner.

"What do you got, Doc?" Jenner turned to me and said, "This is Doctor Wang, forensics. Doctor, this is Dermot Sparhawk, a classmate of mine from BC."

"Nice to meet you." Doc Wang kept his nose buried in his notes. "The cause of the fatality was blunt force trauma to the head. The steel weight fractured his skull, causing instantaneous death." He adjusted his glasses and looked at me. "I take it you're the weight man."

"He shot at me with a gun."

"Thanks, Doc," Jenner said.

Jenner guided me to Hardy's stiffening body as the evidence crew zipped him into a bag. An officer wearing latex gloves handed something to Jenner.

"The victim's wallet," the officer said.

"How much did you snag?" Jenner said. No one laughed. Jenner opened the wallet and pulled out a card. "Lopo D. Gomes, Durfee Street, Fall River. Do you know him?" Jenner held out the license for me to look at. "Ever see him before?"

"Not before tonight."

"Lopo Gomes," Jenner said. "Sounds like a Portuguese name."

"He's from Fall River," I said as they hoisted Gomes onto a gurney and slid him into the ambulance. "Lots of Portuguese in Fall River."

"Father Barboza was Portuguese." Jenner closed his notebook. "Father Barboza's family came from Fall River."

"You think there's a connection?" I actually sounded surprised. "Do you think those men came after me because of Father Barboza?"

"Maybe, maybe not, I'm looking for any string to tug on."

The ambulance drove out of the parking lot and turned left onto Corey Street. The evidence team collected their gear and packed up the van. One by one, the crime personnel wrapped it up and left. The lot was vacant, as if nothing happened. Jenner said he'd call me later. Tomorrow I would visit Fall River. I went home and slept like the dead.

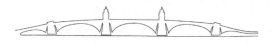

CHAPTER 22

I exited Route 24 at Battleship Cove and found the Durfee Street home of Lopo Gomes. The house was a typical Fall River double-bay triple-decker. The windows needed puttying, clapboard needed painting, and I needed to find out more about Gomes. I stepped onto the porch and read the three nameplates. The name Gomes was etched on each one. I was thinking about which bell to ring when a thin man with a lanky stride and busted face scuttled along the sidewalk toward the house.

"Laurel," I said.

When he saw me on the porch, he ran down Durfee Street and cut into a playground. I chased him, closed the gap, tackled him to the blacktop, pressed his face against the tar, and frisked him. He wasn't carrying a gun, but he was carrying a long folding knife. I tossed it aside.

"Hey man, that's my fishing knife," he said. "I just got it sharpened."

"Shut up." I tore out his wallet and found his license. "Vasco Gomes. How'd you like Charlestown last night, Vasco?" I kneeled on his head to keep him down. "Talk to me, Vasco."

"You're crushing my skull." He squirmed. "Come on, will ya? Lemme up. I won't run. Promise."

"I'll let you up," I said. "And then we're going to walk to that bench over there and sit down. And then we're going to talk." I got to my feet and toed his ribs. "If you run, I'll beat you till the police arrive. And then we'll talk to the cops about Charlestown. Do you understand me?"

"Yeah, yeah, I understand."

We sat on a park bench and caught our breath. I looked at Vasco's face. His right cheek puffed like a trumpeter's hitting the final note of a solo. His sunken brown eyes added sadness to his gaunt face.

"Why were you in Charlestown last night, Vasco?" I waited a second. "You said you wanted to talk to me about Father Barboza."

He reached inside his coat. I grabbed his arm.

"Take it easy, man. Cigarettes." He pulled out a generic pack and lit one with a paper match. "To tell you the truth, Lopo set the thing up. He said he needed some backup, so I went along with him."

Vasco offered me one. I shook my head no. "Backup on what?"

"I don't know a whole lot about it. It was something Lopo had going."

Something Lopo had going. Just last night I had dropped a steel barbell plate on Lopo's head and killed him. It seemed like months ago.

"Sorry about Lopo. He came at me firing." I looked at the glowing tip of Vasco's cigarette. "Was Lopo your brother?"

"He was my cousin." He gazed at the basketball court. "We played hoops here when we were kids, played for Durfee High, too. The Hilltoppers."

The breeze switched and I caught a whiff of something. Vasco reeked of weed.

"Why were you in Charlestown last night?" I asked.

"I already told you, I don't know nothin' about Charlestown. Really man, I'm being honest. I don't know a thing." Vasco flicked the cigarette, and the embers exploded on the tar when it hit. "A guy paid Lopo a grand to scare you off." He lit another one. "I never met the guy, to tell you the truth."

"To scare me off what, Father Barboza's investigation?"

"Yeah, I guess so. We were supposed tell you to—um, I don't know."

"Tell me what?" I waited. "We can always talk to the cops about this."

"Slow down, man. Gimme a second." He waved his cigarette. "We were supposed to tell you to lay off Father Barboza. That's all I know. I don't need the cops here, okay? If I knew more, I'd tell you. What's the difference? Lopo is dead."

"Who hired you?"

"I don't know." He looked away. "Lopo did the deal."

"And you went along for the ride?"

"Yeah, I guess so." Vasco sighed. "Lopo paid me a hundred bucks to go along."

"A hundred bucks? You pulled a gun on me for a hundred bucks?" I stared at his face. "I should kick your ass for that alone."

"I know, man, I know. It was stupid."

I waited until he took another drag.

"Did you know Father Barboza?" I asked.

"Nah, didn't know him, but the name sounds familiar." Vasco shrugged his narrow shoulders. "It was Lopo's gig. When Lopo told you to lay off Father Barboza, it didn't mean nothin' to me, swear to God."

"Father Barboza came from Fall River," I said. "He's one of the priests that got crucified."

"So?" Vasco shrugged. "I don't get to church much these days."

Three teenagers stepped onto the court, bouncing a scuffed Wilson. One of them fired a jump shot from the corner, and it rattled through the chain net. The same shooter dribbled to the top of the key and hit another jumper. Swish. The ball grazed the chains, and it became apparent why it was scuffed. I couldn't think of anything else to ask Vasco Gomes.

"Sorry about your cousin," I said. "He shot at me."

"Lopo's family ain't too thrilled he got killed. They're blaming you, Sparhawk. They're holding you accountable."

"The cops will straighten the Gomeses out. They'll tell them it was self-defense."

"Cops?" His eyes focused for the first time since we sat on the bench. "Do the Boston cops know about me?"

"I don't think so."

"Are you gonna tell 'em? I don't need that kinda trouble right now. I'm on thin ice with my probation officer as it is. If I fuck up again, he'll violate me and, bada bing, back to the can."

"I won't volunteer anything, but if the cops ask, I'll tell them what I know."

"You do that and I'm screwed."

"I'll try to keep you out of it." Something occurred to me, something I hadn't thought of until just now. "How did you and Lopo get to Charlestown?"

"I drove there," Vasco said. "That was part of the deal, we used my car."

"You drove Lopo?"

"Yeah, but he paid for the gas."

I left Fall River and went back to Charlestown.

A tall man wearing a dungaree coat and cowboy boots was waiting on my front steps when I got home. His braided silver hair gave him away; it was Glooscap, my father's half-brother. My insides did a Micmac rain dance. He greeted me on the sidewalk and extended an invitation.

"I want to show you my auto-body shop in Andrew Square and introduce you to your cousin. He works for me." Glooscap paused. "I think you two will get along." He pointed to a new pickup truck. "Hop in, Dermot."

We merged onto I-93 south via the Zakim Bridge and exited the O'Neill Tunnel at Albany Street. We then turned left and took the West Fourth Street Bridge into Southie. Glooscap's shop was set back from Dorchester Avenue, abutting the Red Line tracks behind it. A high, chain-linked fence enclosed the lot. A cinder block building with a corrugated Quonset roof stood to the right. Dozens of newer but dented cars edged the yard's perimeter. Glooscap shifted into park and led me into the Quonset building, where a man wearing a welding helmet was working on a tailpipe with a cutting torch, cussing and spitting as he labored.

"We will wait in my office," Glooscap said with his deliberate cadence.

"Wait for what?"

"For the happy guy working on the tailpipe, he is your cousin."

I never knew about my Micmac relatives until the night of Aunt Agnes's wake, and the surprise of it overjoyed me. Glooscap and I were chatting about Antigonish and Lennox Island when the door flung open and the welder stomped in, still sporting the helmet with the opaque specs. The Darth Vader of dented sheet metal. He unsnapped it and pulled it off like a linebacker who just missed a tackle.

"Dermot Sparhawk," Glooscap said. "Meet your cousin, Harraseeket Kid."

We shook hands like boxers at weigh-in. Harraseeket Kid was about my age, tall, just an inch or two shorter than me, lean but not skinny. Muscles and tendons corded his sinewy neck. His shiny black hair was wound into a ponytail, and his black eyes glowered like an accused schoolboy. I liked him right away, more so when he said, "So you're the spoiled college boy none of us could meet." He shoved a wad of chaw in his mouth. "Am I right?"

"If you say so," I said. "I never knew about you guys till a few days ago."

"Your old man, the so-called Chief—"

"Enough," Glooscap said. "Sit down, Kid."

To my surprise, Harraseeket Kid complied. We drank coffee and talked for a while. I didn't learn much about my father's family, but I was spending time with them, and that was plenty for now. At suppertime I said I had to get back to Charlestown. Glooscap invited me to stay for dinner, but I told him I was tired and wanted to get home.

"I'll grab the Red Line at Andrew," I said.

"I'll give you a ride." Harraseeket Kid spit the chaw into a paper cup. "We'll take the wrecker."

We stepped out of the Quonset garage. The sun had gone down, the air was frosty. I followed Kid to the wrecker and got in.

He shifted into first, popped the clutch, jerked forward, and ground into second. We bounced off the curb onto Dorchester Ave.

"Three hundred thousand miles and she can still outwork any truck out there." He cut off a car and shifted into third. "I always have the right of way."

We ramped onto the expressway, exited at the North End, and crossed the North Washington Street Bridge into Charlestown. I asked Kid to drop me on Main Street at the DAAT Club, short for day at a time. I attended the AA beginners meeting and listened to the speakers. After we said the Lord's Prayer, I grabbed a pamphlet that listed all meetings in Greater Boston.

CHAPTER 23

Saint John's Seminary is located on Lake Street in Brighton, not far from Boston College. Bishop Downey had alerted the seminary staff of my impending visit, and they were waiting for me when I arrived. They provided me with a room to work in and the class records and yearbooks of Fathers Axholm and Barboza. The third victim, Father Del Rio, had been ordained from Blessed John XXIII National Seminary in Weston. I'd visit there later.

As I was browsing Father Axholm's yearbook, I came across Bishop Downey's class picture. He looked young and innocent and ready for ordination. Covering up for miscreants wasn't even an idea for him back then. I studied the class records of both dead priests and discovered nothing that pointed to a killer. I looked at the names and yearbook photos of every seminarian in both graduating classes. Not one of them looked like a maniacal murderer to me.

After a few hours of unproductive labor, my eyes began to cross and I gave up. As I was leaving the seminary, Bishop Downey came out of a classroom and walked toward me. His gleaming shoes clicked on the terrazzo floors and echoed off the barrel ceilings. I waited until he was standing next to me.

"Thanks for not pressing charges," I said. "I was in a blackout. I didn't mean anything by it."

"I know you didn't. Let's forget about the whole thing, shall we?" He sounded sincere. "Is that okay with you, Dermot?"

"That's fine with me."

"Did the class records help you at all?"

"Not really, I couldn't find a connection." I glanced up at a stained-glass window of Saint Michael the Archangel, his sword drawn to slay the dragon. "Father Axholm was in your graduating class here."

"Don't remind me."

"There had to be fifty or sixty seminarians ordained that year."

"That sounds about right. The classes were much bigger back then."

"I hate to bring up a tender subject, but how many of your classmates have died since graduation?"

"Why do you ask?"

"Just curious," I said.

"Too many, I'm sorry to say." He stopped and thought. "Ed Casey died of cancer last year. Thomas Kidwell was killed in a plane crash shortly after he was ordained. A single engine plane, it crashed in Alaska, as I recall, near the Yukon Territory. There was Gerry Gordano, he suffered a heart attack." Bishop Downey named four or five other priests and then he said, "Jack Ahearn committed suicide. He hanged himself a few years after he took his holy vows."

"That must have been sad."

"I celebrated the funeral Mass for his family. God, it was dreadful." A passing cloud blocked the sun and Bishop Downey's coloring went with it. "He was a beautiful man, Jack Ahearn."

"Did his suicide surprise you?"

"It did at first, yes. Jack graduated tops in our class. He was a brilliant man and extremely popular with the seminarians." The bishop hesitated. "Most of the time Jack was an upbeat guy."

"But not all the time?"

"Everyone has mood swings," he said. "Jack Ahearn was no different than anyone else in that regard. But none of us thought him suicidal."

"His death was definitely a suicide?" I asked.

"The police ruled it a suicide, so I suppose it was. But it was so out of character for him. To this day I find it hard to believe."

Usually when a man commits suicide, the people who know him best are not that surprised. They pretend to be surprised, or maybe they want to be surprised, but deep down they're not surprised.

"Did Father Ahearn die in Boston?"

"He died in Sudbury where he grew up, and that's where he was buried, too. I'd bet that half the Sudbury police force attended the funeral." He swallowed hard. "Jack was extremely popular. He had every reason to live."

"You don't seem convinced that Father Ahearn killed himself."

"The police said it was suicide, so I suppose I *should* be convinced," he said. "But it's hard for me to accept it. Perhaps being convinced of Jack's suicide and accepting Jack's suicide are two different things."

Bishop Downey was a smart guy. He'd know the difference between being convinced and finding acceptance.

"If it's okay with you, Bishop, I'd like to look into the death of Father Jack Ahearn."

"You'd be willing to do that?"

"Yes, sir, I would."

"I'd like that very much," he said. "Thank you."

I drove to the Sudbury Police Station and went inside to the lobby. A couple of uniformed cops, far too young to have worked on Father Ahearn's suicide case, milled around. They bantered about police details and griped about civilian flagmen and went out to their cruisers to fight crime. I approached the desk sergeant.

"I'd like to speak to an officer about a suicide," I said. "It took place in Sudbury thirty years ago."

The desk sergeant kept his head down, writing. He was about forty years old with Mediterranean features, Greek or Italian, maybe Lebanese.

"Whose suicide?"

"Father Jack Ahearn's," I said.

"Thirty years ago, that's before my time." He finally raised his head. His puppy eyes contrasted with his heavy beard line. "Let me ask the shift commander. Take a seat."

I walked to the end of the lobby and stared out the window. A few minutes later an older cop interrupted my daydreaming.

"Frank Hollis," he said. "I answered the call for the Ahearn suicide."

"Dermot Sparhawk, thanks for talking to me."

"Sparhawk, that name sounds familiar." He looked me up and down. "Did you play pro ball?"

"A little college ball."

"Doesn't surprise me, the size of you." He joined me looking out the window. "I'm not sure how I can help you. Ahearn's hanging is a matter of public record. The press covered it pretty thoroughly. You can look up the details for yourself online."

"I already did that."

"I doubt I can tell you anything new."

"Maybe you're right, but I still want to talk to someone who was there."

"Why?" Hollis said. "What's your interest in Ahearn?"

"I work for the Archdiocese of Boston," I said. "Three priests have been murdered recently and I—"

"Right, right, they were crucified. It's been all over the news."

"Father Ahearn was a classmate of one of the murdered priests, Father Axholm. I thought there might be a connection between the two deaths."

"A connection between Ahearn and Axholm? One was a suicide, the other was a murder," Hollis said. "What connection?"

"There probably is no connection, but I want to make sure."

"You think Ahearn was murdered?" Hollis asked. "Is that what you're saying?"

"I'm just collecting information."

"Bullshit. I've been a cop for too many years, so don't try to snow me. You think that Jack Ahearn was murdered. Why do you think that?"

Jack?

"When I was talking to Bishop Downey—"

"You know Bishop Downey?" Hollis seemed impressed by this. "I remember Bishop Downey. He said Jack's funeral Mass."

"Bishop Downey was a seminary classmate of Father Ahearn.

Bishop Downey told me about the suicide, and he accepted that the police ruled it a suicide, but I could tell he had doubts about it."

"Is that so?"

"One of the reasons I'm here is to ease Bishop Downey's doubts about Ahearn's death." I waited a second. "The other reason is to satisfy my curiosity."

"Your curiosity?" He stifled a laugh. "Jack Ahearn was *not* murdered, Sparhawk. And I still don't see how I can help you."

"You can answer a question for me."

"Sure, I can do that, especially if it will help satisfy your curiosity. Fire away."

"I know that Father Ahearn was hanged," I said. "Was he wearing anything on his head when you found his body?"

"What did you say?" Hollis stepped backwards. "Be more specific."

"Was Father Ahearn wearing a red hood on his head?"

"Jesus." Hollis grabbed my arm. "Why do you ask? Was the other priest, what's his name, was he wearing a red hood?"

"Father Axholm," I said. "Yes, he was wearing a red hood. Father Barboza and Father Del Rio were also wearing red hoods."

"They all wore hoods?" His face blanched. "Wait here and don't move. I need to make a phone call."

I had struck a nerve.

Hollis returned and told me to take a ride with him.

"Where are we going?"

"To talk to Janice Ahearn, Father Jack Ahearn's sister." We went out to Hollis's squad car. Before we got in, he said, "I want to help you, Sparhawk. But I have to protect Janice. And I want you to protect her, too."

What was Hollis getting at?

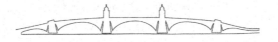

CHAPTER 24

Janice Ahearn lived in a cedar Cape Cod house on Pokonoket Avenue, a sleepy street in sleepy Sudbury. We parked in front and walked up the driveway. Hollis rang the doorbell, but didn't wait for an answer. He let himself in with his own key. A tall woman was standing in the kitchen when we entered. She was wearing a braided, tan sweater and pleated gray slacks. She looked to be in her early sixties and was quite attractive. Hollis hugged her.

"Is everything okay, honey?" he asked.

"Everything is fine, Frank."

"Janice, this is Dermot Sparhawk," Hollis said. "Dermot is working for the Archdiocese of Boston investigating the priest murders."

"Yes, Frank. You told me on the phone." Janice Ahearn looked at me. "Frank said you wanted to ask me about the death of my brother Jack. I fail to see what Jack's death has to do with the recent spate of priest killings. Please tell me."

"Your brother was a classmate of Father Axholm, one of the murdered priests." I decided to keep the discussion general. "As Officer Hollis said, the archdiocese asked me to look into the murders."

"I still don't understand," she said. "Are you interviewing the families of all the seminarians that were in Father Axholm's class?"

"No, I'm not. To be candid I didn't plan to talk to you. I'm here because Officer Hollis drove me here."

"This visit was Frank's idea?"

"Yes, ma'am," I said.

The three of us fell silent, and the silence grew awkward, and after a prolonged stretch of awkward silence, I wanted to get out of there. I looked to Hollis for support. He picked up my cue, and said, "Honey, I think it's important to tell Dermot what we know." Hollis waited, but Janice didn't reply. "If you're not comfortable, I'll tell him." He turned to me. "When Janice found Jack's body—"

"No, Frank, I'll tell him," Janice said. "I don't know why I did what I did back then. I must have momentarily lost my senses. I told Frank about it a few years ago. It has been thirty years since Jack's death. I hate to stir this mess up again, Mr. Sparhawk."

"It's Dermot," I said. "Stir what up again?"

"I tampered with a crime scene." She looked out toward the driveway. "What's the correct word, Frank? Compromised? I compromised an active crime scene."

"What do you mean by compromised?" I asked.

"I removed a hood from Jack's head."

"Honey, sit down." Hollis pulled out a chair for her. "When Janice found Jack's body, he was wearing a red hood, but she didn't say anything about it at the time."

"The hood was covering his head," Janice said. "I didn't want Jack's death to turn into a freak show or some kind of cult thing, so I removed it."

"Janice told me about the hood when she demolished the garage," Hollis said. "That's where Jack died, in the garage."

"I never wanted to believe that Jack killed himself, but, of course, he did." She looked out the window again. "He'd been struggling for months."

"Struggling with what?" I asked.

"With his decision to be a priest, he wasn't sure he wanted to remain in the priesthood. After all the schooling and all the years in the seminary, he still wasn't sure."

"Take it easy, honey." Hollis kneaded her shoulders. "I foolishly used the word compromised when Janice told me what she had done."

"It wasn't foolish, Frank," she said.

"Father Jack Ahearn was wearing a red hood when you found him in the garage," I said in confirmation. "Is that correct?"

They nodded yes. Janice eased the chair away from the kitchen table and stood up. "Does knowing about the red hood help with your investigation?"

Absolutely, it helped. And then I remembered Hollis's words: "Protect her, Sparhawk."

"I won't know for a while," I said. "I'm simply gathering information."

"Well, I hope it helps." She rubbed her elbow. "Wait here, I want to give you something."

She returned to the kitchen holding a brown paper bag and handed it to me.

"What's this?"

"It's the red hood that was on Jack's head. I've kept it all these years. I have no idea why, but I did." She touched my hand. "Please don't open it until you leave the house. I can't bear to see it again."

"Of course," I said. "Thank you."

Hollis gave me my coat. He was already wearing his.

"I'll drive Dermot to the station, and I'll be right back."

I left the house with Hollis. We stopped on the sidewalk out front.

"Thanks for not telling Janice about the hoods on the other priests."

"No problem," I said. "Why upset her?"

If Janice learned about the hoods on Fathers Axholm and Barboza and Del Rio, she might assume her brother was murdered, an assumption that might prove to be true.

Hollis said, "Knowing about the red hoods like we do, I wouldn't be surprised if Jack *was* murdered. For decades everyone assumed he hanged himself. My God, the very thought of someone murdering him is incomprehensible. It doesn't seem possible."

"We don't know anything for sure yet, Frank."

"That's true. It still might be a suicide." He opened the passenger door for me. "By the way, it's okay to handle the hood. For some reason, Janice washed it way back when."

"So there's no DNA on it," I said.

"Even if she hadn't washed it, the DNA would probably be decomposed after all these years. Keep the hood evidence confidential. Janice put herself out on a limb for you, and I don't want her getting hounded by law enforcement."

"I'll be discreet," I said. "She made a gutsy decision."

"Janice is a gutsy lady, and I'll be taking care of her."

"I'm sure you will."

CHAPTER 25

On my drive home from Sudbury, I pulled into a service stop on Route 128 in Lexington and went into a large dining area that had a McDonald's. The place was empty. I ordered coffee and sat at a corner table, away from the restrooms and windows. I opened the bag and removed the red hood. It was made of shiny material and stamped with a diamond pattern. The tie cords were red and knotted at the ends. A white manufacturer's tag was sewn into the seam. The tag read Resnick Clothiers. Criminalist Kiera McKenzie described the exact same hood to me at Doyle's.

The red hood confirmed it. Father Jack Ahearn's death was a lynching, not a suicide. Thirty years ago, the serial killer murdered Father Ahearn inside his own garage. The same man that crucified Axholm, Barboza, and Del Rio, also killed Jack Ahearn. But serial killers don't usually stop in mid frenzy. They continue to kill until they get caught. I drove back to Boston thinking about the decades-long gap between murders, a gap that made no sense to me at all.

Early the next morning I walked from Charlestown to the Boston Public Library in Copley Square to research the long-defunct Resnick Clothiers. The morning sun shimmered low in the east, barely delineating the skyscrapers on the horizon. The forecast warned of an Alberta Clipper sweeping down from Canada, a warning I didn't heed, and I paid the price for ignoring it. The Arctic air frosted my hatless ears to deadened solids, just like the ear on my father's keychain. It also stiffened my knee.

Up Boylston Street I trudged, head down against the wind, the library in the offing. Finally there, I passed beneath the helmeted head of Minerva atop the Dartmouth Street doorway and entered the marble vestibule. The warmth felt good. I asked a woman at the help desk where they archived the telephone books, and she directed me to the Microtext Department in the newer part of the library.

"Go up the stairs and take a left. Walk past Bates Hall and take another left. Take yet another left at the portrait of George Washington, and go right at the delivery desk. You'll know you're in the new building when the floors turn to carpet."

I found the Microtext Department and again went to the help desk, where a man named Henry heard my request.

"I'm looking for a Boston telephone directory from the early seventies," I said.

"Not a problem," said Henry, a pleasant man with steel-rimmed glasses and a receding hairline. "Are you looking for a business or a residence? We have printed volumes of business listings on the shelves behind you, the books bound in red. We have residential listings on microfilm, which I'll be glad to get for you out back."

I told him I'd look at the businesses first.

I browsed the 1973 business volume and, sure enough, I found Resnick Clothiers at 600 Chester Square. I then browsed each volume from 1974 forward. In 1979 Resnick Clothiers was no longer listed. I asked Henry for the White Pages on microfilm for 1979. Ten minutes later he returned with two small boxes.

"Two reels," he said. "What's the last name?"

"Resnick," I said.

"Try the second reel first."

I fed the second reel into a manual projector and turned the handle until I reached the letter R. I found a residential listing for B. Resnick at the same Chester Square address. I returned to the desk and handed the boxes to Henry.

"Where's Chester Square?" I asked.

"It's on Mass Ave. near the Boston Medical Center."

• • •

I walked down Columbus Ave. to Massachusetts Avenue and turned left toward the Boston Medical Center. Chester Square was set back from the street and accessed via a half-circle road in front. I located the 600 building that once housed Resnick Clothiers, a brownstone row house three floors high. Sculpted concrete stairs led to a double front door that had gold-leaf address numbers painted on the beveled glass. The transom above the doorway was also beveled. A woman with long, wiry hair hiked up the stairs carrying two bags of groceries. She took a key from her pocketbook and let herself into the foyer and then through the inner doors. A few minutes later somebody, probably the woman with the wiry hair, drew the shades on the bottom unit. I walked up the stairs as nonchalantly as possible and read the nameplates. Engraved on the top plate was the name H. Schwartz, and on the bottom plate E. O'Burke. There was no middle plate. The middle doorbell had also been removed.

On a whim I checked the row house to the right. It had four nameplates and four doorbells, one for each of the three main floors and one for the garden unit in the basement. I went down and stood on the sidewalk. A blonde letter carrier climbed the same stairs and pushed a few envelopes through the mail slot. She passed me on the sidewalk and started for the old Resnick Clothiers building.

"Excuse me," I said to her. "A friend of my father's used to live at this address. His name was Ed Resnick. Do you know when he moved out?"

"Which unit?"

"Bottom," I said.

"It had to be more than fifteen years ago, because I've had this route for fifteen years. Emmett and Barbara O'Burke have lived on the bottom since I started. For that matter, Harriett Schwartz has been living here that whole time, too. She's up top."

"Do you remember Resnick Clothiers?" I asked. "It was a small business at this address in the sixties and seventies."

"Never heard of them."

She delivered mail to the old Resnick address and went to the next building. I caught up to her again.

"Sorry to bother you, just one more question," I said. "Who had this mail route before you?"

She looked up from the envelopes and stared at me.

"What's going on here?"

"It's important," I said.

"A man named Hickey had the route before me, but he's dead."

I thanked her and walked to the Mass Ave. T stop and rode the Orange Line back to Charlestown. As the train rattled along, I kept thinking about the name on the doorplate, E. O'Burke. Emmett O'Burke, the letter carrier, said. Why did the name gnaw at me? Where had I heard of Emmett O'Burke?

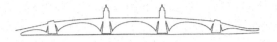

CHAPTER 26

Night had fallen by the time I got home, and when I got there, I saw two men sitting in a workingman's van in front of the house. The stenciled lettering on the side read GOMES SHELLFISH, FALL RIVER, MASS. EST. 1963. Wonderful. I walked up to the vehicle and waited. An older man with a thick build and bowed legs struggled to get out of the passenger side. He stepped onto the curbside and stretched as if from a long ride, doffed his Greek fishing hat, and rubbed his balding head. His forearms, muscled from clamming and blued with tattoos, bulged out of his rolled-up sleeves. A younger man came around the front of the van. His arms were inked with prison tats and so were his hands and neck. The younger man looked up at me. He wasn't used to this, looking up at someone. The older man came forward.

"You killed my son," he said. "Me and Chub are here to settle the matter."

Chub stood next to Gomes.

"It was self-defense," I said. "Lopo and Vasco pulled guns on me. They threatened me on my way to work."

"Vasco?" Gomes turned to Chub. "Vasco was here, too?" Chub shrugged. The old man turned back to me. "How do you know about Vasco? The police didn't say nothin' about Vasco."

"Vasco and I met in Fall River. I went down there to find out why Lopo threatened me." Gomes and Chub looked at each other again. I continued. "I drove to your house on Durfee Street, Mr. Gomes. That's where I saw Vasco."

"I still don't get it. How'd you meet Vasco?"

"He was coming up your walkway. When he saw me, he took

off. I chased him down and caught him in the playground near your house." They both looked confused. I kept going before they got their bearings. "Lopo and Vasco confronted me outside my office at Saint Jude Thaddeus."

"You work for a church?" Gomes's eyes widened. "Jesus, what did Lopo want with a guy from a church?"

I told Mr. Gomes about the crucified priests and how I was looking into their killings. I told him that Lopo fired three rounds, one at me and two at my office door, and that the gunshots prompted my weight-drop response. He listened, but kept shaking his head and looking at Chub. Chub responded with empty shrugs. I told Mr. Gomes that when I caught up to Vasco, Vasco insisted he was only along for the ride.

"Someone hired your son to scare me off the priest killings, or at least Father Barboza's killing," I said. "Talk to Vasco, he'll tell you the same thing."

"Oh, don't worry. I'll be talking to Vasco all right." He adjusted his fisherman's hat. "This don't let you off the hook."

"What hook?"

"Don't move, Spearhead," Mr. Gomes said.

Gomes and Chub stepped away to confer. Their talking was muffled, but their gestures were wild: hands waving, heads shaking. Mr. Gomes turned to me.

"You were defending yourself," he said. "My son came at you with a gun and you defended yourself, which is every man's right."

"I wish it never happened."

"That makes two of us," Mr. Gomes said.

"Three of us," Chub added.

"Drugs. It haunted his mother to watch him." Gomes moved into my face. "I want the man who hired my son. I'll take my revenge on him. That's the way it has to be, Spearhead. Do we have a deal?"

"We have a deal," I said. They went to their van. I started toward my house and stopped. "Before you go, I have a question. Why was Lopo in Charlestown?"

"What do you mean?" Gomes asked.

"Lopo lived in Fall River. Whoever hired him could have hired any number of guys from around here. Why did he hire Lopo? And how did he find Lopo down in Fall River?"

Chub spoke, "Lopo lived in the projects when he fished out of Gloucester."

"In the Charlestown projects?" Something didn't make sense. "The waiting list is endless. How did he get a place?"

"I didn't say it was his place, I said he lived there." Chub scratched his whiskered cheeks with thick fingers. "His friend let him sleep on the couch, charged him ten bucks a night."

"Who was his friend?"

"Don't know his name, but I know he was Portuguese." Chub scratched his cheek again. "And I know he was deaf and dumb."

Deaf and dumb? Blackie Barboza, that son of a bitch.

I went into my apartment, changed into sweats, relaxed on the couch, and clicked on the TV.

Emmett O'Burke. I knew the name. Who was he? And what was up with Blackie Barboza?

The Bruins were skating against the Canadiens tonight at the Bell Centre in Montreal. The referee dropped the puck for the opening faceoff and the Bruins won it. Gigantic Zdeno Chara slapped the black disc into the Montreal zone, and it rocketed around the boards. Semigigantic Milan Lucic chased the puck down in the corner and flipped it to the slot. The puck skipped over the center iceman's stick and was cleared to the neutral zone by a Canadiens defenseman.

Emmett O'Burke. It would come to me.

After a few fruitless rushes up and down the ice, the action picked up again at the Bruins blue line. A Montreal forward with a French surname flicked the puck into the Boston end and the teams changed on the fly. The only surprising part of the game so far was that the Bruins penalty box remained unoccupied.

Emmett O'Burke, I had heard of the name, but where?

My neck prickled. A man named Emmett O'Burke had gradu-
ated in the same seminary class as Father Axholm and Bishop
Downey. I remembered seeing his picture in the yearbook. I called
Bishop Downey's cell phone and he answered on the second ring.

"Go ahead, Dermot," he said, sounding annoyed. "I'm listening."

"What can you tell me about Father Emmett O'Burke?"

"Why are you asking about Emmett?"

"Is he still a priest?" I asked.

"What's this about?"

"It's about finding a serial killer, Bishop."

"Have you lost your mind? Emmett O'Burke is a great guy.
He'd never hurt anybody," he said. "What's going on?"

"Is he still a priest?"

"No, he is no longer a priest. Emmett left the priesthood a few
years after he entered it. As far as I know he was laicized and
moved on with his life. But this happened thirty years ago. What
are you up to, Sparhawk?"

"I'll let you know when I know. I have to do some work first."

The next day Victor Cepeda lent me his car. I drove to the South
End and parked across from 600 Chester Square, the current address of Emmett O'Burke, the former address of Resnick Clothiers.
On Mass Ave. the traffic moved at a slow clip, and so did the
hours, the minutes, the seconds. I sat in the car all day and into
the evening. At ten o'clock, a man wearing a baseball cap came
out of the Resnick brownstone. He looked to be roughly sixty
years old and he walked with his head down. He got into a white
Toyota Camry and pulled onto Mass Ave., heading toward the
Boston Medical Center. It had to be Emmett O'Burke. I bird-
dogged him.

O'Burke turned left on Albany Street and left again on
Frontage Road. He ramped onto I-90 east toward the airport. I
stayed three cars behind him, not as a tailing technique, but as a
necessity. The Acclaim topped out at forty. O'Burke drove into the

Ted Williams Tunnel, and so did I. At the tollbooth he sailed through the Fast Lane. I stopped to pay the toll, and that's where I lost sight of him. Gunning it out of the toll plaza, I guessed Revere and headed north on Route 1A.

A hundred yards ahead of me I spotted the white Camry and stepped on the gas. The car coughed and lurched as I blew through a red light and closed the gap. The Camry turned right on Route 145 toward Revere Beach and Winthrop. Two cars dallied between us, and with heavy oncoming traffic I couldn't pass them. I finally made the turn onto Route 145, but Emmett O'Burke was gone. I lost him near Suffolk Downs racetrack.

CHAPTER 27

The next day I started for Blackie Barboza's apartment to ask him about Lopo Gomes. Gomes used to stay with Blackie when he fished out of Gloucester—at least according to Chub, old man Gomes's fishing partner—and I wanted to find out why Blackie never mentioned this to me.

When I got to his building, an addled junkie wandered out and held the door for me. I walked up to the third floor and knocked. Blackie didn't answer. Down below I heard the outside door open and close. Maybe it was Blackie, or maybe the junkie. Bonita Diaz might know Blackie's whereabouts. I knocked on her door and waited. No answer. I turned to watch the stairwell as the footfalls grew louder. A figure appeared on the landing. It wasn't Blackie, it wasn't the junkie. It was a hooded gunman. He raised a revolver and cocked the hammer.

"You were told to leave it alone, Sparhawk."

He flexed his knees and aimed the gun. Bonita's door opened an inch. I barreled through it like a blitzing linebacker and sent Bonita flying across the room. A gunshot rang out in the hall. I bounded to my feet. Another shot crackled behind me. Bonita slammed the door shut and locked it. Neither of us was hit.

"Padre!" She pointed to an open window and screamed. "Padre, Padre!"

I ran to the window and hung from the sill and dropped onto the metal canopy below. I suspended from the canopy and jumped to the ground.

She screamed out the window, "Padre, he's running down."

I sprinted out of the projects and never looked back.

• • •

Two drinks turned into four at the Horseshoe Tavern. From the Horseshoe I walked to Uncle Joe's Diner and sat at the counter for a late lunch. The drinks dulled my jumpiness, the food fueled my energy, and the adrenaline raced my brain. The booze kicked in, and I slowly calmed down.

I just finished eating my American chop suey when a radio from the kitchen crackled with a news flash. The cook turned up the volume, the customers quieted down. Everyone in the diner was listening. In a booming voice, the radioman said that a fourth priest had been crucified, this time in the Point of Pines section of Revere. The victim, Father Vincent Savold, was fifty-nine years old. He had been serving as pastor of Saint James Parish in Revere for the last five years.

Point of Pines, Revere?

Last night I had followed Emmett O'Burke to Revere and lost him. The son of a bitch killed Father Savold. I should have tailed O'Burke more closely. I should have been welded to his goddamned bumper. He killed Father Savold.

I hustled home and called the chancery, but Bishop Downey wasn't in. I called Detective Adam Jenner, but Jenner wasn't in, either. I was about to call Francis Ennis at the DA's office, but instead I tapped the brakes for a second and thought about the situation. For the first time since I began investigating the priest killings I had a sliver of leverage, and I decided to use it. I called Captain Pruitt. He answered the phone with his predictable grace.

"I'm busy, Sparhawk. What do you want now?"

"I know who killed Father Savold."

"No shit?" When he stopped laughing, he said, "Quit wasting my time."

"Do you want to hear me out or not?"

"Are you a moron or just plain stupid? Didn't you hear what I just said?" He exhaled into the receiver. "I don't have time for your nonsense."

"That's fine, Captain," I said. "I just wanted to give you the first crack at it. I'll take what I know a few rungs up the ladder."

"What's that supposed to mean?"

"It means that if you don't care what I have to say, then maybe the DA's office will, or CPAC. I heard that Lieutenant Staples of the State Police will listen to anybody, even a stupid moron like me."

"Is that a threat?"

"Yes," I said. "Do you want to meet with me or not? I don't give a shit one way or the other, Captain. Like I told you, I'm starting at the bottom rung."

"Fuck you, Sparhawk."

"Are we going to meet or not?"

Pruitt relented, and we agreed to meet at the Pleasant Cafe in Roslindale at six p.m. I had a few hours between now and then, so I called Francis Ennis at the Suffolk County DA's office. Revere is part of Suffolk County. He answered. After a few seconds of bullshitting, I asked Ennis for a contact in Revere, a contact who could tell me about the murder of Father Savold.

"Are you sure you want to go chasing after this, Dermot?"

"I'm positive."

There was a moment of silence on the line.

"It's getting too big for you," he said. "You've done a nice little job uncovering a few minor things, but the case is exploding open. If you get in the way of these guys, they'll stomp you like an ant."

"I'll risk it, Francis. Please give me a name."

"I can't talk you out of it?"

"Nope."

Another moment of silence, this one longer.

"Vito Cotto," Ennis said. "Vito is supposedly the lead homicide investigator in Revere."

"Supposedly?"

"The crucifixion killings are tricky. It involves Revere, Boston, the State Police, and my office. Revere doesn't have a bona fide homicide division, so Father Savold's murder investigation is up for grabs." He stopped. "I'm pushing for the State Police CPAC unit to handle the Savold case."

"CPAC?" I played the Staples card again. "What's the story with Lieutenant Staples?"

"Who told you about Staples?" He paused. "Staples heads up CPAC in Suffolk County, which clearly you know. He's a state trooper, of course. In a perfect world I'd like him to work with Boston Homicide, but it's not happening."

"But Revere is different," I said. "In Revere the State Police outweigh the locals, and in Revere, Boston is out."

"Correct on both, but it presents a dilemma for me, because I like Vito Cotto." Another lengthy pause. "Staples will crush him."

I breezed through the Callahan Tunnel to East Boston and drove along Route 1A past Suffolk Downs and Wonderland Park. I then merged onto Revere Beach Parkway. There was no white Toyota Camry to follow this time, and the regret of losing Emmett O'Burke last night clawed at my gut. I looped the rotary at the south end of Revere Beach, and the sight of the stormy shoreline stilled my angst.

Gray waves exploded off the seawall like bouncing bombs, and high tide was still an hour away. I thought of old man Gomes in his lobster boat with Chub at his side pulling traps. They'd earn their pay today. The Point of Pines neighborhood sat on the north end of the beach, where the Pines and Saugus Rivers emptied into the Atlantic Ocean. I headed that way.

I drove around Point of Pines, staying alert to the backdrop, hoping an aura of karma would enlighten me as to what happened the night before. I navigated North Shore Road and Mills Avenue. No karma occurred, no such luck. All that happened was the fuel gauge pointed lower. What a waste of time. I needed facts not fate. I needed to talk to Vito Cotto. I circled back to Revere Beach Parkway and pulled into Revere Police Headquarters, went inside, and asked for him.

Cotto came out from the behind the front desk. He wasn't tall, but he wasn't small. With trapezius muscles that bowed like leaf springs, he looked like he could grab a pickup by the chassis and shrug it to his ears. His olive face was handsome, his brown eyes were intense. Our handshake wasn't a contest, but it wasn't patty-cake, either. I told him who I was and why I was there.

"Francis Ennis told me you'd be coming," Cotto said. "I'm hungry as a gull. Let's grab a bite to eat."

We got into his police cruiser and drove along Revere Beach and stopped at Kelly's Roast Beef. Cotto ordered fried clams. I ordered a roast beef sandwich and fries. We both drank Cokes. Cotto broke the silence.

"DA Ennis said you wanted to talk to me." He wiped his mouth with a napkin and swigged Coca-Cola through a bendy straw. "He said you were the crime liaison for the Archdiocese of Boston, but he wasn't specific about your role. Are you a consultant of some kind?"

"I guess I am."

"What's your background?"

"I work in Charlestown for Saint Jude Thaddeus Parish." I drained the last of my drink. "It's complicated how I got involved."

Raindrops tapped the windshield in a hypnotic rhythm. Cotto hit the wipers, adding to the trance. The pace of the swipes increased as the rain grew heavier.

I asked, "Who found Father Savold's body?"

"A jogger found him. Father Savold was nailed to a tree in the side yard of the rectory." Cotto faced me. "I answered the call."

"What's the jogger's name?"

"I can't give you that. No reflection on you, Sparhawk, but unless DA Ennis tells me to give you the name, it stays confidential."

We watched the rising tide. Waves hammered the seawall and soared ten feet above the railings before splashing on the boardwalk. Winds howled and blew the rainy deluge into diagonal sheets, a curtain of water that reduced visibility to mere yards. I felt content watching the squall from inside the car, so content that I debated whether to ask the next question.

"Was Father Savold wearing a red hood?"

Before he had a chance to answer, the police radio squawked with a scratchy voice, ordering Cotto back to the station. The State Police were awaiting him. We drove back to headquarters. Cotto pulled into the lot.

"The State Police," he said. "This will get ugly."

"The red hood?"

"Damned State Police." Cotto stepped out on the driver's side and looked at the station house. "Why don't they let us do our jobs?"

"I hear Staples is a dick."

"Aren't we all," Cotto said. "Francis Ennis sent you here, so I'm going to assume it's okay to tell you this. Father Savold was wearing a red hood."

"Thanks, Vito."

Axholm, Barboza, Del Rio, and now Savold. All priests, all crucified, all wearing red hoods. And then there was Father Jack Ahearn in Sudbury, the alleged suicide victim from thirty years ago, also wearing a red hood. All this information and I was no closer to finding the killer than the day I started. How do cops do it? How do they live in the uncertainty?

I still had a couple of hours to kill before my meeting with Captain Pruitt, so I visited the Boston Public Library in Copley Square. To my good fortune, Henry was working behind the Microtext desk. I approached him.

"I need your help again, Henry."

"That's why I'm here."

"Can I get a listing of Boston residents by address? The White Pages list them alphabetically, but I need a listing by address." I thought for a second. "Maybe the post office has something like that."

"Most likely the post office does have something like that, but so do we: voter lists."

"Excuse me?"

"Voter lists are sorted by address, and we have the lists on microfilm. Tell me what you're looking for. Ward, precinct, calendar year, that's all I need."

"How about address and year?"

"That's sufficient."

I gave Henry the information.

CHAPTER 28

When I arrived at the Pleasant Cafe, I saw Captain Pruitt sitting on a stool at the far end of the bar with a drink in front of him. He wasn't difficult to spot; his the only black face in the place. I took the stool next to him and ordered a beer. Pruitt raised his glass for another drink. The barman nodded.

"Okay, Sherlock, what's the big scoop you have for me?"

It's nice to see you too, Captain.

"Last night I followed a man named Emmett O'Burke from the South End."

"Hooray for you, Philo Vance."

"Emmett O'Burke is a former priest, and he was in the same seminary class as Father Axholm." The beer arrived and I drank a third of it. "O'Burke drove to Revere last night."

"So?"

"Father Savold was crucified in Revere last night. Father Savold had a red hood on his head. I tailed O'Burke to Revere."

"How do you know about Father Savold's red hood?" he asked. "I didn't know about Father Savold's red hood."

"I just know." I signaled the barman. "Another beer for me and another drink for my good pal, the captain." I waited for him to leave. "Emmett O'Burke lives at 600 Chester Square, the same address as Resnick Clothiers. When Resnick was still in business they operated out of 600 Chester Square."

"Keep going."

"Resnick Clothiers manufactured the red hoods used in the serial murders, and now Emmett O'Burke, a seminarian classmate of Father Axholm, lives at the same address."

"How do you know about Resnick Clothiers?"

"I broke into the crime lab and analyzed the evidence."

"Go on, wiseass. What else do you have?"

"Emmett O'Burke served as a priest at Saint Cecilia's on Belvidere Street. That's in the Back Bay."

"I know that's the Back Bay."

"Saint Cecilia's isn't far from where O'Burke lives now."

"Yeah, and?"

"I looked up Emmett O'Burke on the voting register from the early eighties. Before he left the priesthood, he was a cleric at Saint Cecilia's."

"You already said that."

"He moved from Saint Cecilia's to 600 Chester Square in 1982. Resnick Clothiers was located at 600 Chester Square—I know, I already said that, too." I finished the beer and tapped my glass on the bar. "Resnick Clothiers closed just a few years before O'Burke moved into the same building. There must have been leftover inventory in the basement or attic or closets or whatever after Ed Resnick died. That's where Emmett O'Burke got the red hoods, 600 Chester Square."

My beer arrived. Pruitt stood.

I said, "Are you going to look into this, Captain?"

He tossed a twenty on the bar and left without saying a word. I stuck around for a few more drinks.

The next morning the telephone roused me from a murky sleep.

"Awake yet, hotshot?"

It was Captain Pruitt.

"Up and at 'em, Captain."

"You were wrong again." He could barely contain his glee. "The former Father Emmett O'Burke now lives in New Orleans with his wife of twenty years, who happens to be a former nun, and they have three very holy children."

"What about—"

"As for the Emmett O'Burke at 600 Chester Square, he works

for U.S. Customs at Logan Airport. His supervisor told me that O'Burke arrived early for his eleven o'clock shift on the night of Father Savold's murder. Emmett O'Burke has worked at Logan Airport for twenty years. They're two different guys."

"I don't get it."

"When you were following the Camry, did you lose it at any time?"

"Yeah, at the toll plaza, but I caught up—"

"You caught up to the wrong car, dummy. Camrys are the most popular car in the country." He waited, no doubt to relish the moment. "Don't take it to heart, good pal. It's not your fault. The booze is rotting your brain."

"How did you find out so fast?" I asked.

"It's what we do, Sparhawk."

CHAPTER 29

I had made a fool of myself with Captain Pruitt.

I got dressed and walked to Saint Jude Thaddeus and sat in a pew, thinking. I might have been wrong about the two Emmett O'Burkes, but I was on the right track. Too many factors overlapped for me to be completely wrong. I just couldn't see the connections yet. Maybe I'd get a fair shake with Detective Adam Jenner. Adam and I played football together at BC. That must count for something. I went home and called him.

Adam Jenner had agreed to meet me at four o'clock at the eight-sided building near Gate 4 in the Charlestown Navy Yard. And that's exactly where I was standing at four o'clock, waiting for Adam. A drowsy pall dampened the late afternoon skies as evening settled on the city. A bevy of seagulls drifted in lazy circles and then flocked up into the ribcage of the Tobin Bridge. To the east, the harbor waters slapped the granite slabs of Dry Dock 2. On Second Avenue, a middle-aged couple walked arm-in-arm to the Navy Yard Bistro. An unmarked police car pulled over in front of me on Fifth Street, forcing the sparse flow of traffic to loop around it. Detective Jenner and Captain Pruitt got out. I hadn't expected Pruitt.

"I thought we put this to bed this morning," Pruitt said, holding a cup of coffee. "I already explained how you flubbed it on Emmett O'Burke." He exaggerated a laugh as he turned to Adam Jenner. "Sparhawk mistook an upstanding citizen named Emmett O'Burke for an ex-priest. He also thought O'Burke was the serial killer. Turns out he was never a priest and he works for U.S. Customs."

"Okay, Captain, I screwed up on O'Burke," I said.

Adam Jenner stared at Pruitt, and I assumed from the stare that Pruitt never mentioned Emmett O'Burke to Jenner. But then I had wrongly assumed that O'Burke was many things that he wasn't.

"I invited Captain Pruitt along." Jenner said this without enthusiasm. "Any new leads, Dermot?"

"No new leads, but I had a thought."

"A miracle," Pruitt said. "Go on, hotshot. Let's hear it."

"We have four victims: Fathers Axholm, Barboza, Del Rio, and Savold." I didn't mention Father Jack Ahearn, not yet. "Three of the four were roughly sixty years old. Father Barboza was only fifty. And we know Fathers Axholm and Savold were in the same seminary class."

"Big deal," Pruitt butted in. "And we know that Barboza and Del Rio weren't in the class. And we know Del Rio was only a priest for six months."

Father Jack Ahearn would have been sixty if had he lived. Father Ahearn was in Axholm's and Savold's class. Four of five victims were in the same age group, and three of the five were in the same seminary class. Father Barboza didn't fit into either category.

"What if the three sixty-year-old priests are somehow linked?" I said, keeping the murder of Father Ahearn to myself. "At first we thought the connection was pedophilia. Because of Axholm and Barboza, we tried to shoehorn the case around pedophilia."

"What's this 'we' shit?" Pruitt actually made quote marks with his fingers. "You aren't one of us, Sparhawk."

"Quit flattering me, Captain. I might get a big head."

"What are you getting at, Dermot?" Jenner asked.

"Why not look at the murders from a different angle, the angle with the most common denominators? Age. Seminary class. Location of murder."

"Location of murder?" Pruitt's black brow compressed. "What do you mean location of murder?"

"Father Barboza was murdered in Boston."

"So what?" Pruitt's coffee splashed on the sidewalk. "All the priests were murdered in Boston, except Savold."

"Dermot, you're not making any sense," Jenner said. "There's only one killer. We know this because of the red hoods. A second killer doesn't fit with the pattern."

I never said anything about a second killer.

"The pattern is wrong." I pushed back. "Father Barboza was serving in a Braintree parish when he was killed."

"So what?" Pruitt yelled.

"The other victims were killed near their parishes, but not Father Barboza. Father Barboza was killed in Boston, nowhere near his parish."

"What about Father Del Rio?" Pruitt said. "Del Rio's parish was in Cambridge, yet he was killed in Charlestown."

"True, but the killer tracked him from Cambridge." It was a reach, but I said, "The killer called Saint Peter's in Cambridge looking for Father Del Rio. He called from a pay phone on Concord Ave."

"How do you know that?" Pruitt flung his free hand into the air. "And who cares? He called from a pay phone, so what?"

"The pay phone was across the street from Saint Peter's parish office." I waited a few seconds. Neither man responded. "Why didn't he simply knock on the office door? If the caller really was meeting Father Del Rio, why didn't he just knock on the door? If you were meeting a friend for dinner, would you call him from a pay phone across the street?"

"How the hell should I know?" Pruitt barked.

"There's only one reason to use a pay phone that I can see," I said. "So the call isn't traced."

"Everyone uses pay phones!"

Who was Pruitt kidding? Almost no one uses pay phones these days. They use cell phones.

"The parish receptionist answered the call. She told the killer that Father Del Rio was at his brother's house in Charlestown. Pete Del Rio, the brother, is listed in the phone book." I found myself pausing to emphasize the point. "And that very same night, the killer nailed Father Del Rio to the base of the Bunker Hill Monument. But the killer first looked for Father Del Rio in Cambridge."

In a quieter voice, Pruitt asked, "Why did the receptionist tell him about Charlestown?"

"Because the caller said he was supposed to meet Father Del Rio for dinner that night, that's why."

"Maybe he was supposed to meet him for dinner," Pruitt said.

"I talked to his brother, Pete. Pete told me that no one else was expected for dinner."

"What's the goddamned point, Sparhawk?"

"Father Barboza doesn't fit with the other victims, that's the point."

"Sure he does."

"Not as far as the location of the murder goes."

Pruitt smiled and wagged his finger at me.

"The killer could have followed Father Barboza from Braintree to Boston. If he followed Del Rio from Cambridge, he could have followed Barboza from Braintree. You didn't think of that, did you?"

He was right, I hadn't thought of that.

"Am I right?" Pruitt chucked his coffee cup to the ground. "Listen to me closely, genius boy. You don't summon us to talk about crime theories, we summon you. We interrogate you. You got that? We're not your advisors. We're in charge." Pruitt stomped on the cup. "Go cry to the DA, because I'm through dealing with you."

"First of all, Captain, I didn't summon you. I asked to meet with Adam Jenner, and you tagged along. Second of all, what are you hiding?"

"Hiding?" Pruitt went nose to chin with me. "Let me ask you the same question, Sparhawk. What are you hiding?"

"Nothing."

"Nothing?" He rocked up on his toes. "How about gunshots in the projects?"

"What are you talking about?"

"Gunshots were reported in the projects. A man fitting your description was observed running from the scene. Anything you want to tell us, hotshot?"

I needed to get out of Charlestown for a while, to a place where nobody knew my name. I browsed an AA booklet and found a meeting in Hull, a desolate locale at this time of year. It took more than an hour to get there and that was fine. Time doesn't matter when you want to disappear. I traveled the meandering road down Route 228 through Hingham and Cohasset and arrived in Hull at West Corner.

I drove along the Nantasket beachfront as the whipping Atlantic gales sandblasted the Acclaim. For some reason I thought of old man Gomes, maybe because of a lobster boat rocking on the whitecaps. I parked at the Knights of Columbus Hall in the Kenburma section and went inside. Whatever the speakers said didn't sink in. After the meeting I drove down Nantasket Ave. and stopped at the penny arcade, a rundown remnant of bygone Paragon Park. I went inside and played Skee-Ball for an hour. The last game I rolled all fifties, a perfect score in this venue. I left the string of tickets where they were, winding out of the slot.

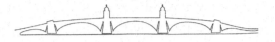

CHAPTER 30

Two Emmett O'Burkes living within a mile of each other? Not likely. It wasn't that I didn't believe Captain Pruitt. My doubt had to do with probability. What were the chances that two *different* Emmett O'Burkes lived so close to one another, but never at the same time? I could buy Pruitt's story if both O'Burkes had been concurrently listed on the voting rolls or in the telephone directory, but they weren't. No overlap existed. I was betting that the former Father Emmett O'Burke moved a few blocks up Mass Ave. I was betting he moved from Saint Cecilia's on Belvidere Street to 600 Chester Square, and not to New Orleans as Pruitt had said.

And then there were the red hoods. The hoods were manufactured by Resnick Clothiers at 600 Chester Square. Emmett O'Burke lived at 600 Chester Square. A member of the seminary class *and* the maker of the red hoods occupied the same building. Despite Captain Pruitt's insistence, I needed more convincing that an Emmett O'Burke tandem actually existed. My gut told me something screwy was going on, and I intended to find out what it was.

I rode the Orange Line to Mass Ave. and walked to the old Resnick address. Standing on the sculpted stoop of 600 Chester Square, I again read the names on the doorbell plates. E. O'Burke was still listed on the bottom. Harriett Schwartz was still listed on top. I rang O'Burke's doorbell and waited, but nobody answered. I tried Harriett Schwartz. A muffled voice tickled my ear. I looked around but saw no one. The voice sounded again. It was coming from an old-fashioned speaking tube. I hollered into the tube, stating my name. Before I had a chance to explain what I wanted, the door buzzed open. I stepped into the vestibule and looked up.

An elderly woman was standing on the third-floor landing. She leaned over the railing and yelled down, "What do you want, young man?"

"Are you Ms. Schwartz?"

"I'm Harriett Schwartz."

"I'd like to ask you a few questions if I could. I'm working for the Archdiocese of Boston, investigating the serial murders of the priests."

"You're investigating the priest murders?"

"I'm trying to catch the serial killer." I looked up to the landing. She was listening. "The trail led me to 600 Chester Square."

"You cannot be serious. The trail led you here? Are you a policeman attached to the archdiocese?" she asked. "I heard they do that on occasion."

"I'm not with the police, but I have been working with Boston Homicide." *Much to their disgust.* "Can I talk to you about the case?"

"Anything to break the boredom. Come on up."

When I stepped onto the landing, she assertively extended her hand and we shook. Her posture was perfect, her hair was styled, and her clothes were tailored. She wore spare makeup and silver earrings. Her nails were manicured and coated with clear polish.

She led me into her apartment, which was Boston brownstone at its finest. The ceiling soared fifteen feet high. The plaster medallion centering it had more swirls than a wedding cake. Sunshine poured through the large bay windows, brightening the Oriental rugs and heavy furniture.

"Obviously, you know I'm Harriett Schwartz," she said. "What is your name? I couldn't understand you through the tube."

"My name is Dermot Sparhawk."

"And you're looking for the serial killer. I can still remember the Boston Strangler from the sixties, scared the daylights out every woman in the city. I was living in this very apartment when he

killed that poor woman on Gainsborough Street. To be candid, I
don't think Albert DeSalvo was the strangler."

"That was before my time, but I saw the movie."

"Yes, with Tony Curtis and Henry Fonda." She looked at me.
"I apologize for venturing off track. It happens at my age. What
do you want to ask me, Dermot? Do you really think I can help
find the killer?"

"I certainly hope so," I said. "I understand that a former priest
named Emmett O'Burke lives downstairs from you. He was a
priest in the eighties."

"Emmett, a former priest?" She hooted and slapped her thigh.
"You are a very funny man, Dermot Sparhawk. Emmett O'Burke
a priest?" She roared with laughter again. "I can see I'll have to
clarify some things for you."

"He wasn't a priest?"

"If Emmett O'Burke was a priest in the eighties, he celebrated
Mass in Ballygarrett, County Wexford. Emmett emigrated from
Ireland in the early eighties. He obtained a Donnelly Visa, that's
how he got into the U.S."

"O'Burke lived in Ireland until the eighties?"

"That's correct," she said. "And he still speaks with a singsong
Irish brogue, such a joy to hear."

"And he works for Customs at Logan Airport?"

"You've done your homework, though clearly not all of it.
Why did you think Emmett was a former priest?"

"O'Burke is not a common name, even in Boston," I said.

"Neither is Emmett."

"A priest named Emmett O'Burke once served at Saint Cecilia's
Parish up the street. The year he left the priesthood, an Emmett
O'Burke appeared on the voting rolls here at 600 Chester Square."

"And you assumed it was the same man. That's understand-
able. I might have leapt to the same conclusion." She looked out
the bay windows. "He had to wait before he could register."

"He had to wait?"

"Emmett was issued a green card right away. The green card

permitted him to work, but he had to wait before he could register to vote. Otherwise, you'd have seen both Emmett O'Burkes on the voting list at the same time."

"He wasn't in the phone book, either."

"He used Barbara's phone."

"Who's Barbara?"

"Barbara is my niece, she lives downstairs." Harriett smiled. "We own this building, Barbara and I. The building has been in our family since 1961, the year before the Boston Strangler went on his rampage."

"A man named Ed Resnick ran a business out of this building."

"You are correct, young man. Ed Resnick was my brother-in-law. He married my sister, Hanna. Barbara is their daughter. Barbara O'Burke was Barbara Resnick before she married Emmett. That's why Emmett didn't get a phone, so he could use Barbara's phone. He was sweet on her right away." She sat on a leather chair and folded her hands on her lap. "I live on the top floor. They live on the bottom two floors. The basement we use for storage. I suppose we could rent it as a garden apartment, but who needs the headaches that come with a tenant?"

O'Burke operated fast.

"Emmett O'Burke moved in with Barbara Resnick when he came here from Ireland?"

"No, no, it wasn't like that. At that time, the first and second floors were separate units. Emmett lived above Barbara in the middle unit. When Barbara and Emmett got married, they combined the first two floors into one condo."

Captain Pruitt was right, there were two Emmett O'Burkes. At least he wasn't here to gloat about it. I thought about the red hoods.

"Did Ed Resnick have any employees?"

"Eddie worked eighty hours a week, mostly alone. As I remember it, he would occasionally hire day help during the holidays.

He'd hire neighbor people, guys looking to earn a few extra dollars. But he never hired a permanent employee."

"Do you remember any of the people he hired?"

"Lord, no."

It felt like I was on the verge of learning something important, and at the same time, Harriett Schwartz said nothing that triggered an aha moment.

"Is there anything left from Resnick Clothiers? Any inventory of stock, anything at all?"

"Not a thing is left. Ed ran his business out of the basement. When he died, we hired a company to clear out everything, the inventory, the machinery, everything. We didn't want any sad memories reminding us that Ed was gone."

"Do you remember the name of the company that did the cleanup job?"

"Not for the life of me," she said. "It was thirty years ago." She looked up from the chair. "Why all the questions about Resnick Clothiers, Mr. Sparhawk?"

I didn't want to tell her about the red hoods.

"I'm just curious." An idea came to me. "Would you mind if I went down to the basement and looked around?"

"As I told you, the basement was cleared out thirty years ago when Ed died. But if you're *that* curious about it, you are welcome to see for yourself."

"Thanks, Harriett."

"The door to the cellar is unlocked. It's tucked in a small alcove on the left side of the entrance foyer. You can check it on your way out. I'd join you, but the stairs are murder on my knees." We walked together to the landing. "I hope you catch the killer."

"Me, too."

I went down to the basement and clicked on the lights. The room was empty. No cobwebs, no dampness, not a box of storage. Even the windows were clean.

CHAPTER 31

The next day I visited the Copley Boston Public Library and read the newspapers for an hour. From the library I walked east on Boylston Street and cut across the Public Gardens and Boston Common to Winter Street. At Arch Street I turned left and went into Saint Anthony Shrine. Some nasty things had been weighing on me, and I wanted to unload them. After lighting a votive candle for Aunt Agnes and splashing holy water on the pant leg of my bad knee, I entered a dark confessional box for an overdue sacrament of reconciliation. The friar opened the screen and listened to my sins. He gasped when I mentioned the weight-drop whacking of Lopo Gomes. He wasn't too thrilled with my verbal assault on Bishop Downey, either, but he hung in there with me.

"Give me a good act of contrition," the friar said.

After I recited an act of contrition, he absolved my sins. I stepped out of the box a bit lighter in spirit and knelt to pray penance. After completing the prayers, I left the shrine and headed for Downtown Crossing. On Summer Street an ambulance raced by and turned down Arch Street, probably to resuscitate my confessor. I entered the subway at Chauncey Street, and an Orange Line train took me to Community College.

As I was walking through Thompson Square, a young black man in a wheelchair rolled up and jingled a tin can. I dropped in a five along with my loose change.

"Dermot?" he asked.

I stopped and looked at him. His face was shaven and his eyes were clear. He wore tattered but laundered clothing. He seemed familiar, perhaps a food pantry client or an AA man. I said hello to him and started to walk away.

"Dermot, it's me, Buck Louis. We played football together at BC, remember?" He wheeled closer. "I got injured my freshman year and had to leave the team. I left school, too."

"Yeah." I studied his face. "Buck Louis."

"You remember me."

I didn't know Buck that well. He had left school shortly after he suffered a paralyzing neck injury, an injury that happened in practice during an Oklahoma drill. Buck never got to play in a game.

"Of course, I remember you," I said. "Let's get out of the cold."

"Sounds good."

We went into Dunkin' Donuts on Main Street and ordered coffee, sat down, and talked about BC football. Buck's face grew serious.

"I'm homeless these days," he said. "But I don't do drugs and I don't drink."

"You're one up on me."

He took off his frayed gloves and laid them on his lap.

"Lucky for me I'm not a quad. I can move my arms and fingers, got good flexibility in them, too. I keep my upper body toned up by wheeling around the city. Sometimes I do pull-ups if I can find monkey bars low enough."

"Where do you sleep at night?"

"Shelters, mostly. My parents died. I got some money from the house in Tennessee, but that's gone now."

That's right, Buck came from Tennessee.

People rushed in from the winter air and went to the counter. A lifelong Townie named Sugar handed Buck a bag with a donut inside.

"Any prospects for a place to live?" I asked.

"None." And then he laughed. "I might not have graduated from BC, but got a master's degree in street survival. Surviving the streets ain't too bad if you're physically handicapped, because people figure you got a legitimate excuse. The poor bastards with mental problems, that's a whole other ball game."

"What about tonight?"

"I'll find a place, always do."

It was freezing outside.

"I own a two-family house on the other side of the hill. My aunt left it to me when she died. You can bunk there tonight if you want."

"I don't know." He looked at the floor. "I don't want to be an imposition."

"It's no imposition, Buck. I have plenty of room and there's even a ramp. My aunt had her own troubles getting around."

"A ramp?" His eyes met mine. "Like I said, I don't want to impose none. And there's another thing."

"What's that?"

"I might smell a little when I take off my coat."

"We have a cast-iron bathtub, holds the heat a long time. I can help you get in and out of it."

"Maybe for a night," he said.

"Good decision."

We humped up to the Bunker Hill Monument and rolled down the other side. Social esteem plummets as you move from the heights of Monument Square to the lowlands of the projects, from the codfish aristocracy to the great unwashed. My house sat on the demarcation line, neither fish nor fowl. When we got home, Buck wheeled up the rickety wooden ramp and into the first-floor unit. Aunt Agnes would have liked Buck.

I drew a bath, helped him get undressed, and eased him into the tub. Buck bathed for more than an hour, running the hot water every so often to reheat the pool. When he finished, I helped him get out and gave him a bathrobe to wear. We went to the parlor.

"Been living in Brooklyn the last couple of years, in the East Flatbush neighborhood," Buck said. "Had a cousin down there, but he's in Afghanistan now, defending us against those terrorists.

He couldn't find a job, so he signed up for the army. And I'm up here in Boston, lookin' to get my footin'. Been doin' okay so far, I guess."

"Glad to hear it."

I asked Buck if he wanted something to drink. He said he'd like orange juice. I didn't have orange juice, but I had apple cider. He said apple cider would be fine. I poured him a glass and a glass for myself.

Buck sipped. "I just thought of something you might get a kick out of." He put down the glass. "I came across it the other day when I was going through my stuff. Pass me my knapsack."

I passed him the bag. He took out a manila envelope and removed a sheet of parched paper from it. It almost crumbled when he handed it to me.

"What's this?"

"It's the football roster from our freshman year." He wheeled up and pointed. "There's my name. Buck Louis, running back, Knoxville Catholic. Never graduated from BC, but I always kept the list."

"Jesus, Mary, and Joseph," I said.

I stared at the roster. There must have been twenty names I didn't recognize, guys that never made it through the four years of college.

"Are you okay?" Buck asked.

"I'm fine. Make yourself at home, Buck. I have to check something out."

I looked at my watch. It was two p.m. There was plenty of time to get what I wanted today.

CHAPTER 32

I called Bishop Downey and told him that I needed two lists of names from his seminary class: the list of incoming freshmen and the list of graduates. The bishop told me it would take a few hours to gather the information. I pressed him on time. He said he would have it for me in two hours, and two hours later I pulled into the seminary parking lot and went inside. A receptionist handed me a folder with my name on it. I opened the folder and found the list of incoming freshmen.

The first name I noticed was Father Del Rio. Del Rio was a member of the incoming freshman class. According to the records, he withdrew from school almost immediately to get married. Thirty years later, after his wife died, Del Rio reentered the seminary, but a different seminary. The list contained the names Fathers Ahearn, Axholm, Del Rio, and Savold.

Four of the five murder victims were incoming freshman in the same class. Four out of five, that's eighty percent. I was no actuary, but eighty percent couldn't be random. Bishop Downey's name was on the list and so was the name of Francis Ennis. My mind sifted the data, and then my arms went cold.

Bishop Downey and DA Francis Ennis, either one of them could be the serial killer—or a potential victim. Bishop Downey was privy to the seminary list. Francis Ennis had the police reports. Both men were in the same class. I tucked the two lists in my pocket and left the seminary.

On the way home I checked again on Blackie Barboza. He still wasn't home. I thought about Bonita Diaz and visited her apartment. Maybe she'd know Blackie's whereabouts, or maybe I was hoping for another breast bump. She didn't answer my knock. I dragged my ass home. Buck Louis was waiting when I came in, and he wheeled over to me.

"I hope I didn't do anything wrong."

"What do you mean?" I asked.

"The phone kept ringing and ringing, so I answered it."

"Don't worry about it."

I flopped onto the couch and rested my feet on the hassock, a simple pleasure that Buck would never again enjoy. He rolled up next to me.

"A guy named Vasco Gomes called you." Buck handed me a piece of paper. "He left a phone number, said it was important."

"Vasco Gomes?"

I dialed the number. Vasco answered and told me he had information about the man who hired his cousin Lopo.

"I can only tell you in person," he said. "Meet me tomorrow in P'town in front of Town Hall at noon."

"Provincetown? All the way down the end of the Cape? Come on, Vasco. Can't we do this over the phone?"

"Bring your wallet," he said. "And make sure you aren't followed."

I drove south for Provincetown on a cold Tuesday morning, supposedly against flow of Boston traffic. No such luck. The HOV lane guaranteed gridlock on both sides of the expressway instead of just one. I finally made it to the Braintree split and things opened up. I cruised down Route 3 through Marshfield and Duxbury and Plymouth. I took the Sagamore Bridge over the Cape Cod Canal and onto Route 6.

The Mid-Cape Highway was a breeze in the winter, and I clicked on the cruise control. An hour later, I parked in Provincetown and walked along Commercial Street to Portuguese Square in front of Town Hall, arriving with ten minutes to spare. Vasco Gomes wasn't there. I sat on a park bench and waited.

After twenty minutes of sitting around, I went to a general store and bought a Cape Cod newspaper and a cup of coffee and took them back to the bench I'd been warming. I was reading about the Celtics overtime win over the Lakers at the Garden, when Vasco Gomes sat next to me. The swelling on his cheek had mostly died down, but the fear in his face had intensified. His sunken brown eyes scanned the square and the street, as if he were a cornered raccoon.

"Anyone follow you?"

"Nobody followed me, Vasco."

"Good, because I'm a little nervous these days." His eyes were bloodshot and his clothes reeked of marihuana. Vasco had probably smoked more bones than a pet cemetery crematorium. "I had to meet you in person, 'cause I need some cash. There are things I know, things you asked me about before. The info is for sale, kinda like an informant."

"Sure, an informant." I played along. "What am I buying?"

"I can help you with who hired Lopo."

"Are you serious?" I asked.

"Yeah, yeah, I'm serious."

"That, I'll buy." We settled on fifty dollars. "Let's hear it."

"It was a cop," he said. "A cop hired Lopo to scare you." He read my face. "It's true, man, I swear. Lopo told me. He said the cop was working on the priest murders."

"What did the cop look like?" I asked. "Was he black?"

"I never met the cop myself. Lopo told me about him, said he was tough, but he never described him."

"It's not much help," I said. "Why didn't you tell me this before?"

"I got scared, man. I thought the cop might kill me if he found out I talked."

"And now?"

"Now, I don't give a shit. I'm desperate. That's why I called you. I need cash."

"For what?"

"For bus fare to Fall River. I've been living here with a gentleman, understand what I'm saying? Nothing committed, just casual, and the bastard threw me out. He said I smoked too much pot. I can't call my family because my family, well, they don't go for the gay stuff. Portuguese are traditional people. Why stick it in their face?"

"They might know anyway."

"Did you know?"

"No, I didn't." I patted my jacket pocket for a cigar, but was fresh out. "Do you know Blackie Barboza, the deaf guy from Charlestown?"

"I met him once or twice, but I don't really know him. Lopo stayed at his place when he fished up that way."

"Do you remember the night that you and Lopo threatened me at the church?"

"Do we have to go through that again?"

"Father Netto Barboza and Blackie Barboza were brothers. Blackie asked me to find Netto's killer. Did you hear me? I said that Blackie and the priest were brothers."

"I didn't know that, honest."

"Quite a coincidence, don't you think? You and Lopo threatened me to lay off investigating Father Barboza. Lopo knew Blackie Barboza. Blackie put me on the case in the first place. And now Blackie happens to be missing."

"I went along for the ride, that's all. It was Lopo's deal." Vasco sighed. "I wish I never took that ride to Charlestown. Between you and that hairy baboon Chub, I wish I never took that ride. My uncle blames me for Lopo's death."

"So it's all a coincidence," I said. "Blackie Barboza and Father Barboza, Blackie and Lopo, Lopo and you."

"Yeah, it's a coincidence."

"I don't think so, Vasco."

I tossed the coffee cup in a town barrel and got up from the bench. Vasco stood, too. Vasco walked away fifty dollars richer. I drove back to Boston with no answers.

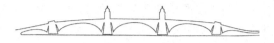

CHAPTER 33

After I finished breakfast at Uncle Joe's Diner, I stepped out to the icy morning air. Yesterday it was Provincetown, today it would be Martha's Vineyard. A former seminarian named Paul Herz lived on the Vineyard, and I wanted to ask him a few questions. Herz had been a member of Bishop Downey's freshman class for a brief time, lasting less than a semester. He was also a classmate of four of the murder victims. According to the school records, Paul Herz left the seminary two months into his freshman year. The reason given for his departure was vague, something about pursuing other ventures.

Meeting with Paul Herz proved a predicament. I wasn't sure whether to warn him or suspect him. As I was contemplating this dilemma, a car pulled up and powered down the passenger window. It was Mickey Pappas from AA.

"Need a ride?"

"I need a ride, all right," I said, "all the way down the Cape."

"I can use a road trip. Get in."

"You serious?"

"I haven't been down the Cape in a long time. And with the weather coming in, the cabin fever will drive me crazy. What part of the Cape?"

"Woods Hole," I said. "I'm going to the Vineyard."

"Let's get moving before the nor'easter hits." He drove away from Hayes Square and maneuvered under the Tobin Bridge. "Hope they don't cancel the ferry on you."

We went over the Zakim Bridge and through the O'Neill Tunnel and stayed south on the expressway. We talked about Charlestown and then the conversation shifted to AA. Mickey did most of the talking. We crossed the Bourne Bridge and picked up Route 28 on the Cape Cod side. When we reached Woods Hole, Mickey stopped at the entrance of the ferry terminal. He was still talking about booze.

"My father was a tosspot," he said. "You remember my old man, stumbling around the projects, slammed on Thunderbird."

"He was a fix-it man."

"I used my father's drinking as an excuse. If you had my old man, you'd drink, too. But today it's different. Today I'm a product of my upbringing, not a victim of it. Today I know that my father had a disease. He was a sick man, not a bad man." Mickey shifted into park. "You don't have to end up like your father, Dermot."

"What do you mean?"

"If I can stop drinking, you can stop drinking." Mickey continued, "Think about what I said. If I can stop, you can stop. I'm heading back to Charlestown before the storm hits. Will you be okay down here?"

"I'll be fine, Mick." I got out of the car. "Thanks for the ride."

"Okay, kid." Mickey wheeled out of the lot.

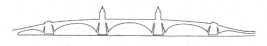

CHAPTER 34

I purchased a ticket for Martha's Vineyard and waited inside the vestibule. Above the pier, two seagulls circled in search of scraps. They weren't having much luck this time of year. After the vehicles were loaded onto the ferry, the passengers were called to board. The whistle blew, the diesels revved, the ship shoved off from the dock.

The ferry carved the choppy waters of Nantucket Sound as the nor'easter encroached from the Atlantic. As we sailed into the deeper channels, the waves gave way to whitecaps, and in the distance the whitecaps shook hands with a darkening horizon. I climbed topside to smell the salt air. A strong swell slammed the portside gunnels. The ferry lurched, forcing me to grab the railing. It was almost Townie overboard.

We docked at Vineyard Haven, where I hailed a cab. But instead of going directly to Paul Herz's house to warn him of potential danger, I told the cabdriver to bring me to an Oak Bluffs bar with a water view. Which one? he asked. Any one, I said. I wanted to watch the nor'easter hit landfall. He drove me to a joint called The Liberty Barge. The place was perfect, a sawdust gin mill.

I was home.

I drank all afternoon and evening and enjoyed the blizzard over Nantucket Sound. The conditions swirled to whiteout. The seas eddied and the waves crashed. The barroom scuttlebutt said that the ferries had been canceled until further notice. I went outside to experience the storm firsthand and nearly fell down the stairs when a squall blew. I went back inside. I had just resettled on my stool when the barman uttered two grave words: last call. I signaled him.

"Three double whiskeys and three large beers," I said.

"Can only serve one drink at last call, partner."

"Three." I slid a C-note into the bar gutter. "Keep the change."

The C submerged and the drinks surfaced, and that's the last thing I remembered.

I woke up strapped in a hospital bed. A nurse told me that I had suffered an alcoholic overdose and that my liver was bigger than a waterlogged buoy. I'd been unconscious for two days. The restraints were for my own protection, she said. And then she said something about pancreatitis. What was happening to me? Not long after the nurse left the room, a uniformed Massachusetts State Trooper came in. He said he wanted to ask me a few questions and sat in a chair next to my bed.

"You were one sick man the other night." His badge read Sergeant Silva. "And one lucky man, too."

"I don't feel lucky."

"You suffered some kind of a convulsion. The bartender tried to hold you down, and then he called an ambulance."

"Is that why you're here, because I had a rum fit at The Liberty Barge?"

"No." Silva paused. "We usually don't care about noncriminal events, and we wouldn't have cared this time either, except you said some things that caused us concern."

My head pounded. "What did I say?"

"You don't remember?" Silva sat back. "No, I don't imagine you could. Did you pop some pills or something?"

"I don't do drugs."

"Of course not." He finger-combed his black hair and took out a notebook. "Tell me about Paul Herz."

"Paul Herz?" How did Silva know about Herz? "Who told you about Paul Herz?"

"Loose lips, Sparhawk. You were talking about Herz at The Liberty Barge, just before you juddered to the barroom floor. What's up with Paul Herz?"

"Nothing's up, I just wanted to talk to him about something."

"Talk to him about what, exactly?" After a few seconds, Silva repeated, "Why did you want to talk to him?"

"I was hired by the Archdiocese of Boston to help find the crucifixion killer," I said. "You know, the serial killer."

"I am well aware of the serial killings, Sparhawk." Silva unbuttoned the cuffs of his pressed uniform and rolled up his sleeves. "What's that got to do with Paul Herz?"

"I'm not sure, maybe nothing. I wanted to ask Herz a few questions and warn him of possible danger."

"Warn him?" Silva's dark eyes opened wider. "What danger?"

"Paul Herz was in the same seminary class as four of the five crucified priests. I believe there's a link between the seminary class and the killings. So I came down here to ask him a few questions about it."

"Paul Herz was a priest?"

"He was never ordained." I squirmed, but my shoulders didn't budge. "Any chance of getting the straps off?"

"Doc's call, not mine." He rubbed his forehead. "What did you want to ask Paul Herz?"

"I wanted to ask him about his classmates." I wriggled my arms. "I suspect that Herz, or somebody that Herz knows, is the serial killer."

"Is that so?"

"But if Herz isn't the serial killer, he could be a target of the serial killer. Either way, I need to talk to him. Why all the questions about Paul Herz?"

"Herz is dead."

"What?"

"Paul Herz killed himself yesterday." Silva sat back in the chair. "He jumped off Gay Head Light. Herz committed suicide."

"Suicide?" If only I had gone straight to his house instead of the bar, I could have saved his life. "Was he wearing a red hood?"

"A red hood?" he asked. "Why?"

I ignored his question.

"Could Herz have been pushed?"

"Anything is possible." Silva's face remained impassive. "He left a suicide note."

"The note could be bogus."

"We checked the note against Paul Herz's signature at Town Hall. The signatures matched." Silva glanced at his watch. "Herz's brother provided letters that Paul had written. We checked the letters against the suicide note. The handwriting matched."

"You sound convinced it was a suicide, Sergeant."

"That's because I am convinced."

"Tell me about his brother." I sounded pushy. "Please."

"His name is Roland Herz, and he is something of a loner," Silva said. "Although he's a loner, he's been very cooperative with us."

"Beyond the letters, did Roland offer anything more?"

"Yes, he did. Roland told me that Paul suffered horribly from mental illness. Paul Herz had been in and out of psychiatric hospitals his entire adult life."

Sergeant Silva's cell phone rang. He stepped out of the room to answer it.

I thought about the suicide note. The handwriting matched the writing samples provided by Paul Herz's brother. And the signature matched the signature at Town Hall. I thought about murder, and I thought about the red hood. Could the hood have fallen off Herz's head and been blown away in the nor'easter? Possibly, but not likely.

Sergeant Silva said that Paul Herz had a history of mental illness. Maybe suicide fits. Maybe Herz succumbed to the emotional pain and ended it. I felt relieved by his suicide. If Paul Herz had been murdered, it would have been my fault for not warning him in time. As it stands now, there was nothing I could have done about it.

I nodded off.

CHAPTER 35

The following morning Glooscap walked into the hospital room and sat in the same chair that Sergeant Silva had sat in the day before. The restraints were now off my arms and legs, and it felt good. I cranked the bed to raise my head.

"How did you know I was here?"

"I got a call." He clutched my hand. "Are you okay?"

Wow, someone holding my hand.

"I don't know." The skies outside were now peaceful in the aftermath of the nor'easter, but a grayness of clouds remained. "I thought I had the booze thing figured out. I went to a bar for a few beers, not to get drunk."

"Some people cannot stop after a few beers, Dermot. Some Micmac Indians cannot even have one drink without placing themselves in danger."

"I'm half Irish, too."

"You are beautiful." He tapped his knee and smiled. "Imagine that, using your Irish heritage as a defense to drink. That is the disease of alcoholism for you."

"I don't know what to do about it."

"It is simple, but it is not easy." Glooscap draped his dungaree coat on the back of the chair. "Your father tried to stop drinking before. He attended AA meetings. Fits and starts, he never quite got it, but he never gave up. Chief brought me to my first meeting."

"You're in AA?"

"Yes, I am," he said. "Your father needed more than meetings. He needed a place to meditate."

"Is that why he disappeared for weeks at a time, to find a place to meditate?"

"There is much you do not know," Glooscap said.

"Do you know Mickey Pappas?"

"Mickey is a good man."

"Did he call you?"

"Mickey and I talk occasionally." Glooscap pointed his cell phone at me. "I am taking a picture of you. It will be a good re-member-when."

After sitting through the required consultation with a doctor, who strongly recommended that I enroll in a thirty-day treatment pro-gram, I signed myself out of the hospital. Glooscap was waiting for me in the lobby. He brushed the barroom sawdust off the back of my coat as we were walking out of the building.

I said, "Let's go to the lighthouse." I told Glooscap about Paul Herz. "I want to see where he jumped."

We drove in Glooscap's truck to Gay Head Light, which sat atop a clay bluff overlooking Vineyard Sound. A flock of seagulls glided in the windless sky, and the leaden seawater lay flat as glass. Glooscap parked at a gate that barricaded the road leading to the lighthouse, but it was easy enough to step around it. We got out of the truck and walked to the edge of the cliff and looked out to the sound. The smell of salt air stimulated me out of my funk. Glooscap and I looked back to the lighthouse.

"Quite a fall," Glooscap said. "Paul Herz landed on frozen turf. It must have been like hitting concrete."

I glimpsed over the edge again.

"The drop to the shore below must be a hundred feet. No way to survive a jump from that height. Look at the boulders at the bottom."

"Take a gander at this." Glooscap walked to the tower and pointed at the recently cut hasp. "Herz had tools with him. Where are they now?"

"The police must have collected them."

"Why bother with tools at all?" Glooscap asked. "Why not jump off the cliff? It is a much bigger drop than the tower."

"If Paul jumped off the cliff, the tide might have washed away his body."

"So what if it washed away his body? Paul Herz would be dead. Why would he care if his body was taken to sea?"

"Maybe someone wanted Paul's body found. Maybe Paul Herz didn't jump off the lighthouse. Maybe he was pushed."

"You and your conspiracies."

"Let's get out of here," I said.

Glooscap and I went back to the truck to warm up. We listened to a crackly Martha's Vineyard volunteer radio station while we waited for the heat.

"Let's visit Roland Herz," I said.

"The recluse brother?" Glooscap cupped his hands on the defroster. "Why?"

"To express our sympathies for the loss of Paul."

"We do not know Roland, and we did not know Paul."

"We'll get to know Roland, and then we'll ask him some questions, and maybe he'll tell us some things we don't yet know."

"I do not like it, Dermot. I do not like the idea of bothering a grieving brother, especially under the guise of sympathy, when the real motive is personal gain."

"I'm trying to find a killer, Glooscap. Let's talk to him."

"It could backfire."

Glooscap acquiesced and looked up Roland Herz's address on the Internet using his cell phone. Roland resided on Osprey Lane in Chilmark, a short distance from Gay Head Light. We drove between Menemsha and Squibnocket Ponds on State Road and snaked our way into Chilmark. Roland lived in a cedar-shingled saltbox house near Lucy Vincent Beach, a stretch of unspoiled oceanfront on the Vineyard's south coast. We parked in front and knocked on his door.

A long minute later a hunched man answered. He craned his neck and looked up at us with rheumy eyes. I thought he might fall over.

"Yes?" he asked. "Can I help you?"

"My name is Dermot Sparhawk and this is Glooscap, my uncle. We are sorry for your loss, Mr. Herz. It was an awful tragedy."

"Thank you for saying that. It was undeniably tragic. I appreciate your stopping by to offer condolences. Call me Roland," he said. "Neither of you look familiar to me. Where are you from?"

"Charlestown," I said. "Glooscap lives in Dorchester."

"Charlestown and Dorchester, that's quite a distance away. Well, if you were friends of Paul, you may as well come in."

We stepped into the small room. Roland closed the door behind us.

"So, you came all the way the way down from the big city, how nice," he said. "Please sit down, both of you. May I offer you coffee?"

"No, thanks," I said. "We just stopped by to pay our respects."

Glooscap's cell phone must have vibrated, because he opened it.

"Damned telemarketers." He fiddled with it and closed it. "Forgive me, Roland. It is shut off now."

"No need to apologize," Roland said. "I thought I knew most of Paul's friends."

I looked at Glooscap, who looked down at the floor.

"Paul and I never met," I said. "Neither of us knew Paul."

"Is that so?" Roland's eyes focused for the first time. "If you never met Paul—"

"I'm investigating a murder, Roland, more precisely multiple murders. I'm investigating the serial killings of the priests, and I wanted to ask Paul a few questions."

"Questions about what?"

"Paul attended Saint John's Seminary with most of the serial victims. I wanted to ask him about his time in the seminary with them. And then — "

"And then Paul finally ended his misery, the poor soul." Roland nodded to himself. "You are correct, Mr. Sparhawk. Paul was a seminarian. He stayed at the college for less than a semester." He paused. "But that must be thirty years ago. Is that why you wanted to talk to Paul, because he was in the seminary thirty years ago?"

"That's pretty much it, yes. I had hoped Paul might offer some firsthand knowledge about his classmates, some clues to help me find the killer."

"Are you saying that the serial killer was a member of Paul's seminary class?"

"It's possible," I said. "At the very least, I think there's a connection to the class."

"There is something amiss." Roland stroked his soft chin with a smooth hand. "You didn't know Paul, you don't know me. You didn't come here to offer condolences. What are you doing in my house, Mr. Sparhawk?"

I stood up from the chair and put my hands in my pockets. To my surprise, Roland waited for a response instead of throwing me out.

"I apologize for coming here under false colors, Roland. The idea of barging in and asking questions seemed wrong."

"So you pretended to be a mourner."

"I'm sorry for that. I came here because I was hoping you could help me."

"How on earth can *I* help *you*?"

"You can answer a few questions for me. If you're not up to it, I'll understand."

Roland got up from his chair and joined me standing. He walked around the room once and then looked at me.

"If you really think it will help find the killer, ask your questions. I'll answer them out of respect for Paul."

"Thank you, Roland. To your knowledge, did Paul stay in touch with any of his seminary classmates?"

Roland rubbed his throat with an open palm. "No, Paul never stayed in touch with his classmates. He wanted to, but he scared them off. Mental illness does that to relationships. His schizophrenia drove them away." Roland started to cry as he spoke. "Paul wasn't always sick, Mr. Sparhawk. There was a time when Paul had his head on straight. He was a very intelligent man once." His shoulders shook. "I don't think I can talk any longer."

"Dermot." Glooscap leaned forward. "We should leave Roland to his grief."

"Yes." I patted Roland's shoulder. "I'm sorry I upset you." I wrote my address and phone number. "Call me if you need anything."

We left the house and left Chilmark. The conversation with Roland Herz troubled me. He was a weak man who was mourning the death of a sick brother, but instead of easing his pain, I worsened it. My thoughts then turned to the suicide of Paul Herz. Something wasn't right.

I said to Glooscap, "I know what you said about my conspiracy theories, but my gut tells me that Paul Herz didn't jump off that lighthouse."

"I am listening."

"His supposed suicide is too convenient for me to accept. The whole thing is too much of a coincidence, and I'm getting sick and tired of tidy little coincidences."

"What if Paul Herz was the serial killer?" Glooscap speculated. "What if the guilt got to him? Perhaps he could no longer handle the guilt and jumped to end it."

"Serial killers don't feel guilt. Guilt has been conditioned out of them."

"I must agree with you," Glooscap said. "Maybe it was something else, not guilt but some other reason."

"Like what?"

"If Paul Herz was in fact the serial killer, maybe he sensed that you were closing in on him. Perhaps the very thought of a trial and prison time proved too much for him to handle, and so he jumped to his death instead."

"Maybe, but it sounds farfetched."

Glooscap drove to Vineyard Haven, where we boarded the ferry to Woods Hole.

CHAPTER 36

The next morning I visited Blackie Barboza's apartment again. He still wasn't in. I went home to chat with Buck Louis, who was making coffee when I got there. He poured me a cup, and I carried it to the parlor couch. Buck wheeled in behind me. I placed the cup on the coffee table.

"I'd like to talk to you about the house, Buck."

"I understand," he said. "I'll leave today if you want me to."

"What do you mean?"

"I don't want to overstay my welcome."

"That's not what I meant. You can stay as long as you want. In fact, I have a proposition for you. Why not live here permanently?"

Buck rolled back a few feet and looked at me.

"Are you pulling my leg?" He laughed. "Not that I'd know."

"There's no sense in your living out on the street when I have an extra apartment right here. No matter what you decide, I'm moving upstairs to my aunt's old unit anyway, so you might as well stay. Think it over."

Buck popped a wheelie.

"Don't need to think it over. I love living here." He wheeled up and shook my hand. "Now that I have a mailing address, maybe I can get some benefits."

"Maybe you can."

"You mind if I get cable?" He backed up. "I don't want to push it."

"It's your place, Buck. If you want cable, get cable."

• • •

A man named Robert Iverson was another classmate of the crucified priests, and as with Paul Herz, Iverson lasted less than a semester at Saint John's Seminary. I wanted to talk to Robert Iverson,
and I hoped my visit with him would go better than my attempted
visit with Paul Herz. Iverson lived in the central part of the state,
in Gardner. Victor needed his Plymouth Acclaim today, so I called
Glooscap at his shop.

Glooscap told me that he had a car I could use for the Gardner
trip and for me to come by and pick it up. I arrived in Andrew
Square thirty minutes later on the Red Line and walked to the
auto-body shop. When I got there, Harraseeket Kid was standing
next to the hydraulic lift with his arms crossed, assessing a dented
fender.

"I have a favor to ask," I said to Kid.

"What's that?"

"A paralyzed man named Buck Louis is living with me. Can
you shore up a handicapped ramp for him?"

"Of course, I can." His shiny black hair was twisted in a ponytail. "I'll have to pull a permit to do the job right. Do you own the
house?"

"I do."

"You do?" Kid picked up a torch from the workbench. "I'll
weld a steel frame for him, won't warp or rot. For the platform,
I'll use diamond tread plate." He put down the torch without looking up. "I need a place to live, myself. I've been staying in a rooming house near the *Herald*, and they just condemned it." Kid's eyes
remained riveted to the workbench. "I have to be out soon."

I knew the rooming house he was talking about. My old man
crashed there on prolonged drunks. The place wasn't fit for bed-
bugs.

"How soon?"

"Next week."

"You're cutting it close, Kid."

"I could live with Glooscap, but we'd drive each other crazy."

He looked up from the workbench. "What about your cellar? I've lived in cellars before. The noise from the boiler helps me sleep."

"I don't know about the cellar. There's no sink or toilet, the place is dank. You don't want to live down there. Stay in my apartment until you find a place."

"I like cellars. The dampness is easy to fix, and I can treat the mold. I'll build a bathroom and replace the windows. I can mortar the walls. I'll have the place livable in no time." He stopped talking and kicked at the floor. "I'm not looking to barge in. If you don't think it's a good idea, I'll find another place."

It sounded as though Kid wanted a place to call home, not a place to hole up.

"I'd love to have you move in." I took a spare key off the key chain, the one next to the petrified ear. "Take it, the house key."

"Thanks, Dermot."

Glooscap came out of his office and tossed me a key.

"The black Navigator near the gate, you can keep it for two days. The tank is full, the alignment is perfect."

"Thanks, Glooscap."

I revved the engine, pulled out of the lot, and ramped onto I-93 north. I took the Mystic Valley Parkway through Somerville and picked up Route 2 west in Arlington, and stayed on it halfway across the state.

At four o'clock, I rang the doorbell of former seminarian Robert Iverson in Gardner, Mass., Chair City of the World, hometown to an assortment of furniture outlets, and home to a state prison that Townies called The Farm. I rang the bell again.

A scarecrow of a man answered. I told him who I was and why I was there, and said, "I'd like to speak with Robert Iverson."

"I'm Robert Iverson." He let me inside. "So, the Archdiocese of Boston hired you to find the serial killer. I must say, I'm not at all impressed with your progress thus far. I read the newspapers each day. You've made little to no headway."

"I'm working at it."

"No doubt you are." He closed the door and led me to the den. The house was filthy. The dust bunnies rivaled tumbleweed. Adding to the ambiance of louse, Iverson scratched his sideburns as if he had fleas. "Why exactly are you calling on me?"

"Another one of your seminary classmates died recently," I said.

"I didn't hear of another one dying. Which one was he?"

"He lived on Martha's Vineyard. His name was Paul Herz."

"Paul is dead?" Iverson's gray face flushed. He almost looked alive. "I've known Paul Herz for thirty years. We kept in touch after our seminary debacle."

A thirty-year acquaintance? Robert Iverson contradicted what Roland Herz had told me. Roland said that Paul didn't stay in touch with any of his classmates.

"What did you mean by debacle, Robert?"

"The seminary claimed that neither Paul nor I was priestly material, which was their loss. They reaped what they sowed, didn't they? Look at the mess they are in now." He scratched the sideburns again. "How did Paul die? Not suicide, I hope."

"The official cause of death was suicide. He allegedly took his own life." I studied Iverson's face. His eyes darted side to side, as if he were watching a Ping-Pong game on fast forward. "Paul Herz supposedly jumped from a lighthouse."

"Allegedly? Supposedly?" His eyes stopped darting. "Did Paul Herz commit suicide or not?"

"As far as the police are concerned, he did." I paused. "Does suicide fit with what you know about Paul?"

"Paul Herz is dead. I can't believe it." Iverson walked to the end of the den, turned, walked back toward me, and jerked his head up as if surprised to see me. "I didn't mean to be rude. Please, sit down. I expected but a brief chat with you." Iverson lowered himself into a fabric chair, sending dust motes aloft. "What did you ask me again?"

"It was about Paul Herz." I remained standing. No sense getting munched by mites. "In your opinion, would Herz commit suicide?"

"Paul and suicide." He scratched and brainstormed. "It doesn't shock me. As you doubtlessly know by now, Paul struggled with schizophrenia. Worse, he had difficulty staying on his medications. Defiance defined Paul Herz. Hence, he had great difficulty with life in general."

"So I've gathered."

"Paul would sometimes arrive at my doorstep unannounced when he ventured off his meds." Iverson scraped his sideburns with both hands, setting off a scaly blizzard. "Roland must be heartsick."

"You know Roland Herz?"

"Roland and I conferred from time to time vis-à-vis Paul's emotional frailties." He fidgeted with his frayed sleeves. "Paul received care from numerous mental institutions across the state. Did you know that?"

"I heard something about it."

"His was a sad life."

"When did you last see Herz?" I asked.

"Pardon me?"

"Paul Herz," I said. "When did you last see him?"

"Hmm, when was the last time." Iverson rested his chin on his fist: The Thinker. When he spoke again, the top half of his head rose instead of his jaw dropping. "I saw Paul two months ago when he was discharged from a state hospital. I picked him up upon his release and drove him to the ferry terminal, where I coordinated with Roland to meet Paul on the Vineyard side. Since that time, I've spoken with Paul several times on the phone, but the ferry terminal was the last time I actually saw him."

I couldn't tell if Iverson was hiding something or if he was simply soft as shit. He continued to stare straight ahead. His chin remained on his fist, and then his eyes closed.

I said, "Is there anything else you can tell me about Paul?"

"Pardon me?" His eyelashes fluttered. "What did you say?"

Iverson was a space cadet, doped into a prescription stupor.

"I said thanks for your time, Mr. Iverson."

"Yes, yes, of course, I'm always ready to do my moral duty. Paul's death is a stunning revelation indeed, most stunning." He walked to the door with me. "Roland Herz is a good man, a saint of a man, really—the way he took care of Paul. I plan to visit Roland to console him."

Why didn't Roland tell me about Robert Iverson?

"I'm sure Roland will appreciate that." Iverson didn't strike me as a killer—a moron, perhaps, but not a killer. "About the serial killer, Mr. Iverson, I need to give you a warning. There's a possibility you're in danger."

"What do you mean?"

"The killer might be targeting seminarians as well as priests. Specifically, he might be targeting seminarians in your class. I went to Martha's Vineyard to warn Paul Herz of a potential threat, and now he's dead. If Paul jumped off the lighthouse, that's one thing, but if somebody shoved him off, that's another."

"Father Barboza wasn't in our seminary class," Iverson said. "How do you explain his death?"

"I can't explain it."

"A copycat killer?" he asked.

"The serial killer murdered Father Barboza."

"Has the serial killer actually killed a seminarian yet?"

"Not unless Paul Herz was a victim."

"Happy trails to you, Mr. Sparhawk."

I stepped outside. He shut the door in my face. Saint John's Seminary got it right with Robert Iverson. He wasn't priestly material; he was nuthouse material. I got in the car and drove back to Boston.

CHAPTER 37

A few days had passed and nothing happened on the priest murders. I threw on my coat and walked down Bunker Hill Street to Uncle Joe's Diner. I thought about something Glooscap said to me on Martha's Vineyard. What if Paul Herz was the serial killer; what if Paul Herz suspected someone was closing in on him? Glooscap speculated that Paul might have jumped off the tower to avoid prosecution.

It didn't seem likely.

I went into the diner and sat at the counter and read a *Boston Herald* that someone left behind. I read the sports page, the obituaries, and filled in the crossword puzzle. I find the *Herald* crossword harder than the *Globe*. After finishing the omelet and home fries and toast, I flipped the page, and a headline caught my eye: Ferry Passenger Drowns.

According to the article, a man's body washed ashore on Martha's Vineyard yesterday morning. The drowning victim, a ferry passenger named Robert Iverson, had drifted onto a beach at Oak Bluffs, where a local fisherman discovered the body. The article quoted Silva. "We were lucky that Robert Iverson wasn't swept out to sea," said Sergeant Silva, commander of the Massachusetts State Police in Martha's Vineyard. "If he had floated beyond the point, we would not have found him. The currents would have taken him away."

The article implied that the drowning might not have been an accident. Iverson's sister told a reporter that her brother Robert had struggled with mental illness his entire adult life. Although the word suicide was never mentioned in the piece, it seemed to be a logical conclusion. I folded the newspaper on the counter and signaled the waitress for more coffee and then called Glooscap on my cell. I asked him if he'd like to take another ride to the Vineyard.

"I cannot today, but Kid is restless. He will drive down with you."

Harraseeket Kid picked me up at Uncle Joe's twenty minutes later. I handed him an egg-and-cheese bagel sandwich and a large cup of coffee. He ate and swigged as he accelerated over the Zakim Bridge.

"I started work on the ramp yesterday," he said. "Did you see it?"

"I got in late."

"I tore out the old ramp and poured concrete footings for the new one. I'll weld it of structural angle iron. Don't worry about Buck. I built a temporary ramp for him. The new one will stand up to anything."

"Thanks, Kid."

"I'm fencing in the yard, too, a chain-link fence with razor wire."

"Razor wire?"

"We need to defend ourselves, Dermot. Buck is handicapped and he needs protecting." He finished the sandwich. "With the projects across the street, we need fortification."

"I don't know about a fence."

"Lots of houses have fences."

"No razor wire," I said.

Kid steered the pickup off the ferry at Vineyard Haven. He had insisted on bringing the truck over, saying it would be cheaper than hiring a cab. We drove out of the lot and onto the empty downtown streets. Martha's Vineyard rested this time of year, recovering from the onslaught of summer vacationers. Most of the stores were closed, and the ones that remained open were run by islanders.

Harraseeket Kid parked in front of the State Police barracks in Oak Bluffs and let me out.

"I'm grabbing another coffee," Kid said. "I'll meet you back here in an hour."

I went inside and waited in the lobby. Twenty minutes passed before Sergeant Silva saw me and waved me into his office. He told me to sit. He sat behind his desk.

"What do you need now, Sparhawk?"

"I spoke to Robert Iverson a couple of days ago."

"You get around."

"And now Robert Iverson is dead. The last time I was down here I wanted to talk to Paul Herz, and he's dead, too." I paused to give Silva a chance to speak, but he didn't. "Any thoughts, Sergeant?"

"No foul play with Robert Iverson as far as we can tell."

"So I've read."

"You don't buy it?"

"Paul Herz and Robert Iverson are both dead," I said. "Do you think that's a coincidence?"

"It is a coincidence," he said. "But I'm betting you don't see it that way."

"I get drunk and shoot off my mouth at The Liberty Barge about Paul Herz, and Paul Herz jumps off a lighthouse. I go to Gardner to talk to Robert Iverson, and Robert Iverson washes up on a beach. Both deaths are attributed to suicide. Does any of this strike you as odd?"

"Odd, yes. Criminal, no. We have no evidence that a crime took place. But it smells fishy, I'll grant you that."

"Are you looking into it?"

"Yup." Silva took a pad of paper from the middle drawer and read from it. "Wednesday: Robert Iverson purchased a round-trip ferry ticket to Martha's Vineyard online. Thursday: According to two crew members, Robert Iverson boarded the ferry at Woods Hole at noon. Nobody remembers Iverson exiting the ferry in Vineyard Haven, but nobody can say for sure he didn't. That's all we've got. How's that for a timeline? Oh, one more thing. We found Iverson's return ticket in his wallet." He placed the pad back in the drawer. "Why did you talk to Robert Iverson?"

"Robert Iverson and Paul Herz were in the same seminary class. Neither of them lasted long, but they stayed in touch over the years."

"Is that so?" Silva sat up a bit. "Paul Herz and Robert Iverson knew each other?"

"Quite well, from what Iverson told me. Iverson knew Roland Herz, too."

"They knew each other." He was on his feet. "Then the two deaths can't be a coincidence." He stifled his enthusiasm. "I mean, it's not very likely."

That's what I've been trying to tell you, Sergeant.

"My cousin's truck is outside," I said. "I'm driving out to Chilmark to talk to Roland Herz."

"We're driving to Chilmark to talk to Roland Herz," he said, "in my car."

I told Harraseeket Kid that Sergeant Silva and I were off to see Roland Herz. Kid said that he had never been to Martha's Vineyard before, and that he planned to take an island tour. We agreed to meet again in a couple of hours at the barracks. I got into Silva's cruiser, and we drove to the Herz house on Osprey Lane in Chilmark.

Roland answered the door and invited us inside.

After a hasty exchange of pleasantries, Silva started talking. "Did you know Robert Iverson?"

"Robert Iverson." Roland stroked his retreating chin. "Yes, I knew Robert, but he was much closer to my brother Paul than to me. Robert called me the other day after he learned of Paul's death."

"What did he say?"

"He said he was coming here to visit and to stay a few nights.

He had done this in the past to spend time with Paul. When I read about Robert's drowning, I um—"

"Yes?" Silva leaned forward. "You what?"

"Well, it didn't shock me. Both Paul and Robert suffered horribly from mental problems. I suppose they connected in mutual sickness. Does that make sense?"

"Maybe." Silva sat back. "Do you think Robert Iverson committed suicide?"

"Sadly, I do. The mere news of Paul's death could have sent Robert over the edge." Roland caressed his chin some more. "Neither Paul nor Robert had many friends. Robert treated Paul with such love."

"Did you see Robert Iverson?"

"Oh yes, I've seen Robert many times."

Silva rolled his eyes.

"Did you see him after he called to say he was coming down?" Silva shook his head. "Did you see him within the past few days?"

"Oh, I understand what you mean now. No, I didn't see him, but I was awaiting his phone call. I told Robert I'd pick him up at Vineyard Haven when he arrived on the ferry. But he never did call me."

"He never called you." Silva looked at me. I shrugged. Silva said to Roland, "If you think of anything else, call me."

"I will do that, Sergeant."

Roland accompanied Silva and me to the door. I stopped when we got there.

"The last time I was here, you said that Paul never kept in touch with any of his seminary classmates."

"Did I say that? Yes, I suppose I did." Roland opened the door. "You're referring to Paul's kinship with Robert. It was an oversight on my part, Mr. Sparhawk. It had been years since I'd thought of Robert Iverson. Maybe I'm just getting old."

We left Roland's house and headed back for the State Police barracks.

"What do you think?" I asked.

"I think Roland Herz belongs in a booby hatch, that's what I think." The roads were free of tourist traffic, and Silva cruised at a wintertime clip. "Too much inbreeding on this island."

"Two mentally ill guys, both committing suicide, maybe it is a coincidence."

"Yeah, maybe it is at that."

Harraseeket Kid met me at the barracks. We ferried back to the mainland and drove north to Boston.

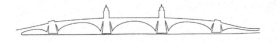

CHAPTER 38

Blackie Barboza knocked on my door the next day. Looking tanned and refreshed, he sported a big smile on his Portuguese face. He stepped into the hallway and wrote on his lined pad, *Are you looking for me?*

"Yes, I'm looking for you. Come in." I led him upstairs to the kitchen. "Where have you been?"

He sat at the kitchen table and wrote, *Florida. My cousin's wedding. I took a bus. Got back today.*

I sat across from Blackie at the kitchen table.

"Tell me about Lopo Gomes."

He wrote, *Why?*

"Lopo Gomes is dead."

Blackie dropped the pen and picked it up, *What happened?*

"I killed him."

He squirmed in the seat. *Why?*

"Lopo Gomes and his cousin Vasco threatened me with guns. They told me to stop looking into the death of Father Barboza." I walked to the stove and lit the gas under a teakettle. "I was on my way to work when they came at me."

How did you kill Lopo? They had guns. Vasco was the other one?

"Vasco was the other one. He pulled a gun first. I knocked Vasco down with a punch then ran for my office. Lopo shot at me." My heart rate quickened in the retelling. "I dove inside the building and raced up to the roof. Lopo shot at the lock, trying to get inside. That's when I dropped the weight on his head."

What weight?

"The forty-five-pound York weight, I use it to hold down the table."

Lopo was my friend.

"Are you sure Lopo was a friend? He told me to lay off your brother's killing." The teakettle whistled, and I mixed a cup of instant coffee. I offered Blackie a cup, but he shook his head no. "How well did you know Lopo Gomes? Why would he tell me to lay off Father Barboza's, sorry, Netto's killing?"

Blackie played with the pen and wrote, *I met Lopo at a Portuguese club. East Cambridge. We got friendly. He slept at my place when he fished in Gloucester. Lopo hated to drive back and forth to Fall River. He stayed a few nights a month.*

That squared with Chub's account.

"Did Lopo know your brother Netto?"

No. I don't think so.

"But he might have known him," I said. "It's possible."

Blackie wrote, *Lopo never talked about Netto. Netto never talked about Lopo. I never saw them together.*

"How do you know Vasco Gomes? Did you meet him in East Cambridge, too?"

I met Vasco in Fall River. A bar. Lopo took me there.

"Are you telling me everything you know?"

Blackie didn't answer. He stood up from the kitchen table and left the house, apparently indignant. I'd hit him with a lot of information, perhaps too much at once, and it was nasty stuff. I didn't chase after him.

I was eating reheated macaroni and cheese from Uncle Joe's Diner when Harraseeket Kid came up from the cellar and sat at my kitchen table. We talked about cable TV and the Internet. Kid told me that Buck wasted no time in getting us connected. A team from the cable company had worked most of the afternoon, linking us to the worldwide web. Kid said that an inspector returned at the end of the day to double-check the work. We were now online. I'm not sure how Aunt Agnes would've felt about that.

I rinsed out my mug and refilled it with coffee and filled a mug for Kid. It was good he was here. I needed to talk to somebody about the deaths of Paul Herz and Robert Iverson. Harraseeket Kid drew the short straw.

"The last two seminarians I talked to are dead," I said. "Both of them apparently committed suicide."

"You have that effect on people."

"There's another seminarian I want to visit, but—"

"But you're afraid you'll get him killed, too."

"Yeah, something like that." I drank coffee and ate mac and cheese. "The police think the suicides are legitimate. Both victims suffered from mental illness."

"But you're not as sure as the police that the suicides are legit." Kid sipped his coffee. "Hey, that's good joe."

"Food pantry coffee," I said.

The deaths of Paul Herz and Robert Iverson bothered me. Both men were unbalanced, both were emotionally fragile. I feared that my drunken rant at The Liberty Barge got back to Paul Herz, prodding him to jump off Gay Head Light. I also feared that my visit to Robert Iverson proved too much for him, prompting his Nantucket Sound channel dive. Both men were vulnerable to the merest distress.

"I don't want to get anyone else killed, and yet I need to talk to this man."

"Who is he?"

"His name is Pollard," I said. "He's a former seminarian."

"Then talk to him."

"It's not that simple, Kid."

"Why not?"

A strange sensation came over me, a feeling of rage. Where did it come from? Why? My stomach knotted, my hands clenched, I pounded the kitchen table.

"Goddamn it, I'm not following my instincts."

"What are you talking about?"

"I *know* that Paul Herz and Robert Iverson were murdered. I just know it, I know it in here." I punched my chest. "They didn't commit suicide, they were murdered. I feel it in my gut."

"Slow down, big fella. How can you be so sure? Your gut might be wrong. The cops are calling them suicides."

"The cops are wrong." I pounded. "They are wrong."

"Take it easy." He grabbed my arms. "You're making me nervous pounding. Friggin' cups are hopping. Tell me about Pollard. What's eating you about Pollard?"

"I don't want to get him killed, that's what's eating me about Pollard, okay?" I thought about it. "If I talk to him, he might get killed like Herz and Iverson."

"Then don't talk to him."

"And if I don't talk to him, he might get killed, like Fathers Axholm, Barboza, Del Rio, and Savold." *And Father Jack Ahearn from Sudbury.* "It's a dilemma."

"You're jumping to conclusions. Paul Herz and Robert Iverson probably committed suicide, but let's pretend they were murdered. If they *were* murdered, it wasn't because you visited them. And if they *did* kill themselves, it wasn't because you visited them, either. On the other hand, the priests were definitely murdered."

"And?"

"I say you talk to Pollard. If you're worried about seeing him, call him on the phone." Kid looked at the stove. "Any mac and cheese left?"

"The phone is out." I prepared Kid a plate of mac and cheese with a chunk of cornbread. "I need to look people in the eye when I talk to them." I set the plate in front of him with a knife and fork. "There's something else."

"What's that?"

"I'd like to set a trap."

"A trap?" Kid took a bite of the cornbread. "What kind of trap?"

"A foolproof trap, where Pollard is protected from danger. If I decide to talk to Pollard, I'll need a man to protect him afterward.

The situation is complicated, Kid. Pollard could be the serial killer or he could be the serial killer's next victim."

"Or neither." Kid ate. "I know a man named Ike Melkedae. He lives up in Nova Scotia, in Antigonish. Ike is the best crossbow man in the Micmac tribe, can handle a rifle, too. Not to mention a tomahawk."

"Tomahawks? Crossbows? That's great for cowboys and Indians, but we're dealing with a serial killer."

"I know what we're dealing with." Kid's black eyes gleamed. "Ike is the right man to protect Pollard. I'd guard Pollard myself, but Glooscap needs me in the shop. Besides, if I kill someone, I'm known in these parts. If Ike kills someone, he'll disappear to where nobody can find him, not even me." Kid pushed his chair away from the table. "Ike is smart and tough. He can protect Pollard and he can protect himself."

"He sounds perfect for the job."

"One more thing," Kid said. "If Pollard is the serial killer, Ike will catch him. No one gets the drop on Ike Melkedae. He's a Micmac Indian."

I liked the idea of a Micmac watching Pollard. Indians have an attentiveness that whites can't muster. They interpret events in a circular manner, seeing all the dimensions. White men interpret things in a linear way, seeing only the plane they're on. I wanted Pollard protected, but I didn't want to place his protector in jeopardy. Harraseeket Kid assured me there was no need to be concerned about Ike Melkedae's safety.

"I'll call Ike right now," Kid said. "He'll be here in twelve hours."

The next day I drove to Pollard's Wellesley estate, and when I got there I debated whether to gas up the car before I ventured in. His plantation of a lot could have had its own zip code. I pushed the intercom button at the entrance and waited. Pollard was expecting me, and the steel gates opened to allow me in.

I drove to the top of a tall knoll and saw the house, a Tudor mansion with massive chimneys and half-timbering. Taken together it rendered a medieval flavor. To my surprise there was no moat, no drawbridge, no knights on duty. Scotch pines and balsam firs edged the property in a green curtain that isolated the manor from public view. Not a good thing.

Pollard, not a butler, answered my knock. I told him that I worked for the Archdiocese of Boston. He said he already knew that. I asked him for a moment of his time. Pollard didn't smile, but he did let me in. He was a no-nonsense guy, so I got right to it. I told Pollard about the serial killer. I told him about the possible connection to the seminary class that he had once been a member of.

"I was never ordained," said Pollard, whose iron-gray hair was combed straight back from his prominent brow. He was a shorter version of Mike Ditka. "I only completed two years of studies."

"Do you remember Paul Herz or Robert Iverson?" I asked. "They were classmates of yours for a brief time at the seminary."

"I remember Paul Herz but not Iverson. Herz got thrown out of school," Pollard said. "He literally left the seminary kicking and screaming. An ugly scene, they dragged him out in a straitjacket. Why do you ask?"

"Herz and Iverson are dead."

"Both of them?"

"Yes, both of them. Do you remember anything else about Paul Herz?"

"That's all I remember. Herz was devastated by his dismissal. He desperately wanted to be a priest." We were still in the front foyer. Pollard had never invited me inside. He stepped toward the door and said, "I knew all the murdered priests, except Father Barboza. Good guys, I hope you find the killer."

His body language was unambiguous. He wanted me out of there. I got in the car to drive home. I didn't warn Pollard of potential danger. Although my instincts told me that Pollard and his classmates were in danger, my experience told me that my instincts were sometimes wrong.

• • •

Ike Melkedae arrived in Boston, just as Kid said. He was in the cellar with Kid, and I went down to meet him. Ike was of average size and outdoorsy looking. Or maybe I just wanted him to be outdoorsy looking. His hair was dark and short with no ponytail. His eyes were deep set and alert. We shook hands and sat down. I told Ike about the priest killings, not that he needed much prepping. Kid had already talked to him.

I said, "I want you to watch over Pollard."

"Got it," Ike replied. And without another word, he walked out of the cellar and went out to his truck.

"Why did he leave?" I looked at Kid. "Did I offend him?"

"If you offended him, you'd have a hatchet in your head. Ike is a quick study. Tell him something once and he gets it. He's on his way to guard Pollard's house."

Ike Melkedae stayed on Pollard's tail for seven days, taking breaks when Pollard went to the office to work. Ike's stakeout routine became predictable. Pollard went to work each day, came home each night, and attended Mass with his wife on Sunday. After a week of shadowing him, Ike knocked on my door and came in.

"I don't think Pollard is in any danger," he said. "And I don't think he presents a danger to anyone else. He is not the serial killer, not in my judgment. What do you want me to do?"

"I'm not sure." I clicked off the TV and invited Ike to sit down. "How much longer can you stay?"

"Three days."

"Give me three more days, just to play it safe."

After Ike left my apartment, I clicked on the DVD player and inserted a Three Stooges disc. The boys, dressed in flannel shirts and caps, discussed their upcoming fishing trip.

Larry said, "You know fish is very good brain food."

Moe replied, "You know you should fish for a whale."

Slap!

CHAPTER 39

The city of Fall River was enjoying a late January thaw. The snow was melting and the sidewalks around Battleship Cove showed more black than white. The I-195 overpass added drama to the already dramatic setting of World War II naval vessels in the harbor. The decommissioned fleet was so fascinating that I almost forgot the reason for my trip.

I walked along Water Street to Anawan Street to an old munitions' depot that housed a dust hole of a joint called Hal Valente's Ringside, which sat on the corner like a trash can on collection day. Valente's had escaped the federal facelift that renewed the rest of Battleship Cove, but it also escaped the motif that came with it, leaving it strangely historic. A taproom from the whaling days of yore.

I stepped inside and waited for my eyes to adjust to the darkness, and when they did, I saw Vasco Gomes sitting on a bar stool sipping a mixed drink. He slackened when I came toward him.

"Give my friend another drink," I said to the barman, who wore a tee shirt that said "Paddle faster. I hear banjos." "And I'll have a Coke."

The barman repaired to his work without a word. Valente's was one of those bars where the patrons said nothing and the barmen said less.

"I have a question for you, Vasco."

"How'd you find me?" He swished the ice cubes around the bottom of his glass. "Blackie Barboza told you. What do you want?"

"Lopo's fishing gig in Gloucester," I said. "Who was he working for?"

The barman returned with the drinks. Vasco drained the old one, took a swig of the fresh one, and began poking the ice cubes with the stirrer. He stared at the clock on the wall, and I couldn't blame him. The second hand was the only thing in the place moving.

"Why should I tell you?"

"I helped you out in Provincetown." I dangled a twenty in front of him. "Maybe I can help you out here."

"A lousy twenty bucks," he said, and stirred his drink. "Andrew Jackson ain't got a twin brother by chance, does he?"

"He might." I dug out another twenty. "But he's not a triplet."

He snatched the two twenties.

"His name is Joe Souza. He owns a fishing boat, docks it on the main pier in Gloucester." He stopped with the stirrer and drank more aggressively, now that he had forty bucks in the kick. "Souza is a tough son of a bitch, tougher than you, Sparhawk."

It took me two hours to reach Gloucester and find Joe Souza's fishing boat, which was right where Vasco said it would be. I watched from the dock as Souza's crew sifted the day's catch. They looked like prospectors panning for gold. Out of the boat's cabin came a muscular man with a concrete chin. He reminded me of the shark hunter in Jaws. He looked up at the dock and smiled at me with fewer teeth than a jack-o-lantern.

"You like to buy fish?" he asked.

"I'd like to talk to you about Lopo Gomes."

The man stepped onto the dock and moved closer to me. He was tall and wide. I was taller and wider. But he had one advantage. He could knock out more of my teeth than I could his.

"Lopo Gomes is dead." He peered at the fading sun. "I miss Gomes. He worked hard, even on drugs he worked hard. He's dead."

"I know he's dead."

"I hear a big Indian killed him." He paused. "I didn't catch your name."

"Dermot Sparhawk," I said.

"Joe Souza." He remained quiet for a moment. "Fishing is dying out. The work is hard, the pay not so great. The men I hire, they got problems. I don't question. I watch. If they work hard, they work for me. Gomes worked hard."

The fishing crew had nearly finished their chores. They shed their rubber gloves and unbuckled their yellow overalls. One of them winched the fishing net into a spool and tied it off.

"I'm looking for a little help, Joe."

"With what?"

"Somebody paid Lopo Gomes to threaten me, and I'd like to know who that person is."

"Yeah? And?" He rolled his head. "How do I help?"

"You can tell me why you hired Gomes."

"Why should I?"

A gold cross hung around his leathery neck. Our Lady of Fatima was tattooed on one forearm, a string of rosary beads on the other.

"The Boston Archdiocese hired me to find Father Netto Barboza's killer," I said. "He was crucified."

"So were other priests."

"Right now I'm working on Father Barboza. Lopo Gomes threatened me to leave Father Barboza's killing alone. He told me to stop looking into his murder. Gomes shot at me. One thing led to another and now Gomes is dead. It was self-defense."

"You're the big Indian that killed him."

"I want to find the man who paid Lopo Gomes to scare me off."

"Barboza, that's a Portuguese name, yes?"

"Yes."

The sun melted into the horizon, the seawater darkened to gray. Bright barroom lights circled the pier, their neon signs winking Schlitz, Pabst, and Budweiser. I stared at them. Joe Souza interrupted my thoughts.

"I see the AA pamphlet in your back pocket," he said. "Are you sober?"

"I'm trying."

Souza yelled to a skinny kid on the boat to join us. The kid dropped the lanyard he was reeling, climbed onto the pier, and stood next to Joe Souza. The kid had strong hands and lots of ink on his arms.

"Yes, Uncle Joe?"

"This is my nephew Squid," Souza said to me, and then to Squid, "Tell Sparhawk why you spoke for Lopo Gomes."

"We were friends."

"Are you from Fall River?" I asked.

"We're from Gloucester," Joe Souza said. "We fished here many generations."

"How did you meet Lopo Gomes, Squid?" I asked.

"Yeah, how did you know Gomes?" Souza asked.

Squid looked down at the pier. "We were cellmates in Concord."

"That's why you got him the job?" I asked. "Because you were cellmates?"

"Why didn't you tell me Gomes came from prison?" Joe Souza looked hurt. "I would still hire him. Why didn't you tell me?"

There was a length of silence. Souza and I waited. Squid finally spoke.

"It wasn't just prison. It was my probation officer. He knew about the fishing boat and told me to get Gomes a job." He faced Souza. "I flunked a piss test. My PO said he'd bust me back to Concord if I didn't get Gomes a job. I'm sorry, Uncle Joe."

"What's your PO's name?" I asked.

"No way, man, I don't want to get jammed up with him. The guy's an asshole, and I'm already on his shit list." Squid's hands flopped against his sides. "He'll fuck me over if I tell you."

"I won't say I got Lopo's name from you."

"He's gonna know it was me," Squid said. "He knows that Gomes and me were friends. He knows I got him the fishing job."

"Tell him," Joe Souza said. "Give Sparhawk the PO's name. If the PO gives you trouble, we will deal with him together, me and you." Souza waited a few seconds. "Tell him the name, Squid."

"Do I have to?"

"Tell him!"

"His name is Malone, a fat fuck in a wheelchair. He works in Dorchester District Court."

"Dorchester Court?" It didn't make sense. "Lopo Gomes lived in Fall River."

"Yeah, but he got bagged in Dorchester stealing cars," Squid explained. "They busted him in a chop shop near Fields Corner."

CHAPTER 40

From the pier, I called Ike Melkedae to check on the Pollard situation. I didn't like what he told me.

"Something is wrong, Dermot. We need to talk. I'll meet you in Charlestown in a couple of hours."

"What's wrong?"

"We'll talk in Kid's cellar."

Kid's cellar? I thought it was my cellar.

"I'll see you at Kid's, Ike."

When I got back to Charlestown, I saw Ike's pickup with a rifle rack parked in front of my house. I knocked on the downstairs door to say hi to Buck Louis before I went to the cellar. Buck wheeled over to me.

"What do you think of this?" He slapped a leather scabbard on the side of his wheelchair then unsheathed a sawed-off shotgun. "Kid rigged it up for me. Nice, huh? Anybody breaks in, I'll blast 'em."

"Is that thing loaded?"

"Not yet," Buck said.

"Keep it that way."

Ike and Kid were in the cellar smoking cigars. The room looked good. Kid had swept the cobwebs from the rafters and mopped the floors clean. Four new casement windows let in the outside light, which at this time of the evening was a streetlight. A Remington rifle leaned against the middle Lally column, the barrel pointing up. Kid tossed me a Phillies Blunt and a book of matches.

"Dermot," Kid said as he blew smoke to the ceiling. "We got a problem."

"A serious problem," Ike said, "otherwise, I wouldn't have asked for this meeting."

Kid and Ike looked at each other. Ike talked.

"It has to do with Pollard. Everything was going fine, and then this thing happened." Ike blew a smoke ring. "A car slowed down in front of Pollard's house. It didn't stop, it just slowed down. No big deal, right?"

"Okay," I said. "No big deal."

"An hour later the same car drove by again and stopped at the front gates. I had a perfect view of it. I was hidden across the road in the woods and could see everything." Ike tapped his cigar in an ashtray. "The windows were tinted, the license plates were caked in mud, the headlights were off."

"Go on," I said.

"The driver was casing Pollard's place. I'm positive about that." Ike puffed. "The third time he drove by, I crept to my truck and followed him, and I, um—"

"What's wrong, Ike?"

"He *knew* I was following him. More than that, he suckered me into following him. The bastard is smart." He looked at the cigar tip. "He ran a red light near Wellesley College, and I lost him on Route Nine."

The killer was stalking Pollard, or was I jumping to yet another conclusion?

"What do you think?" Kid said to me.

"I'm not sure," I said.

Kid plugged in a teakettle and the cellar lights dimmed. The furnace kicked on with a hum. I crushed my cigar in a tire rim that contained other dead butts. I didn't question Ike's read on the situation.

"We have to get Pollard out of town," I said.

"The sooner the better," Ike agreed.

I walked to the foot of the stairs.

"Kid, can I have a word with you?" We walked up to the landing. "I'm worried about Buck having a shotgun. He knows nothing about guns."

"There's nothing to worry about, Dermot. I'm gonna load it with buckshot. All he has to do is point the barrel and pull the trigger. He's bound to hit something."

"That's not what I meant." I didn't have the energy to explain. "Let's tone down the fortification for a while."

For a second time, I drove to Pollard's house in Wellesley, this time to warn him of real danger. Glooscap was keeping guard tonight, nowhere in sight, but he was out there somewhere watching. Pollard answered the door.

"Sparhawk?" He looked up at me. "It's late. What are you doing here? And how did you get past the gate?"

"It's important that I talk to you," I said.

Pollard didn't like the intrusion, but allowed me inside. I followed him into a huge living room, where a woman was lounging in a chaise, sipping a drink from a lowball glass. Maroon blemishes pied her neck. Red lipstick smudged the rim of the glass.

"This is my wife, Vivian," Pollard said. "Frankly, I'm surprised to see you again, Sparhawk. And how did you get past my gate?"

"I believe you're in danger," I said.

Vivian started to say something, but Pollard stared at her, and she closed her mouth. "What do you mean by danger?" Pollard asked.

"Someone is casing your house."

"What are you talking about?"

I told Pollard what Ike had told me, and then I told him what to do.

"Leave town for a while," I said. "Take a cruise. Visit the grandkids, whatever. But get out of your house."

Pollard got in my face.

"Who the hell are you to have someone watching my house?"

"I'm trying to protect you." I paced to the fireplace and

stopped. "I went to Martha's Vineyard to talk to Paul Herz, and a day later he was dead. I went to Gardner to talk to Robert Iverson, and less than a week later he was dead. I think they were murdered, and I think you're next."

"Oh, please." Pollard laughed. "All because a car slowed down and an Indian got goose bumps? Are you serious?"

"I'm dead serious."

"A red alert, eh?"

Pollard walked to the bar to mix himself a drink. Vivian held out her glass, and he mixed another for her. He didn't offer one to me. I had to convince Pollard his life was in peril, and I had to convince him before he drank too much. Booze can make people fearless—and stupid.

"What's the harm in staying in a hotel tonight?" I asked. "If not for yourself, do it for Vivian."

"Not a chance." His voice grew hoarser. He aggressively drank another mouthful. "I'm not going anywhere, Sparhawk. The serial killer doesn't even know who I am."

"What if you're wrong?"

"I am rarely wrong. Besides, if anyone threatens me, I'll handle it myself. No one fucks with me, understand?" He drank more. "You'd best be moving along."

"You're taking a needless risk," I said, "a risk that could have a fatal outcome."

"Nonsense," he said with less bite, and then the bite returned. "Leave now. Move it, sonny, get out of my house."

I buttoned my coat and walked to the front, and as I was walking, Vivian placed her drink on the end table and got up from the chaise.

"I'm going with you," she said.

"No you're not." Pollard's face shook. "You aren't going anywhere, little lady." He grabbed her arm and jerked her back to the living room. "You're staying put until further notice, got that?"

"Hey." I stepped in. "Let go of her."

"What did you say?" Pollard released Vivian and turned on

me. "Get the fuck outta here before I have you arrested. You are fuckin' with the wrong guy, kiddo. You have no idea who you're screwing with."

"Don't I?" I took him by the collar and eased him against a chimney. His arms thrashed harmlessly. I pushed my fist into his throat, increasing the pressure. "We're not in some Wall Street boardroom, asshole. And I'm not one of your bootlicking employees. Call the police. Tell them you're holding your wife hostage. Tell them you grabbed her and yanked her. Go on, shithead, call them. We'll wait for the cops together."

"I can't breathe." His face darkened. "Stop, please."

I let go of him. He bent over, gasping for air. Vivian and I went to my car. She didn't make a fuss when I opened the rotting door of the Plymouth Acclaim, and that told me something about her. I dropped her at her brother's house in Dedham.

CHAPTER 41

I stood on the sidewalk outside Packy's Liquor Store. Should I buy a jug or go to an AA meeting? The jug won out tonight. I went to make the purchase and a woman bumped into me.

"Dermot," she said.

I recognized her voice. It was Gladys Foley and she was shaking. I put my arms around her and hugged her, and that's when I noticed the bruises on her face.

"What happened to you?"

"Nuthin'."

"I'll call an ambulance, get you to a hospital."

"I don't need no hospitals. I'm fine. What I need is ten bucks. Can you lend me ten till tomorrow? I wanna get cigarettes."

"I'd rather get you some help."

"Help me with a ten, Dermot. The cigarettes'll calm me down. Just gimme ten and I'll be fine."

I handed Gladys ten dollars. I decided against Packy's and went home.

The morning began battleship gray. I had just rolled over to go back to sleep when I heard pounding on the door. I put on my bathrobe and answered it. Harraseeket Kid and Ike Melkedae were standing on the landing, Ike looking at the floor, Kid shaking his head. They followed me into the kitchen.

"Bad news," Kid said. "Pollard is dead."

"What?"

"I'm sorry, Dermot." Ike said. "I don't know what happened.

I was watching Pollard's house and all of a sudden I got zapped by a Taser or a stun gun. I thought I got hit by lightning. The son of a bitch snuck up on me from behind. He never snapped a twig or rustled a leaf. He knew I was in the woods."

Kid said, "He zapped Ike and handcuffed him to a tree."

Ike nodded. "I couldn't free myself. The tree was forty feet high. I was stuck."

Kid said, "I drove to Wellesley to relieve Ike and found him shackled to the tree. I snapped the cuffs with bolt cutters. Then we checked the house. Pollard was nailed to the fireplace mantel, dead."

Ike's face contorted. "Something doesn't make sense, Dermot. I had the perfect hiding place, deep in a thicket. Nobody could see me in there. I was covered like a duck hunter in a blind. Not only did the bastard know where I was hiding, he was prepared enough to bring handcuffs. He planned it out."

"Was Pollard wearing a red hood?" I asked.

Kid said, "Yeah, he was wearing one. How did you know that?"

"It fits the serial killer's pattern," I answered.

Ike said, "I am not shifting the blame, this is my fault, but the killer knew exactly where I was hiding."

"You mentioned that," I said. Pollard was dead, and I still had no clue to the killer's identity. "Something screwy is going on."

Kid asked, "What are you going to do about it?"

"I don't know yet." The eight o'clock bells of Saint Jude Thaddeus gonged. "Pollard refused to listen to me. What about the police?"

Kid said, "We got out of there before the cops came. I'd bet they still aren't there. Pollard's property is enormous."

"Yeah, it is enormous."

Ike walked up to me. "I blew it, Dermot. You hired me to do a job and I blew it. This never happened to me before. Boston is crazy. I'm going home to Antigonish."

"I don't blame you." I shook Ike's hand. "Thanks for the help. Something weird is going on. What happened to Pollard isn't your fault."

Ike Melkedae left the apartment, but Harraseeket Kid stayed behind. We remained standing in the kitchen.

"Did you hear sirens when you left Pollard's house?"

"Nothing," Kid said, "not a thing."

At nine o'clock I called 911 from a pay phone in Hayes Square and reported the Pollard murder to the police. After I hung up I went into Packy's to borrow the van.

"Sure, take the van." Packy rubbed a scratch ticket. "I was sorry to hear about Gladys Foley."

"What are you talking about?"

"You didn't hear?" Packy tossed the losing ticket into the barrel. "Gladys died last night. She overdosed, heard it was heroin."

"Overdosed?"

"Yup, she overdosed." He tore off another scratch ticket. "The police found her in a hallway with a needle in her arm, over on Walford Way. You know something, Dermot? You were the only guy in the neighborhood that gave a shit about her."

It was my fault Gladys was dead. If I hadn't given her the money, she couldn't have gotten the drugs, and she wouldn't have overdosed. Pollard and now Gladys, both dead in one night. I took the van keys from Packy.

I let myself into the lower church of Saint Jude Thaddeus and knelt down. After a feeble attempt at prayer, I went into the sacristy and grabbed a bottle of altar wine from the cabinet. I sat in the front pew and drank the hooch and thought about my chat with a Gloucester fisherman named Squid. Squid told me that his probation officer was named Malone. He said that Malone worked in Dorchester District Court. I grabbed another bottle of wine and drove to Codman Square. It was time for a court appearance.

I found Malone's office on the second floor of the courthouse. His fellow workers must have been in session or out to lunch, because Malone, a fat man in a wheelchair, was the only person in the room. His hair was gray, his cheeks were puffy. He looked up from his desk when I walked in.

"Malone?" I asked.

"Do we have an appointment?" he asked. "I said do we have an—"

"Tell me about Lopo Gomes. Why did you get Gomes the fishing job in Gloucester?"

His eyes blinked.

"Get out of my office." He rolled back from his desk. "You're drunk."

"You're right." I stepped around the desk and backhanded his head. "Tell me about Lopo Gomes."

"What are you doing?"

I wound up. Malone covered his face. I dropped down and thumped him in the ribs. Spittle blasted from his mouth. His eyes welled as he wheezed for air. It was tough beating a man in a wheelchair, but it wasn't as tough as I thought it would be.

"Gomes," I said. "Tell me about Gomes."

"I can't." Malone's face purpled. "I'm dead if I tell you."

"You're dead if you don't." I rolled him out of the office and into the hallway. "We're going for a trip, Malone."

His hands flailed for the wheels. He yelped when the spokes pinched his fingers. I kicked open the fire door and pushed him into the stairwell. I sped up when I hit the landing.

"So long, Malone."

"Stop, stop." His scream echoed off the hollow structure. "I'll tell you."

"Let's hear it."

"It was a cop," he said.

"Keep talking."

A cop ordered Malone to get Lopo Gomes a job. You don't

screw around with cops, Malone said. And so Malone did as he was told. He found Gomes a job. Malone's description of the cop proved nondescript—a middle-aged white man with thinning gray hair. I didn't believe him. I pressed him further, but when I smelled shit and urine drifting from his trousers I stopped. I rolled him back to his office and left the courthouse.

CHAPTER 42

The next morning, half drunk and fully ashamed, I confessed my sins to Father Dominic. We spoke quietly, sitting in a pew with parishioners around us. I told him that I assaulted a paralyzed man and threatened to roll him down a flight of stairs. Father Dominic responded like an expert poker player, showing no expression in his face. After contemplating, he said, "You're still drunk, Dermot."

"I know."

"Your penance is twofold. Get to more AA meetings, and pray to Saint Jude Thaddeus, the patron saint of lost causes." Father Dominic granted me absolution, and said, "Stick around for morning Mass."

I skulked home after Mass, and when I got there, I saw two men sitting in a car in front of my house. The windows were tinted, making it impossible to see their faces. They got out when I reached my front door. I recognized Suffolk County DA Francis Ennis. I didn't recognize the other man, but he was a cop.

"Dermot Sparhawk," DA Francis Ennis said. "This is Lieutenant Staples, head of the State Police CPAC unit in Suffolk County. Lieutenant Staples is investigating the serial killings, the most recent one being the Pollard murder. You're familiar with the Pollard murder, are you not?"

"I heard about it on the news," I said.

"The news, huh?" Staples said.

He wore his brown hair in a tight flattop. His shoulders were square. His jaw was square. I bet his office was squared away, too. We all shook hands like politicians, went up to my apartment, and stood in the kitchen in a quasi huddle. Staples called the signals.

"I'm told that an Indian from Canada was watching Pollard.
What happened to this man?"

Ennis said, "Pollard's wife told us about the Canadian. She
overheard you and Pollard arguing about the protective measure
you took, hiring the Micmac to watch over Pollard."

"He's back in Canada," I said. "He watched Pollard for a
week, thought the coast was clear, and went home."

"Your man was dead wrong," Staples said.

"You're dead right."

"Are you a wise guy, Sparhawk?" Staples inched closer to me.
"We got a murder victim in Wellesley and you're cracking jokes?"

"I shouldn't have said that. How can I help you, Lieutenant?"

Staples took off his suit coat and carefully draped it over a
kitchen chair. I was about to offer him an iron when he said,
"What's the man's name? The Canadian Micmac, what's his
name?"

"I don't know his name. He came here under the condition of
anonymity."

"Why anonymity?"

"In case he killed the serial killer."

"I don't believe you," Staples said. "But it doesn't matter. We
don't need your help to find him. We'll check at the border crossing
and get his name that way."

"There won't be any record at the border."

"Really?" Staples decided to let that one go. "You figured out
that Pollard was a potential mark for the serial killer."

"It was mostly guesswork."

"You figured Pollard for a target, because he was in the same
seminary class as the other victims."

"Except for Father Barboza," I said. "Barboza wasn't in his
class."

DA Ennis said, "Dermot not only looked at the ordained
priests, but he also looked at the dropouts and expellees."

"Expellees?" Staples stared at Ennis, then looked at me. "Pretty
good work on the seminary connection."

A compliment?

"But now it's time for the professionals to take charge, right, Lieutenant?"

"Wrong, Sparhawk. We were already in charge," he said. "But you've made some progress, so I'll allow you to keep working on the case."

Thanks, dickhead.

Staples said, "But keep me in the loop. If you keep me in the loop, I won't hunt down the Canadian." He took me by the elbow and led me into the parlor away from Ennis. In a low tone he said, "Don't think for a second that I swallowed that crap about the Canadian insisting on anonymity. I know he's one of your tribesmen." He released my elbow. "Want to see something funny, Sparhawk?"

"Do I have a choice?"

"Look outside." Staples pointed out the window. "The 911 call, the call that reported Pollard's murder, it came from that pay phone in Hayes Square. Can you see the pay phone? It's right there on the corner."

"I see it."

"And yet you claimed that you heard about the killing on the news. Quite a coincidence, don't you think?" Staples slapped me on the back. "I'll be in touch."

Buck Louis wheeled out from behind a TV dinner table when I came into his apartment. Something must have shown on my face, because Buck asked me what was wrong.

"I need to talk to you, Buck."

"About what?"

"Did you hear about the murder in Wellesley last night?" I asked. "A man named Pollard got killed."

"Sure I heard about it. Who hasn't?"

"A Micmac Indian from Nova Scotia named Ike Melkedae was protecting Pollard. Ike was a friend of Harraseeket Kid."

"A friend of Kid's?" Buck popped a wheelie. "He didn't do too good a job. It must have been the guy with the truck, the one with Nova Scotia plates."

"That's Ike. The killer snuck up on him. Ike never heard him coming." I eyed the scabbard on Buck's wheelchair. "The sawed-off shotgun, can you shoot it?"

"Sure, I can shoot it. Kid showed me how."

"Got ammo?"

"Yeah, I got ammo." He rolled back a few inches and looked up at me. "Kid gave me a box of shells yesterday. What's goin' on, Dermot?"

"Keep it loaded." I sat on the couch. "The serial killer thinks I'm on his trail. He's wrong, of course. I don't have a clue who he is, couldn't venture a guess."

"If you don't know who he is, why does he think you're on his trail?"

"That's a good question." I thought for a second. "Maybe I have it backward, Buck. Maybe the killer is on *my* trail."

"What do you mean?"

"Each time I visit a man, the man ends up dead." I didn't want to scare Buck. "Not every man, just former seminarians. Were you in the seminary, Buck?"

"No way, too many women out there."

"I'm kidding, but I'm not kidding about keeping your guard up." I looked around the apartment. Harraseeket Kid had installed a security grate on the back door. "Kid's got the place buttoned up pretty tight, so we should be okay."

"I can tell you're worried, Dermot."

"You're right, Buck. I am."

CHAPTER 43

I was about to turn in for the night when the doorbell rang. I went downstairs to answer it and saw Detective Adam Jenner standing on the porch. For a change, Captain Pruitt wasn't with him. I let him in, and we went up to my apartment. Adam wasted no time in getting to the reason for his visit.

"I understand that Staples and Ennis paid you a visit."

I said nothing in reply.

"What did they want?"

"We just talked," I said.

"Just talked? The Suffolk County DA and the head investigator for CPAC dropped by just to talk?"

"That's what I said."

"I'm trying to solve a multiple homicide, Dermot. The killer is a complete sicko. Let's put our heads together on this thing." He unbuttoned his overcoat and sat on a kitchen chair. "I helped you earlier."

"I know that, Adam." He didn't help me at all. "What do you need?"

"I need to know one thing. Was Pollard wearing a red hood?" He waited a second. "We're jammed up on Pollard. We can't get any information on him because he was murdered in Wellesley. Ennis is using Pollard's murder to get CPAC into the mix. Boston Homicide will look like idiots if we don't figure it out first. Help me out here."

"CPAC got into the mix with Father Savold's murder in Revere." I sat and leaned forward. "What is it with cops? Why don't you work together?"

"You don't know how it is, no idea," he said. "Just help me out. Was Pollard wearing a red hood or not?"

"What makes you think I know about Pollard?"

"Don't play me for a jackass. You know about Pollard. Why else would Ennis and Staples come here after his murder?"

Adam and I had known each other a long time. We played football together in college. We sweated in August and froze in November. I didn't like Adam as a player, but he was on the team.

"Pollard was wearing a red hood," I said.

"Thanks, Dermot. I mean it." His cell phone rang. "Jenner, here." He waved his free hand. "Handle it until I get there. No, no, O'Dell is out on medical. Wait till I get there. Tell him I'll talk to him then." Jenner hung up. "Another murder in Dorchester."

"It never ends for you guys."

I didn't sleep well that night. Something that Adam said ate at me, but I couldn't figure out what it was. After a few restless hours, I nodded off, and when I did, Astrid Bordeaux's face came to me in a dream. I awoke with a start.

I knew what Adam Jenner said that bugged me.

Astrid Bordeaux and I hadn't talked since my initial visit with her. I had told Astrid I'd call, but I never did. She'd understand. Women always do. I drove to her house in Billerica and rang the bell. Astrid opened the door, looking better than ever. Her throat flushed when she saw me.

"Dermot, what are you doing here?"

"I need to talk to you about Father Barboza."

"What?" A reddish tint colored her face. "You came here to talk about Barboza?"

Oops.

"I'm sorry I didn't call you. I meant to but forgot."

"Forgot? Are you kidding me? You are unbelievable, you know that? You slept in my bed, Dermot. You slept in my bed and I never heard from you again, not even a measly phone call." She kicked the doormat. "And the only reason you're here today is to ask me about Father Barboza."

"Maybe I should go."

"Maybe you should at that."

Astrid began to close the door. I stopped her.

"Please talk to me for a minute. I wouldn't ask if it wasn't important."

She didn't say yes, but she went into the house and left the door ajar. I followed her inside. She turned around and said, "What do you want?"

"I meant what I said, Astrid. I like you and I've been meaning to call."

"Anything else?"

Why hadn't I called her? She was stunning and I really liked her. We were great together. And then it came to me.

"The reason I didn't call had nothing to do with you. It has to do with me. I wouldn't be good for anybody right now, especially a classy woman like you."

"Why not?"

"Lots of reasons. For one, I drink too much. For another, I'm chasing a serial killer." I shuffled my feet on her thick carpeting. "I'm getting people killed."

Astrid sat on the couch where we first kissed.

"I'm not looking for a husband, Dermot, not even a commitment. I'm just looking for a little respect. A phone call would have been nice."

"I should have called you."

"I hadn't had sex since my husband died, and I haven't had sex since that night with you." Her eyes filled up. "I'm not a tramp."

"I know you're not a tramp." I sat on the couch next to her, but not too close. Fluffy, the dog, trotted into the room and wagged her tail. I patted her head. "I'm sorry I didn't call. I really am."

"Fine." Astrid stood and wiped away a tear. "You said you wanted to talk about Father Barboza."

I stood up, too. "The last time I was here we talked about Bill O'Dell and Bill Jr. I didn't realize that O'Dell was a Boston homicide cop."

"So?"

"This isn't easy to talk about, Astrid."

"Oh, please, Dermot. I'm tired of your fencing. Just say it."

"Okay, was Michael's behavior consistent with that of a pedophile victim?"

"Why do you ask?"

"Do you think it is feasible—" I stopped and tried again. "Is it possible that Bill O'Dell manipulated your Michael and Bill Jr. into falsely accusing Father Barboza?"

"What are you saying?"

"I think Father Barboza was falsely accused, that's what I'm saying."

"Where on earth is this coming from?"

"It's a feeling, Astrid. I want to find the truth about Father Barboza. One way or the other, I want to establish his guilt or innocence."

"He's guilty."

"Maybe you're right, I just want to be sure."

"What do you want from me?"

"I want you to consider two things. One, is it possible that Father Barboza was falsely accused? Two, is it possible that Bill O'Dell manipulated the boys into accusing him?"

"Are you crazy? Do you realize what you're saying?" Astrid walked to the front door and opened it. "Please leave my house."

"Think about what I said."

I drove back to Charlestown with my head up my ass.

A day later and to my great surprise, Astrid Bordeaux left a message on my answering machine, telling me to call her immediately. I dialed the number. She picked up on the first ring.

"I need to see you right away," she said.

"Is everything okay?"

"If okay means learning the truth, then yes, everything is okay. But if okay means the truth will set you free, then no." She paused. "Get over here as soon as you can. I'll make sure Ellen O'Dell is here, too. What time shall I tell her?"

"Three o'clock?"

"See you at three."

At three fifteen on a dusky afternoon with cloud cover building and the temperature dropping, I arrived at Astrid's house. She opened the door and led me to the kitchen where another woman was sitting at the table drinking tea. Astrid extended one hand toward the woman and the other toward me.

"Dermot Sparhawk, Ellen O'Dell. Ellen, Dermot."

We said hello with forced sincerity, and then Astrid and I joined her at the table. Astrid poured a cup of coffee for me from a carafe on the lazy Susan.

"I'll start," Astrid said. Her ash-blonde hair was pulled back in a ponytail, making her face look fuller. "I talked with my Michael last night, and he finally told me the truth. Father Barboza never touched him." Astrid's gray eyes remained steady. "Michael told me that Bill O'Dell coerced him into accusing Father Barboza of those awful things."

"Father Barboza never touched either boy?" I asked.

"I'm only speaking for my Michael," Astrid said. "He never touched Michael."

"Billy, either," said Ellen O'Dell, whose wiry, brown hair framed her puffy face. "Bill Jr. lied, too. He made up the whole thing. Father Barboza never laid a hand on him."

It seemed like a good time to say nothing. I waited for what seemed an appropriate period and broke the silence.

"Why would the boys do such a thing?"

Astrid looked at Ellen, who pushed away her teacup.

"I was having an affair." Ellen stared at the Formica table. "I started feeling guilty about it because of my son, not Bill. Bill is such an asshole." Her words ran flat. "I sought Father Barboza for guidance. Netto was great to me, a wonderful counselor."

Netto?

Ellen looked at me. "Netto urged me to end the affair, which I did. He encouraged me to go to Mass, which I did. Our counseling sessions continued. As time went by, I developed feelings for Netto, and Netto for me. We never acted on them, not even a kiss." She blew her nose into a tissue. "But the feelings were real."

"What happened next?"

"Bill got suspicious. He thought Netto and I were having an affair. Bill said he knew we were having an affair because of the way I looked at Netto. I told Bill that I was seeing Netto for spiritual direction, which was true."

"But not the whole truth," I said. "Sorry, I shouldn't have interrupted."

"Want to hear something funny?" Ellen said. "When I was having an affair, Bill didn't have a clue. When I stopped, Bill grew leery, probably because I became emotionally attached to Netto."

The pieces of the puzzle assembled.

"And that's why Bill stage-managed the boys' accusations," I said. "He wanted to bring down Father Barboza."

Ellen said, "Bill manipulated Bill Jr. into accusing Netto. He told Billy that Netto was trying to break up our family. Bill told Billy that I wanted a divorce so I could be with Netto. It was a lie. He told Billy he'd have to move away from Billerica. Billy would have to leave his school and his friends. Bill scared him into making the accusations."

"And that's when my Michael got sucked in," Astrid said. "Bill became a father figure to Michael after my husband died. When Bill told Michael the O'Dells would have to move, Michael panicked. Bill played on Michael's panicked state, and pressured him into accusing Father Barboza."

"Bill pulled the strings," Ellen said. "He destroyed a good man."

"He sure did," I said. "Why didn't you protect Father Barboza, either of you?"

"I didn't know about the lies," Ellen said. "Bill told Bill Jr. I was having an affair with Netto, but I didn't know. When I finally heard about the accusations—the pedophilia, not the affair—I got confused. I wondered if something had happened to Billy. My mind played tricks on me. I remembered Netto shooting hoops with the boys in the backyard. He played cards with them on the picnic table. I began to wonder."

"How long has Bill been a homicide cop?" I asked.

"Twelve years." She wiped away tears. "He's out on medical leave right now, emotional stress."

"How long has he been out?"

"A few weeks," Ellen said, "maybe a month."

I got up and walked around the kitchen and stood at the sink.

"Who did you have the affair with, Ellen?"

"I'm not saying. He has nothing to do with any of this. Besides, we're finished. The affair is over. I'm keeping him out of it."

"Okay." I sat again. "We can leave him out of it if that's what you want."

"What should we do?" Astrid asked.

"Don't do anything until you hear from me," I said. "I'll call you soon."

I left Astrid's house and thought about Bill O'Dell. I thought about him as the murderer of Father Barboza. O'Dell had access to the evidence. Who but a homicide cop would know about the red hoods? O'Dell had motive. Who but a betrayed husband would want to kill the man he suspected of shacking up with his wife? O'Dell conned his son and another boy into lying about a good priest, accusing him of the vilest crime.

Any man capable of that is capable of murder.

CHAPTER 44

My handling of Bill O'Dell required a careful touch. I didn't want to spook him, and I didn't want to alert Boston Homicide that I suspected him of murder. There was no question that Bill O'Dell was a copycat killer, the man who killed Father Netto Barboza. O'Dell must have been thrilled with the way the murders rolled out. The killing spree began before the murder of Father Barboza and continued after it. O'Dell couldn't have planned it any better.

The timing of the first murder was perfect. O'Dell had pulled off the pedophilia charade against Father Barboza *before* Father Axholm was murdered. When Axholm was killed, everything lined up for O'Dell to crucify Father Barboza. And now it made sense why Father Barboza was murdered in Boston, so that Boston Homicide, not CPAC, would handle the case. The scheme was ingenious.

But there was one question I couldn't answer. Where did O'Dell find a red Resnick hood? The hood on Father Barboza's head was an exact match to the others. Criminalist Kiera McKenzie, an evidence expert, convinced me the hood could not be duplicated. Where did O'Dell get the hood?

I parked in front of Bill O'Dell's house in Billerica. Ellen O'Dell wasn't there. She was staying at Astrid Bordeaux's place with Bill Jr. for the short term. Ellen had told me that Bill Sr., who was still living in the family abode, usually got home around six. And that's where I was, in front of Bill O'Dell's house at six o'clock, with the car engine idling. Huddled against the cold in the borrowed Plymouth Acclaim, I waited.

O'Dell pulled into the driveway at seven and turned off the engine. He rocked out of the car on the second heave forward, using the door as a fulcrum. O'Dell was all belly, no brawn. He probably wore his wristwatch on the tightest notch and his belt on the loosest. He was the most dangerous kind of cop there is, a fat boy with a badge.

Scant strands of gray hair were combed across his balding dome and slicked in place with plenty of Brylcreem. His overcoat screamed at the seams, the belt that went around it stretched like a drawn slingshot, a cigarette jiggled in his thick mouth. O'Dell waddled down the driveway in my direction. He paused when he reached me, took a drag, and blew smoke in my face. "Do I know you?"

"Not yet, Detective." His breath smelled of booze. "My name is Dermot Sparhawk. I'm investigating the murder of Father Barboza for the Archdiocese of Boston."

"Father Barboza?" O'Dell undid the belt, revealing a holstered gun on his right hip. He unsnapped the catch. "Get off my property."

"Not until we talk."

He kept his hand on the gun butt. "Okay, choirboy, we can talk for a minute." He wiggled the gun, but didn't pull it out. "You got ten seconds."

"You conned your son Billy and Michael Bordeaux into accusing Father Barboza of molesting them. Bill Jr. came clean and so did Michael Bordeaux. Your wife told me the story."

"That bitch." He loosely belted his coat and tossed the cigarette into the street. "Ellen was whoring around with that priest." He paused. "Wait a minute. I don't have to say a thing to you. Get off my property."

"You manipulated those boys."

"Get away from here."

"You destroyed a good man. Father Barboza wasn't having an affair with your wife." I poked him in the chest. "He was trying to save your marriage."

"Hey, watch the hands."

"It wasn't enough you ruined the man's reputation, you killed him, too."

"Whoa, hold your goddamned horses. I didn't kill him."

"Come on, O'Dell. You're a homicide cop. You work with Captain Pruitt and Adam Jenner, which means that you knew about the red hoods."

"Did you tell them?"

"Not yet," I said.

"Sure, I knew about the hoods. Everyone in Homicide knew about them, the lab too. That doesn't mean I killed Barboza. You can't make that jump."

"Then why did you hire Lopo Gomes to scare me off Father Barboza's case?"

"How did—" He stopped himself. "You can't prove that."

"I already proved it." I lied. "I showed your picture to a Dorchester probation officer named Malone. You remember Malone. He's the guy in the wheelchair you bullied. Malone told me you threatened him to get Lopo Gomes a job."

"That doesn't mean anything."

"And then there's Lopo's cousin, Vasco Gomes." I lied again. "Lopo told Vasco that you paid him a grand to threaten me off the case." What I said was part bluff, part truth, but there was enough truth in it to carry the bluff. "You murdered Father Barboza."

"I didn't."

"It's as simple as one, two, three. You knew about the Resnick hoods. You hired Lopo Gomes to scare me off. You used your own son as a stooge." I warmed my hands in my pockets. "You killed Father Barboza."

"I didn't kill him, and I'm through talking to you. Get off my property now. Get outta here before I blow your fuckin' head off."

"We're not finished, O'Dell."

"Then why haven't I been arrested yet?"

"A visit to CPAC is next on my list," I said. "Lieutenant Staples will be visiting you tomorrow morning."

• • •

It was late when I got home to Charlestown. Somewhat hungry, I satisfied my sweet tooth with raisin toast and chocolate milk. I went to the parlor after eating and sat on the couch. The TV didn't appeal to me and neither did the radio. Across the street in the projects the stillness was noticeable. No ambulances howled, no tires squealed, all of which boded for a peaceful night in the bricks.

Inside my bedroom I opened a library book, reclined on the bed, and commenced to read. I didn't finish more than a page before my eyelids drooped, dropped, and closed. And just as they closed, a gunshot shattered the silence. It rang out from downstairs, and it was followed by a cacophonous blast that shook dust from the ceiling. I raced down the back stairs and ran into Harraseeket Kid on the landing.

"What was that?" Kid asked.

"Shotgun."

Kid and I charged into Buck's apartment and sprinted down the hall to his bedroom, where we found Buck Louis lying on his bed with the sawed-off resting on his lap. On the floor beside him lay Bill O'Dell, his mouth agape, his eyes awaiting pennies.

"I couldn't help it," Buck said. "He shot at me, so I shot back."

"It's a good thing you did," Kid said. "He'd a killed you sure."

"Is he dead?" Buck asked.

I could have answered Buck's question, but I let Harraseeket Kid do his thing, feeling O'Dell's jugular for a pulse.

"He's dead all right," Kid looked at me. "Who is this guy?"

"He's a Boston Homicide cop named Bill O'Dell. I spoke to him earlier today and accused him of killing Father Barboza." I looked at Buck. "O'Dell came here gunning for me, not you. He must've assumed I still lived on the first floor."

"It's a good thing he came in here instead of upstairs, because you don't have a gun," Buck said.

"I never thought of that."

I called 911—I could almost dial it blindfolded now—and walked back to Buck's bedroom and eased the sawed-off out of his hands. Kid and I lifted Buck onto the wheelchair and the three of us waited for the police.

"I told you Buck needed a gun," Kid said. "You thought I was overdoing it with the way I armed him. What do you think now?"

"What do you think I think? You were right."

Kid walked to the front hallway, rattled something, and came back.

"O'Dell got in through the front door," Kid said, "the only door in the house without a security grate. I shored up the back door and the bulkhead. I'll grate the front door tomorrow."

Everybody showed up. Captain Pruitt, Detective Adam Jenner, even DA Francis Ennis. When a cop gets killed, everybody shows up. The lab crew worked without stopping until dawn. They bagged evidence, brushed for prints, dug a bullet out of the wall, sniffed O'Dell's gun, and seized Buck's sawed-off. The forensics team zipped O'Dell into a bag and carted him to an ambulance. Adam Jenner grilled Buck Louis for an hour. Buck showed Jenner his FID card, which cleared him of gun charges. When Jenner was done, Captain Pruitt took a shot at him. After Buck, they double-teamed me.

"What happened, Sparhawk?" Pruitt said. "What the hell was Bill O'Dell doing in your house?"

"Yeah," Jenner echoed. "What's going on, Dermot? You killed a cop on our watch."

"I didn't kill anybody," I said. "O'Dell broke into my house and started shooting up the place. Buck Louis defended himself. That's all there is to it."

"That's your story?" Pruitt said. "Buck Louis was defending himself?"

"Bill O'Dell was looking to kill me, not Buck. I talked to O'Dell earlier today."

"Talked to him about what?" Pruitt asked.

"It's a long story, Captain."

"A long story? A cop got killed, Sparhawk. I don't give a shit if it's *War and Peace*. Let's hear it, and don't leave out a god-damned thing."

"Bill O'Dell suspected his wife of having an affair with Father Barboza. O'Dell was wrong, but that's what he thought." The windows brightened with the rising sun. "Because Bill O'Dell thought his wife was seeing Father Barboza, he manipulated two boys into accusing Barboza of molesting them. One of the two boys was O'Dell's son."

"How do you know this?" Pruitt asked.

"I talked to Bill O'Dell's wife, Ellen."

Jenner asked, "You talked to Ellen O'Dell?"

"I did." I then stated my theory as if it were fact. "Bill O'Dell hired Lopo Gomes to scare me off Father Barboza's killing."

"O'Dell hired Gomes?" asked Pruitt.

"A probation officer named Malone can link Lopo Gomes to Bill O'Dell. I talked to Malone at the Dorchester Courthouse."

Captain Pruitt leaned closer. "You yourself talked directly to Malone?"

"Yes, I did. Malone told me that Bill O'Dell threatened him to get Gomes a job. Malone in turn threatened one of his parolees, a kid named Squid, to get Lopo a job on the same fishing boat that Squid worked on. Squid got Lopo the job. Check it out. The boat is in Gloucester. The boat's captain is Joe Souza. Squid is Joe Souza's nephew."

Pruitt told me to keep talking.

"I told Bill O'Dell about my talk with Malone at the courthouse. I told O'Dell that Malone connected him to Lopo Gomes. O'Dell asked me if I had reported this information to law enforcement, and I stupidly said no. Bill O'Dell came here tonight to kill me. He wanted to keep me from talking."

Pruitt said, "You think you were the target?"

"Why else would he come to my house armed with a gun?" I asked. "Odds-on, O'Dell thought I lived on the first floor. My name is still on the bottom plate."

"Your name's on the bottom plate," Pruitt said. "That doesn't prove anything."

"Sure it does. It proves that O'Dell assumed I lived on the first floor. And because O'Dell assumed I lived on the first floor, he broke into the first-floor unit; and because he broke into the first-floor unit, it is reasonable to assume that he broke in to kill me. After all, he came in here firing his gun. And because O'Dell broke in to kill me, it is reasonable to conclude that he killed Father Netto Barboza."

Pruitt's head was shaking. "Slow down, Sherlock. Why would I conclude that?"

"Bill O'Dell wanted to shut me up about Father Barboza, about Malone, too."

Jenner groused. "Are you saying that Bill O'Dell killed Father Barboza just because Barboza was drilling his wife? Come on, Dermot. And then O'Dell tried to kill you, just to shut you up about Malone?"

"That's exactly what I'm saying, except you have one part wrong, Adam. It's true that Ellen O'Dell was having an affair, but it wasn't with Father Barboza." I addressed both Pruitt and Jenner. "You had a bad cop on your hands, plain and simple. A bad cop who murdered a good priest, and he murdered him copycat style."

"Copycat?" Jenner chortled. "And I suppose Bill O'Dell admitted to killing Father Barboza."

"Not in so many words, but his actions confirm it, don't they? He came here tonight to kill *me* because I accused *him* of killing Father Barboza."

Pruitt, who was still shaking his head, said, "I'm not convinced."

Of course you're not convinced. You're a Boston Homicide cop, and Bill O'Dell was one of yours.

"Why aren't you convinced, Captain?"

"O'Dell was on medical leave."

How is that relevant?

"O'Dell was a copycat killer," I said. "He knew about the red hoods, and he knew about the Taser. He was smart enough to kill Father Barboza in Boston, where Boston Homicide would lead the investigation."

Pruitt and Jenner looked at each other.

I said, "The serial killer is still at large."

After the cops left I walked around the projects, treading a rectangular path in the snow from Chelsea Street to Medford Street to Polk Street to Bunker Hill Street. With each lap my thinking deepened. Something didn't fit together, and it had to do with Bill O'Dell. The conversation in front of O'Dell's house gnawed at me, but I didn't know why. It was the tenor of the talk, not the content. The tenor didn't ring true. I circled under the Tobin Bridge again to complete a third lap, but my thoughts regarding Bill O'Dell were anything but complete. I was probably thinking too much.

CHAPTER 45

A Boston police officer stood outside Bishop Downey's office in the chancery. Another one stood downstairs in the lobby. The bishop futzed with a fountain pen as he sat behind his big, oak desk and stared at a brass crucifix that hung on the wall. The cross must have been a yard long.

"The police don't have a clue as to the serial killer," he said. "Not a blessed clue."

His white hair was parted on the side, his Roman collar centered in place. At first glance you wouldn't know he was distraught. I was sitting in a chair against the wall.

"Have you warned all your seminary classmates?" I asked. "Have you told them what's going on?"

"I have, every one, ordained or not."

"Good."

"I wish I had listened to you earlier. You were right about the seminary connection." He tossed the pen on the desk. "It sounded crazy when you suggested it."

"I wasn't a hundred percent sure myself at the time." I looked out his office window. "We'll get the bastard."

"My prayers will be answered if you do."

I left the chancery and drove home.

Harraseeket Kid and I joined Buck Louis for a Fat Tuesday corned beef dinner, with turnip, potatoes, beets, and cabbage. We devoured pastries for dessert and quaffed coffee to cap it off. We cleared the table and washed the dishes and sat in Buck's parlor and lit cigars. Our conversation turned to the serial killer and to Bill O'Dell.

Kid blew a plume of smoke to the ceiling. "Thank God you had a gun, Buck. I'd hate to think what would've happened if you didn't."

I got my cigar lit and dropped the match in an ashtray.

"I still can't believe O'Dell came here," I said. "Although I believe that O'Dell killed Father Barboza, I'm more confused now than when I started looking into the serial killings."

"You shouldn't be more confused," Buck said. "You figured out that Bill O'Dell was a copycat killer, so you know about one killing for sure."

"Something still bothers me about O'Dell. I don't know why, but I'm not convinced I got it right with him."

"What more convincing do you need?" Kid pointed his cigar at me. "O'Dell came here to kill you. He fired at Buck, thinking he was firing at you. Isn't that proof enough?"

"You're right, Kid. I should be convinced."

We talked about the killings of the priests and the seminarians who didn't become priests. We talked about Pollard's murder, the red hood on Pollard's head. For some reason, I told Kid and Buck about Father Jack Ahearn, the priest who supposedly hanged himself thirty years ago in Sudbury. I showed them the red hood that Father Ahearn's sister Janice had given me. Buck gasped when he saw it. Kid simply nodded, which meant he wanted to gasp but was too cool to do so. I talked about my trip to Martha's Vineyard, and when I did, Kid perked up.

"Two suicides, one after the other?" Kid said. "What are the chances of that happening?"

"That bothers me, too."

"Yeah." Buck jumped in. "Paul Herz jumped off a lighthouse. And the other guy, what's his name again?"

"Robert Iverson."

"You tried to talk to Herz and he jumped off a tower," Buck

said. "You talked to Iverson and he dove into the water. Two suicides in a row? That's too weird for me."

"They were mentally ill," I said.

"Mentally ill, my ass," Kid said. "You need to go back to
Martha's Vineyard. There's something more there."

"Agreed," I said.

The next morning I drove to Woods Hole in Victor Cepeda's rust
bucket and took the ferry to Martha's Vineyard with the Acclaim
onboard. I steered off the ship and motored along East Chop
Drive, wishing the speedometer went up faster than the fuel gauge
went down. I parked behind the State Police barracks on Tamahi-
gan Avenue, went inside, and asked for Sergeant Silva. Silva came
out and escorted me to his office.

"Nothing's changed since the last time you were here," he said.
"Paul Herz and Robert Iverson's deaths are still ruled suicides. The
cases are closed, practically speaking." Silva spoke without con-
viction, as if he wanted me to refute his claim. He emphasized
"practically speaking," and that told me he wasn't satisfied with
his findings. Silva continued. "The deaths were tragic, but explain-
able, Sparhawk." He ran a hand through his dark hair. "The cause
of death in both cases is suicide."

"I want to talk to Roland Herz one more time."

"Paul's brother?" Silva looked at me. "Why?"

"I want to ask him about the other seminarians in Paul's class."

"It sounds like a waste of time." He looked out his office window to the parking lot. "Let me know if you find anything."

I left the barracks and drove to Chilmark to visit Roland Herz. I
parked in front of his house and knocked on the door. Roland didn't
answer. After a drive around West Tisbury and Edgartown, I returned
to Chilmark and knocked again. No answer. I visited the Gay Head
Light, where Paul Herz had jumped to his death, and drove to the
beach where Robert Iverson had washed ashore. I returned to Roland
Herz's house and tried one more time. He still wasn't home.

That night I stayed at a hotel in Edgartown. At eleven o'clock I turned on the news, and as soon as I did, I wished I hadn't. Another priest had been crucified, this time in Quincy. The killer nailed him to the basement floor of the rectory. The live shots showed the police pacing the church grounds. I clicked off the TV and went to bed.

I tried Herz's house the next day, and again nobody answered. For a recluse, he sure wasn't home much. And, at that moment a feeling of dread came over me. Something happened to Roland. I looked for a way to get into the house. All the windows were latched. The bulkhead was locked. I went to the back door and kicked it open.

I searched the house, not knowing what to look for, not knowing what I'd find. The one thing I didn't find was a dead body, and that gave me solace. I went to the sitting room where Glooscap and I had first talked to Roland. A framed picture of Paul and Roland Herz sat on an end table. I picked it up and studied it, and when I did, some thoughts swirled and some inferences formed. My body reacted, an involuntary reflex, like a doctor tapping a knee.

I had solved the case.

I couldn't put words to it yet, but I had the answer to the serial murders. I took the framed photo of Paul and Roland Herz and drove back to the State Police barracks in Oak Bluffs, where Sergeant Silva humored me one more time.

"Make it fast, Sparhawk. I have a meeting."

"The serial killer is Paul Herz."

"Are you off your rocker? Paul Herz is dead. He jumped off Gay Head Light."

An idea had been brewing in my head. I filled in the blanks as I spoke.

"Suppose it was Roland Herz's body at the lighthouse, not Paul's."

Silva didn't bother to respond.

"Humor me, Sergeant. When I visited Robert Iverson in Gardner, he showed me a photo of Paul Herz from their seminary days.

I have another photo of the Herz brothers here." I showed Silva the picture. "Remember the day we drove to Herz's house?"

"Of course, I remember."

"We talked to Paul Herz, pretending to be Roland."

"Oh, come on."

"What if Paul Herz suckered Roland to the lighthouse and pushed him off?"

"Are you crazy?" Silva paused. "He could never pull it off."

"But what if he did? Paul could have written the suicide note, which would pass muster because it was his own handwriting. The signature would match the one at town hall because it actually *was* his signature. And Paul could have easily switched wallets with Roland."

"What are you saying?"

"I'm saying that Roland Herz got shoved off the lighthouse by his brother, Paul."

"What's the motive?"

"Look what Paul gains. He is no longer a suspect in the priest murders because he is presumed dead, thus he can operate at will. Last night, for example, I'd bet anything that Paul murdered the priest in Quincy."

"I saw that on the news."

"Paul is whacko, you said so yourself. He got booted out of the seminary, and he's been in and out of nuthouses ever since. Paul Herz is alive, masquerading as his brother, Roland."

"It's an interesting theory, I'll give you that much. But how do you explain Robert Iverson? Why would he jump off the ferry?"

"Robert Iverson told me he planned to visit Roland, to console him on Paul's death." I walked to the window. "Suppose Iverson called Paul Herz, thinking he was talking to Roland. Suppose Iverson told Paul, not Roland, that he was coming down for a visit. Paul knew that Iverson would recognize him."

"Go on."

"Iverson tells Paul the ferry he'll be on, and they agree to meet in Vineyard Haven." I turned from the window. "But Paul is a step ahead of him. Paul goes to Woods Hole and boards the same ferry as Iverson. Paul somehow subdues Iverson and throws him overboard. And Robert Iverson washes up on Oak Bluffs the next day."

"Interesting."

"Take a look at this." I held up the photo of Paul and Roland Herz again and pointed out one of the men. "This is the man we talked to, remember?"

"I can't tell them apart. I didn't know either of them."

"We talked to this man." I pointed to the man I presumed to be Paul Herz. "He's an older version of the man I saw in Robert Iverson's photo."

"Are you positive?"

"Yes, I am," I said, even though I wasn't.

"I don't know." Silva stood by the window and looked at the bleak skies. He shoved his hands in his pockets and seemed to be thinking. He turned to me, and said, "You've convinced me to take a second look."

Silva called a judge and requested a court order to exhume Herz's body. The judge contested Silva's request before finally relenting.

"Yes, Your Honor," Silva said to him. "Send me the paperwork and I'll fill it out immediately." He hung up. "Okay?"

"Thanks, Sergeant."

"Don't thank me yet. As far as I'm concerned, Paul Herz is buried in that grave." He stepped out from his desk. "But you've raised enough doubt that I want to be sure, if for no other reason than to get you out of my hair and off this island."

"How soon will you know?"

"Soon enough, Sparhawk, soon enough."

Before I boarded the ferry home, I called the Boston Public Library at Copley. I reached the Microtext Department and asked for Henry, and a second later he came on the line.

"Henry, I need to call on your expertise once again," I said. "Will you look up a name for me in an old Boston telephone directory?"

"Not a problem," he said. "Give me the name."

"The name is Herz, spelled H-E-R-Z. I need a listing from the sixties or seventies, even the early eighties." Harriett Schwartz of Chester Square had told me that Ed Resnick of Resnick Clothiers would occasionally hire day labor from the neighborhood. "I'm looking for a South End address, somewhere near the old Boston City Hospital."

"Hold the line." Henry came back on. "I found a man named Carl Herz listed in Dorchester, nineteen seventy-nine. Let me try the late sixties. Hold the line again." Less than a minute later he was back. "I think I found what you're looking for. A man named Everett Herz lived on Northampton Street, a block from the hospital."

"Thanks, Henry."

I called a Townie named Eddie Reeder, who works in the registry division of Boston City Hall, and asked him to look up a birth certificate. He said he'd be glad to and asked for my phone number. Fifteen minutes later he called me back.

"Paul Herz was born in Boston, nineteen fifty. His father was Everett, mother Helga née Fuchs. Everett's occupation, bartender."

"Thanks, Eddie."

CHAPTER 46

I called Astrid Bordeaux from my apartment and asked her if she'd like to go out to dinner.

"Dinner, as in a date?" she asked.

"Yes, as in a date."

"Um, well, okay." She waited a moment. "What should I wear?"

Wear? "Jeez, I don't know."

"Where we going?" she asked, "What type of restaurant are we going to?"

This was harder than I thought. "It's, ah, a nice restaurant. You know, with menus and napkins."

"No plastic forks and knives?" She laughed. "What time are you picking me up?"

"How about seven?"

"I'll see you at seven."

I arrived at Astrid's house at seven sharp. I was wearing gray gabardine trousers, a cordovan belt with matching shoes, a powder-blue shirt, and a navy blazer with brass buttons. I'd never grace the cover of GQ, but nobody would hand me a quarter if I stood on a corner, either.

Astrid answered the door and my mouth dropped. She was wearing a purple silk blouse that was as clingy as Velcro, giving static electricity a good name. The blouse was tucked into high-waisted black pants.

"You look beautiful."

"Thank you," she said, and took my arm.

We dined at a Greek restaurant in Lowell. After dinner, we

walked to a cozy café. The small circular tables were draped in linen tablecloths and centered with candles. We ordered coffee and dessert.

"I notice you're not drinking tonight," Astrid said. "Is it because of me?"

I stared out the window. An older couple walked along Merrimac Street and stopped on a canal bridge.

"The booze is getting to me lately."

I looked at Astrid's face in the flickering light. The glow came from the candle in the middle of the table. The flame played with Astrid's pupils, ballooning and deflating them, as the wax and wick wrestled for oxygen.

"I'm glad you're watching it tonight, the drinking I mean." She moved her lips slowly when she spoke. "I can take or leave the stuff."

The older couple moved away from the canal and continued up Merrimac Street. Astrid arched in her chair, pushing her breasts against the blouse. I held her hand.

"I wish I could take it or leave the stuff myself." I drank some coffee. "One taste and I'm gone. I can't stop once I start."

"I noticed." She laughed a little. "I didn't want to say anything, but I haven't had a drink since the night we slept together. God, I was sick the next day." Astrid finished her coffee. The candlelight shadowed her cleavage. "Dermot, I like you. You're easy to be with, and I'm having a nice time tonight."

"I'm glad you gave me a second chance."

We left the café and walked to an independent bookstore that devoted an entire wall to Jack Kerouac, Lowell's most noted son, the King of the Beats. One bookshelf consisted of *On the Road*, both hardcover and paperback. There was a photograph on the wall of Kerouac smoking a cigarette with his Beat chums: Allen Ginsberg, Hal Chase, and the dubious William S. Burroughs. That's what the tag said, dubious. Next to the photo was an obituary that clarified why Burroughs might be deemed dubious.

According to the obit, Burroughs, while drinking heavily at a party in Mexico City, said to his wife, Joan, "It's time for our William Tell act." Joan, an eager participant in the act, balanced a glass of water on her head. Burroughs took out his pistol and fired. He missed the glass but not her noggin. The article said he was devastated by her death after a week on life support.

Astrid and I browsed the books and read the dust jackets and looked at the photo plates. We drove back to her house, where the lights were burning.

"Let's go to your place," she said. "Ellen O'Dell is staying over with Bill Jr. She'll watch my Michael. I already told her we might not be home tonight."

"I don't know, Astrid. It's a guy's place, not what you'd call romantic."

"Take me there."

We made love twice that night, and it was love making. Astrid and I stayed in bed all morning, holding each other, listening to music on the radio, neither of us in a rush to start the day. Lucinda Williams's "Passionate Kisses" came on the air, and two turned into three. I'd never drink again, she was my narcotic.

We lay on the bed afterward and talked.

"I have this recurring fantasy," Astrid said, "that in another life I'm a mermaid."

"In another life?" I kissed her neck. "You went mermaid on me last night."

"Oh, you." She hit my shoulder. "Stop that."

We showered and dressed and ate at Uncle Joe's Diner. The cook gave me the thumbs up when I walked in with Astrid on my arm. After breakfast we drove back to Billerica and parked in front of her house. I started to get out of the car to walk her to the door, but she told me to stay put because of the neighbors.

"I feel like I've known you my whole life," she said.

"When can I see you again?"

"Soon," she said, "very soon."

Astrid got out of the car and walked to her house.

"I'm in love," I said to myself.

Two phone messages awaited me when I got home. The first was from Sergeant Silva in Oak Bluffs, the second from Lieutenant Staples, who called from DA Francis Ennis's office. I called Silva first.

"You were right," he said. "Roland Herz was buried in the grave. We haven't officially confirmed it yet, but it was Roland Herz all right."

"How can you be sure?"

"Doc Taylor used dental charts. When Doc saw the mouth, he claimed he didn't need the charts because of Roland's overbite, but he compared the teeth to the chart anyway. They matched."

"We have to find Paul Herz."

"I have a man covering his house, but Herz hasn't shown up yet, not that I expected him to. Paul is foxy, I'll give him that much."

"He's gone," I said. "Paul is in the wind."

I then called Lieutenant Staples at the DA's office. Francis Ennis's secretary told me that Staples had left. I'd no sooner hung up the phone when a loud rap shook the downstairs door. I went to answer it. Staples stood there like a Beefeater on duty.

"Come in, Lieutenant," I said.

Staples looked the same way he looked the last time I saw him. Suit pressed, hair clipped, face scorned. He followed me upstairs and into the kitchen.

"Kudos on Paul Herz." He shoved his hands deep into his pants pockets and shook the loose change. "I told you to keep me in the loop. I gave you wide berth because you were supposed to keep me in the loop."

"I just found out."

"You should have called me immediately from Martha's Vineyard. Instead I had to find out from Sergeant Silva, and I look like a fringe player."

"I gave Silva your name." I drew a glass of water from the kitchen faucet and drank it. "He's a fellow trooper. It's not like he's with the FBI or Boston Homicide."

"You're missing the point, Sparhawk. You're my guy. I gave you free rein because you are my guy out there." He paced from the kitchen to the parlor window. "You were supposed to be my source on the street."

"I figured you and Silva would team up."

"Listen to me closely. When you find something or suspect something or dream something, anything, call me first."

"Yes, sir."

"Are you being funny again?"

"No, sir." I walked with Staples to the door. "Before you go, it might help if you gave me your cell number."

"Sure, Sparhawk, I can do that." Staples handed me his card. "Be at Francis Ennis's office tomorrow afternoon at five."

"Why?"

"Just be there, understood?"

"Yes, sir."

CHAPTER 47

"We're setting a trap," Lieutenant Staples said. Staples, Ennis, and I were sitting at a conference table in the Suffolk County DA's office. It was five p.m. "We're going to decoy Paul Herz into the trap and snare him."

Francis Ennis took a bottle of Jameson 12 from his desk drawer and poured a few ounces into a crystal tumbler. Ennis eyed Staples, Staples nodded yes. Ennis turned to me. I shook my head no, even though my mouth salivated yes. He poured a glass for Staples.

"How are you going to trap him?" I asked. "Paul Herz is a clever bastard."

"It won't be easy." Staples stood from the table. "We know Herz is stalking Bishop Downey, because Downey was in his seminary class."

"He's stalking everybody in the class, not just Bishop Downey," I said. "Herz has gone mad. He killed his brother."

"He killed his brother so he could keep killing his classmates." Staples swirled the glass. For Staples the whiskey was more of a prop than a requirement. "We've contacted every member of the seminary class, and every member has vacated the area, including Bishop Downey."

"That's a good start," I said.

"I'm going to pose as Bishop Downey," Staples said. "We've devised a comprehensive trap, and I'm the decoy. Sharpshooters will be placed around the perimeter of the chancery. Troopers will be posted at every door. We'll either apprehend Paul Herz or kill him off." Staples sat down. "One way or the other, he will be stopped."

"I'm worried." I reached for the whiskey bottle then stopped. They both looked at me. "What's my role in this?"

"You have no role, Sparhawk. I'm heading this operation," Staples said. "I'm posing as Bishop Downey, I'm baiting Paul Herz into the trap, and I'm nailing him to the wall with his own damn nails." He drank a small sip. "We have one major advantage."

"What's that?"

"Paul Herz doesn't know we know about him."

"That's bullshit. Herz knows something is up," I said. "He left Martha's Vineyard and hasn't returned."

"I'm executing the plan starting tomorrow," Staples said. "I'm catching the sick son of a bitch."

"You're making a mistake," I said.

To say that Lieutenant Staples's trap didn't work would be an understatement. It would be better to say that it went kaput, that it fatally failed. And as a result of the failure, Staples was dead.

Francis Ennis called me and told me what happened. Simply put, the ambush backfired. Paul Herz was ensconced in the chancery long before Lieutenant Staples and the State Police ever got there. Herz conceived a strategy that proved ingenious. By being conspicuous, he became inconspicuous. Dressed as a priest, Paul Herz waited in a library down the hall from Bishop Downey's office. He even said hello to Lieutenant Staples, who was dressed as a bishop, when the troopers escorted him to Downey's office, the site of the trap.

Except the trap was rigged the wrong way round, and Staples was the quarry.

Horn-rimmed glasses changed Paul Herz into Clark Kent when everybody was looking for Superman. Nobody recognized him, probably because he donned a Roman collar and carried a breviary. According to the trooper stationed at Bishop Downey's door, Paul Herz humbly asked Staples for a blessing. Staples reportedly looked at the trooper and awkwardly complied.

The exact order of events after that is sketchy, but this much we know:

Using a blackjack, Paul Herz knocked out the trooper guarding Bishop Downey's office, damn near killing him. He then zapped Lieutenant Staples with a Taser gun and shoved a Knights of Columbus sword into his heart. He nailed Staples to Downey's oak desk. He tied a red Resnick hood around Staples's head and smashed his face to mush with the brass crucifix he yanked off the wall.

Before the sharpshooters adjusted their scopes, before the troopers took their places, Lieutenant Staples was dead and Paul Herz was gone.

Herz had been planning the murder of Bishop Downey for months, and the plan was fairly elaborate for a nut job. Using letterhead from the Archdiocese of Montreal, Paul Herz, pretending to be a Montreal priest, began a correspondence with Bishop Downey. He told Bishop Downey that he would be studying at the Harvard Divinity School and asked for access to the chancery as a home base. Granted access, Herz became a familiar face among the staff. They issued him keys to the building and a parking space.

The fox had outfoxed the foxhunters. Paul Herz, posing as a priest, walked out of the chancery unscathed. Lieutenant Staples, posing as Bishop Downey, got carried out in a plastic bag. Herz fooled everyone.

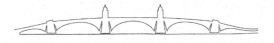

CHAPTER 48

I called Astrid Bordeaux and we went to a movie. This time we stayed the night at her place, her Michael being at his grandmother's house in Dracut. Ellen and Billy Jr. had moved back home. The next morning Astrid and I held each other. We loved to hold each other in the morning.

"Are you enjoying this as much as I am?" she said.

"Yes, ma'am."

"I am alive again thanks to you. I never thought I'd feel alive again after my husband died." She rolled on her side. "Am I scaring you?"

"Not a bit," I said. "I'm falling in love with you."

"Me, too. I want you to get to know my Michael." She wiggled closer. "I mean, if things keep working out for us."

"I'd like that." Getting close to Michael didn't scare me. Nothing scared me with Astrid in my life. "He sounds like a good kid." I pulled her tight against my skin. Our bodies bonded.

We made love again.

We ate scrambled eggs and toast in her kitchen, not saying a word. Words would have spoiled the perfection. Fluffy the dog curled up at my feet and rested her nose on my foot. After breakfast I drove back to Charlestown and slept on the parlor couch until three in the afternoon. I awoke, laced my boots, and went for a walk around the neighborhood. God had put a woman in my life, a beautiful and smart woman. When I got home my cell phone rang—Astrid's number—and I answered.

"Hey, honey."

"Is that you, Sparhawk?" It was a man's voice, and the voice sounded familiar. "You fucked things up for me on Martha's Vineyard. You broke into my house, illegally I might add."

"Herz?"

"I enjoy watching people suffer. It gives me pleasure to inflict pain on my victims, and pain on those left behind. It's so poetic. Save your pennies, Sparhawk. Caskets are expensive. I'm going to enjoy watching you suffer."

I hung up and called Francis Ennis at the DA's office, telling his receptionist it was an emergency. She patched me through.

"What's going on, Sparhawk?"

"Paul Herz called me from Astrid's phone."

"Slow down. Who's Astrid?"

"A woman I'm seeing." I gave Ennis Astrid's full name and address. "Herz is there now. Should I call 911?"

"I'll take care of that. I'll meet you in Billerica."

I ran out to the car, except I didn't have a car. Victor needed the Acclaim today. I ran to Packy's, but Packy needed the van. I ran to the rectory just as Father Dominic was pulling into the parking lot. He looked at my face.

"What on earth is wrong?"

I told him about Astrid and that I needed to borrow his car to see her.

"I'll drive you there," he said. "Get in."

Father Dominic drove north to Route 3. When I told him about the call from Paul Herz, he stomped on the accelerator and drove in the left lane until we exited in Billerica.

A State Police car was parked in front of Astrid's house when we got there. I ran to the front door, but a trooper blocked it.

"Crime scene," he said. "You can't go in."

Father Dominic caught up to me. The trooper stood in the doorway calm and distant, as if the crime were jaywalking. His body language showed no urgency.

"What's going on in there?" I asked.

"Who are you?"

"My name is Dermot Sparhawk. I'm Astrid Bordeaux's friend." I tried to look around him. "I made the 911 call. I mean, I called Francis Ennis."

"Wait here, sir," the trooper said.

The trooper came back with DA Francis Ennis, whose face was a darker shade of maroon today.

"Astrid is alive, the boy is alive, neither was harmed," Ennis said. He cleared his throat. "The dog was stabbed."

"Herz killed Fluffy?" I asked.

"He didn't kill the dog, he stabbed it. The dog is getting stitched up at the vet. Fluffy will live." Ennis didn't give a damn about Fluffy. He had bigger issues to contend with. "CPAC is inside collecting evidence. When Ms. Bordeaux saw the dog carved up she became, well, she left."

"Where did she go?"

"I'm not at liberty to say. We are hiding her in a safe place until we apprehend this madman."

"She's okay, right?"

"Astrid is okay." Francis Ennis gestured for me to follow him inside. "I want to show you something."

We followed Ennis into the house. When we reached Astrid's bedroom, Ennis stopped and said, "You might not want to see this, Father."

"I'm here to support Dermot. Show me what's in there."

We went in. Written in blood on the wall were the words "Michael is next."

"Nobody was home when we got here," Ennis said. "Astrid and her son arrived later. We kept the boy away from the dog, but Ms. Bordeaux insisted on seeing it." Ennis guided us out to the hallway. "Her shriek probably scared the boy more than the sight of the dog would have."

"She shrieked?"

"This is terrible," Father Dominic said, "absolutely terrible. Are the mother and son doing all right?"

"No, Father," Ennis said. "Both of them are quite upset."

"I'll keep them in my prayers."

Father Dominic and I left Astrid's house and drove back to Charlestown. Neither of us spoke during the ride home; neither of us spoke in the church parking lot, either. I got out of his car and walked to Finbar's Saloon and sat on a stool. Tall Ed sauntered over, showing no more urgency than the state trooper in Billerica. He then exerted himself, flipping the bar towel over his shoulder. And then I exerted *myself*.

"Whiskey," I said. "Double."

"Want a beer to wash it down, Dermot?"

"Just whiskey, Ed. I need room in my stomach for whiskey."

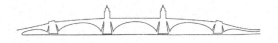

CHAPTER 49

When I came to the next day, I called Astrid Bordeaux's cell phone. She answered on the first ring, which seemed a good sign. We talked a few minutes. Astrid assured me that both she and Michael were doing fine. My shoulders unknotted when she told me this. And then her tone grew serious.

"This is difficult for me to tell you, but Michael and I are moving. This was not an easy decision to make. I've been going over and over it in my head, and I can't find a way to make it work for us."

"What do you mean?"

"I don't feel safe anymore," she said. "This whole escapade has rocked my Michael and me, too—the pedophilia sham, the knifing of Fluffy, the threat written in Fluffy's blood—it's too much, Dermot. We're leaving the state."

"Where are you going?"

"I'm not telling you or anyone else. This is the wisest decision for all of us."

"I can protect you, Astrid; Michael, too."

"I have to put my son first, Dermot. Michael comes first."

"Maybe I can help with Michael."

"I'm sorry. It's over."

She rang off. I sat like a fool holding the phone. I went back to Finbar's Saloon to walk the plank. Two days later I awoke on the parlor floor, rum sick.

CHAPTER 50

I went to my office and logged onto the computer and searched for articles on Paul Herz. A *Boston Globe* story chronicled his recent killing spree. Another front-page piece talked about law enforcement's search for him, a team that included the FBI, Boston Homicide, and CPAC. A manhunt was afoot that included everybody but me. I wondered if Herz had left town. The police had cast a dragnet that a minnow couldn't squirm through, and yet nobody could find him.

Where was Paul Herz? I left the office and walked home. Harraseeket Kid had installed a security grate on the front door in response to the O'Dell incident. I didn't have the key, so I rang the doorbell. Buck Louis let me in and wheeled backward into his apartment. I followed him.

"Harraseeket Kid told me to give you this." Buck tossed me a key. "Nobody gets in without a key."

"Good," I said. "And keep the shotgun loaded just in case."

"It's loaded." Buck held up a box of ammo. "Armor-piercing rounds, blows away the confetti shells I was using before."

"Those confetti shells killed Bill O'Dell."

I went up to my apartment and had just turned on the news when Harraseeket Kid's diesel churned into the parking space behind the house. I went down to meet him in the hallway.

"I have a request," I said.

"Me first." Kid removed his cap and rubbed his forehead. "I want to get a watchdog for the house. A friend of mine in New

Hampshire breeds Alaskan malamutes, and he's got a year-old female. Okay if I get her?"

"Good idea, Kid."

"What's your question?"

"I need a ride to Gardner," I said. "That's where Robert Iverson lived."

"Iverson, the guy that drowned."

"That's him. I want to break into his house."

"All the way out to Gardner, huh?" Kid zipped his tan Carhartt coat and pulled on his bump cap. "Let's go."

We drove west on Route 2 and pulled into Gardner an hour and a half later. Kid turned into Iverson's driveway and parked behind the house. I knocked on the door, waited ten seconds in case someone was inside, and then kicked it open.

"Work fast," I said. "Look for anything that might help find Paul Herz."

Kid worked downstairs while I worked upstairs. Iverson's bedroom was crammed with crap. He had trinkets and ashtrays from gift shops, parched postcards, a 1967 Red Sox pennant, refrigerator magnets. I took the postcards. I emptied the dresser and tossed the closet. Nothing I found helped. I tipped the dresser on its side and jumped on it, splintering the dried pine. Nothing fell out like it does in the movies.

We'd been at it an hour. It was only a matter of time before a neighbor noticed a wrecker in a dead man's driveway. I went downstairs.

"Find anything, Kid?"

"I found a diary in the basement."

"Good, let's get out of here."

We got into the wrecker and drove back to Charlestown.

That evening I went to the basement to talk to Kid, and that was the first time I saw the Alaskan malamute. She was curled up near the sump pump. She had coarse gray fur and a head the size of a basketball. I leaned over and scratched her back and then sat in a folding chair. The dog padded over and sniffed my leg, apparently liked what she smelled, and padded back to the pump. Across the street in the projects a police siren wailed. The malamute raised her head and pointed her nose at the rafters and answered the siren with a mournful howl.

"Are you sure she's not a wolf?" I asked Kid.

"Her name is Sled Dog, a purebred Alaskan malamute."

"Hey." Buck yelled from upstairs. "Did I hear a dog? What are you guys doing?"

"Just talking," I said.

"Come up here and talk," Buck said. "I'll throw on some coffee."

We went up to Buck's apartment and sat in the parlor. Buck rolled in from the kitchen to join us. Sled Dog charged up from the cellar and snuggled against Buck's side, butting him with her brow.

Buck inched back. "That dog is huge."

Kid said, "She's a beauty, well bred, too. Her name is Sled Dog."

"A fitting name." I rested my feet on the hassock and watched Sled Dog. She never moved from Buck's side. Smelling the brewed coffee, I went to the kitchen and poured myself a cup and sat again, and said, "Kid and I broke into Iverson's house today."

Buck asked, "The seminarian who drowned?"

"Right, the man who washed up on the Vineyard," I said. "We were searching for clues, anything to help find Herz." I held up the diary. "Kid found this. While Kid drove to New Hampshire to get Sled Dog, I read the diary. I found something, but it's not very much."

"What did you find?" Kid asked.

"Two years ago Paul Herz and Robert Iverson stayed at some kind of commune or retreat house in the Berkshires."

"Two years ago?" Buck said. "Is it worth checking out now?"

"I'm not sure. I have nothing else to go on, so I probably will check it out."

Kid gestured with a nod. "Let's go to the Berkshires in the morning and see if Paul Herz is out there."

"We'll go in the morning," I said. "Can you and Sled Dog watch the house, Buck?"

"It's covered. Anyone breaks in, either I'll shoot him, or Sled Dog'll bite the shit out of him." Buck wheeled up to me. "I'm kidding 'round with ya."

Going to the Berkshires probably wouldn't do much good, but I needed to do something. Paul Herz was running wild, while I was running in neutral.

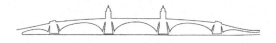

CHAPTER 51

The next morning Kid and I headed for the western part of the state and found the commune, which abutted October Mountain State Forest. It was a dilapidated mansion that looked like the hotel in *The Shining*, with turrets and gables and steeply pitched roofs. A gravel driveway led from the country lane to the front of the house. Kid crunched to a halt at the farmer's porch. A man in a rocking chair rose to his feet. Kid and I got out of the truck. The man stood on the top step and crossed his arms. He wore woolen pants and a plaid shirt, but no coat.

"What do you people want?"

"I'd like to talk to you," I said.

"This is private property. You can't just drive up here."

"I'm looking for a man named Paul Herz." I showed plaid man a picture. "This is Paul Herz. Have you seen him?"

"Evidently, I didn't make myself clear. I suggest you leave here at once. If you don't leave at once, I shall call the police."

"Call them." I handed plaid man Lieutenant Staples's card. "I'm working with them on the priest murders." I held up the picture of Herz again. "This man is a serial killer. He has stayed here in the past. I suggest you call the police so we can straighten out this mess."

Plaid man waved his hands.

"There's no need to involve the police. We can work this out like adults."

"I thought we could." I handed him the picture. "Take another look."

"Yes." Plaid man didn't need a second look. "I know of this man, though I never knew his name."

"His name is Paul Herz and he is dangerous," I said.

"He's not here anymore. Herz, or whatever his name is, left." Plaid man swallowed hard. Maybe the thought of having a serial killer under his roof threw him. "He was only here for a night. He checked out early this morning, but I don't know where he went."

"Can anybody here help us?" I asked. "We need to stop him."

"You have my permission to talk to the residents."

"Thank you."

We talked to the commune dwellers, but none of them knew where Paul Herz might be. Kid and I drove home to Charlestown.

That night Mickey Pappas and I attended The Bottom of the Barrel meeting at Mission Church. One of the speakers said that the healing begins when the blaming ends. Another one talked about acceptance. After the meeting Mickey drove me home. He sailed through red lights and cut off cars. If he heard the horns, he didn't show it. We arrived in front of my house unscathed.

Aunt Agnes's old rotary telephone was ringing when I stepped into the apartment. I had forgotten it was still connected. A thought came to me. God forbid it was one of Ag's friends who hadn't been told of her passing. I picked up the Bakelite receiver and heard nothing but a dial tone. Then my cell phone rang. The man on the other end was already speaking before I got the phone to my ear.

"Nice try at the commune, Dermot. I'm impressed that you tracked me down there. How did you know about the Berkshires?"

"Herz?"

"Tell me how, I seriously want to know."

What difference would it make if I told him?

"I found Robert Iverson's diary in his basement. That's how I knew about the commune."

"Sometimes they call it a retreat house."

"What?"

"Still hot on my trail, are you?"

"I am. And when I find you, I will kill you."

"You'll never catch me, Dermot. Nobody will ever catch me."

A city bus roared down Bunker Hill Street and stopped in front of my house to pick up passengers. The diesel engine echoed in the receiver as it accelerated away. The echo came from the receiver, not the street. Herz was in front of my house.

"I'm glad you're still after me," he said. "I like you pursuing me."

"Yeah, me too."

I glanced out the window to the sidewalk below. There were parked cars but no pedestrians. No one stood in the project doorways or alleys. Paul Herz had to be in one of the cars. Or he could be in a doorway on my side of the street, a doorway I couldn't see from my window.

I crept down the back stairs while Herz babbled and let myself into Buck Louis's apartment. Buck saw me and was about say something, but I placed my finger across my lips. He nodded. I wrote on a shopping bag "Call 911. Herz is outside."

"You sound quite angry," Herz said, "Was Astrid's loss too much for you to handle?"

"It was tough."

"My, you're angry."

I went out the back door and walked down the alleyway to the front of the house, working to keep Herz on the phone. "I was wondering something, Paul. Were you and Robert Iverson lovers? Was Robert your boyfriend?"

"Tsk, tsk, Sparhawk. You can't rattle me."

"The cops figured you for a rape victim. They figured you went after Father Axholm, because you were molested as a kid. Was it your father? Or was it one of your mother's boyfriends?" I glimpsed around the corner at the front of the alley. "How did you become such a freak?"

"You are wasting your time, Sparhawk."

"Why did you kill Robert Iverson?" I said. "He was the only person alive who could stomach you. Why?"

I saw a man sitting in a car parked a short way up the hill. How could I get close to enough to see if it was Herz? A bus came up Bunker Hill Street bound for Sullivan Square and stopped to let out passengers. When the bus accelerated, I jogged next to it, keeping it between me and what I assumed to be Herz's car.

I guessed the location of the car and rolled to the gutter, keeping out of Herz's sightlines. But I had misjudged the distance. He must have seen me. The engine revved. I sprinted after him, but you can't outrun a car. Herz drove over the hill out of sight.

"Adios, Sparhawk," Herz said. "You lose again."

I stood on the sidewalk and gasped for air. Paul Herz had outflanked me, but it was more than that. He was playing me. Something he said bugged me. What was it? I crossed Bunker Hill Street and thought about Herz, and as I was thinking, a car raced down the hill and pulled up next to me. Two men jumped out. Captain Pruitt and Detective Adam Jenner.

"A 911 caller said Paul Herz was out here," Jenner said. "The call came from your house."

"I know, Adam. I told Buck Louis, the paraplegic who lives on the first floor—"

"We know all about Buck Louis," Pruitt said. "Get to the point. What's going on with Paul Herz?"

"Herz called me from his car outside my house. I was closing in on him when he saw me and drove off."

"You got a good look at him, I suppose," Pruitt said.

"I didn't actually see him, but it was Herz."

"How do you know it was Herz if you didn't see his face?" Pruitt asked. "He could have been calling from anywhere."

"Herz said 'Adios, Sparhawk' as he sped away."

Pruitt and Jenner looked at each other.

"What kind of car was he driving?" Jenner asked. "Did you get the license plate?"

"I didn't get the plate," I said. "It was too dark. And I didn't get a good look at the car, either. It might have been a newer sedan."

"That's a lot of help," Pruitt said.

I told them everything I could remember about the phone call. They radioed the information to the station, got back in their car, and drove off.

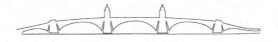

CHAPTER 52

Early the next morning the cell phone woke me. Buck Louis said he needed to talk to me right away, that it was urgent. He was waiting for me when I got to the landing. Buck wheeled to his computer and pointed at the monitor.

"The police released a composite of Paul Herz," Buck clicked on the sketch to enlarge it. "Is that a good likeness of him?"

"It's pretty close."

"That's the guy who inspected the cable work the other day."

"What?"

"That's him, that's the guy."

"Are you sure about that?" I asked.

"I'm positive."

I was sitting in Glooscap's office at the auto-body shop. He poured me a cup of coffee and sat at his desk. Harraseeket Kid, wearing coveralls and a Dropkick Murphys tee shirt, lounged on the couch against the wall.

"I called Francis Ennis at the DA's office." I sipped the coffee. "I asked him to scan my house, and he found something I suspected he might find: three listening devices, one in the cellar, one in Buck's apartment, one in my apartment."

"Everything makes sense now," Glooscap said. "That is how Paul Herz got the drop on Ike."

"Herz was listening to us," I said. "He knew about Ike Melkedae at Pollard's house. He probably knew about Lieutenant Staples at the chancery."

"It's my fault," Kid said. "House security is my responsibility."

"It's nobody's fault," I said.

Glooscap asked, "How did you catch on?"

"Herz called me. Hey, that's another thing. Herz knew my cell phone number. Remember I told Ike the number in the cellar? That's how Herz knew it." I sat back and thought. I might have given Herz my number in Martha's Vineyard. "Herz said something about the commune. He said the owners sometimes call it a retreat house."

"He was listening to us in Buck's parlor," Kid said.

"When Herz heard we were going to the Berkshires, he shot out ahead of us, stayed the night, and left before we arrived the next day," I said. "I wouldn't be surprised if he watched the whole thing from his car."

"The bastard." Kid leaned forward. "Did the DA remove the bugs?"

"The bugs are gone."

Glooscap said, "Maybe you should have left them in place."

"Use the bugs to set up Paul Herz," I said. "I thought of that, but I thought of it too late. I called Francis Ennis from Buck's apartment, which turned out to be bugged. Herz probably heard the call."

"It might be for the best, Dermot," Glooscap said. "Using the bugs to trap Herz might have proved risky. Herz is not a man to play games with."

Kid said, "I wonder how Herz knew we were getting cable. He posed as a cable guy, so he knew we were getting cable."

"I don't know."

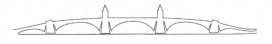

CHAPTER 53

Thanks to Henry's research at the Boston Public Library, I now knew that Paul Herz had grown up on Northampton Street, one block from Chester Square, the home of Resnick Clothiers. Although I couldn't prove it, I was certain that either Herz or someone Herz knew worked for Resnick Clothiers as a day laborer. Perhaps his father or brother, or even Paul Herz himself. And the person who worked there stole the red hoods that were used in the murders. The way Herz got the hoods seemed trivial at that point.

But trivial or not, I had no idea how to find Paul Herz, and Northampton Street seemed to be as good a place as any to start. With Henry's help, I assembled a list of residents that had lived on Northampton Street in the sixties and that still lived there today. There were seven names in total. Maybe one of them would remember Paul Herz.

I drove Victor's clunker to the South End and parked at a meter on Washington Street and began to canvass. The first two addresses yielded nothing, because no one was home. At 28 Northampton Street an elderly man named Curley answered my knock. He smoked a Pall Mall red and spoke with a croupy growl. I asked him if he remembered his old neighbor Paul Herz from the 1960s. Curley vaguely remembered the Herz family, the father and mother and two sons.

"It looks like Paul Herz is famous now," he said. "He's been on the news."

"I saw that." I sniffed the aroma of the burning tobacco. "What can you tell me about the Herz family?"

Curley dropped the butt on the steps and crushed it out.

"The wife was backward. I think she escaped from Germany after the war. It was so long ago. One of the boys loitered at the train station. It might have been Paul or maybe his brother, I can't say which. But he was always up there. I used to wonder if he got a job working for the T. He'd fit right in, the way he loitered." Curley placed an unlit cigarette in his mouth with a liver-spotted hand. "The boy loved it up there on the El train, before the city went and tore it down. That's about all I can tell you."

Nobody answered at the next three addresses.

The last name on the list was Lucius Bethune. I probably should have started with Bethune, because he lived nearest to the Herz home. I rang the bottom bell of a three-story brownstone and waited. A tall, black man with a shorn head answered the door. He looked to be about sixty years old, and he looked to be in excellent shape. A wrought-iron security gate was locked between us. Lucius Bethune, if that's who was standing in front of me, seemed to be in no great rush to open it. He waited for me to speak.

"My name is Dermot Sparhawk," I said. "Are you Mr. Bethune?"

"I'm Lucius Bethune." His face remained expressionless. "Is there something you want?"

"I'm looking for information on an old neighbor of yours named Paul Herz. Do you remember him?"

"Why are you looking for Paul?"

Shouldn't it be obvious? It's been all over the news.

"Paul Herz is a serial killer," I said. "He killed the priests."

"I saw it on TV."

"Did you know him?" I asked.

"I knew him, knew the whole screwy family." He stared at my face. "What do you want with Paul?"

The gate remained between us.

"I want to stop him," I said. "I work for the Archdiocese of Boston. Herz killed a lot of priests, so they hired me to look into it."

Bethune nodded, apparently satisfied with my explanation. He

unlocked the gate and led me inside. His apartment was what re-
altors called a floor-through, a unit that ran from the front of the
building to the back. And it consisted of one commodious room.
The ceilings were as high as Harriett Schwartz's, and the bay windows were just as bright. The kitchen consumed a third of the
space and was outfitted with commercial equipment.

"Your place is huge," I said.

"The building's been in my family for three generations. I live
here alone now, so I removed the interior walls. None of them were
weight bearing anyway. The unit used to have three bedrooms, but
I like openness. Fifteen hundred square feet, that's more than some
houses. I own the two units above, pays me some nice rental in-
come."

Lucius leaned against a built-in bookcase. On the top shelf was
a faded photo of two black men in gray suits shaking hands. A
banner behind them read "Brotherhood of Sleeping Car Porters."
Lucius pointed to a chair and invited me to sit. He sat on a couch
across from the coffee table. After a minute or two of chitchat, he
nodded for me to begin, and I did just that.

"What can you tell me about Paul Herz?"

"Paul had a miserable childhood. His father was abusive and
his mother was out of step."

"When you say abusive?"

"Old Everett Herz kicked the crap out of Paul. He wore engi-
neer boots and literally kicked Paul around the apartment." Lucius's eyes glazed over. "Everett would come home drunk from
work and start in on him."

"He tended bar."

"Not a chance. He worked at a bar called Bernstein's over by
City Hospital, but not as a bartender. Old Everett was known as
the broom. He swept the barroom floors. He might get a drink for
his efforts, maybe some jingle from the patrons."

"The broom," I said. "No wonder he came home angry."

"Drunk and angry," Lucius said.

"The mother?"

"Helga came from Austria or Germany, one of those places. She lacked maternal instincts. Motherly things didn't register in her head. Helga would stand at the stove frying Wiener schnitzel, while Everett booted field goals with Paul's ribs. She was numb to the whole thing."

"She never protected Paul." There is always a reason to explain why someone becomes a psychopath. "Paul is a serial killer, you know."

"Like I said, I saw it on TV."

"I'm trying to find him."

"I imagine a lot of people are trying to find him." Lucius got up and walked to the stove. "Coffee?"

"Thanks."

"I haven't seen Paul since the late eighties." Lucius talked louder from the kitchen area. He scooped coffee into the basket and poured water into the pot. "That's when he got released from the hospital and came back to the neighborhood."

"The late eighties, that was a long time ago."

"When Paul came back, he went crazy. An ambulance had to take the poor guy away." He turned the gas on high. "They should've never let him out in the first place."

"Do you remember why he went crazy?"

"If I told you, you wouldn't believe me." Lucius watched the pot. When the first jet of water squirted through the glass knob he lowered the gas. "He went crazy because the elevated train was gone. The city dismantled it while Paul was in the sanitarium. The poor bastard couldn't handle it."

"He couldn't handle the dismantling of the tracks?"

The coffee finished percolating. Lucius served it on a stainless steel tray, with cream and sugar, mugs and spoons and napkins.

"That's right, he couldn't handle it. Paul hung out at Northampton Station. It became a refuge for him. Whenever his father started in on him, Paul ran and hid in the station. After a while, he practically lived up there. Northampton Station was Paul's idea of a tree house. He ate up there, slept up there, even in winter. Paul had one of those thermal sleeping bags. I think a neighbor gave it to him."

"Sounds bad," I said.

"When Paul got out of the hospital and saw the elevated train gone, well, he went bonkers. He had a meltdown, right there at the corner of Mass Ave. and Northampton Street, right where the old station used to be."

"Paul was a pretty messed-up guy."

"He sure was." Lucius put down his mug. "You haven't heard the worst of it yet. It happened a decade earlier, in October of nineteen seventy-nine. The El was still there when the incident took place."

"What incident?"

"I remember the year because the Pirates won the World Series. Willie Stargell and those guys beat the Orioles. 'We Are Family.' Do you remember the song? It was a big hit for Sister Sledge. Anyway, that was the Pirates' theme song that year, "We Are Family." Talk about a double whammy. Paul gets kicked out of the seminary and a day later Everett Herz hangs himself. What a horrible spectacle. There was old Everett Herz dangling from Northampton Station with a rope around his neck. When I first saw him I thought he was a Halloween dummy."

"Why's that?"

"There was a hood covering his head."

CHAPTER 54

I became obsessed with the elevated Orange Line and Northampton Station. I searched the Internet for everything I could find on the subject, and there was plenty. I found photographs and diagrams, and printed every one of them. The photos were mostly black-and-white stills that aroused a lowdown sentiment, as if you were looking at an urban hobo camp. I found city plans and old maps. One map showed Chester Square when it was still a circle, before Mass Ave. cut it in half.

I tacked the prints to the walls and hallways. Stacks of prints covered the kitchen table. Hour after hour I stared at the city collage and waited for it to tell me something. I read an article by Sal Giarratani titled "Next Stop: Northampton Station." The article mentioned Bernstein's bar, and I wondered if Sal had ever met Everett "The Broom" Herz there.

The hours turned to days. I didn't drink.

After Mass one Sunday I went to the office computer and searched again for images of the El train. The pages scrolled by hypnotically, and if not for the vivid quality of one particular image, I would have missed it. A color photo. The colors were from a recent photograph, probably from a digital camera. For some reason the previous searches hadn't hit on it.

The picture showed an abandoned train station in the middle of a grassy meadow. The copper siding had oxidized and the tin roof sagged. It sat on an I-beam that could have been part of the original elevated structure. Attached to the station was a sign. The sign had two horizontal stripes, one orange, one white. Written in white on the orange was NORTHAMPTON. Written in black on the white was OUTBOUND.

I was standing on my toes.

According to the photo credits, the picture was taken in 2003 by John Bay. The caption read: "This elevated train station used to tower over Northampton Street and Massachusetts Avenue in Boston. It now resides at the Seashore Trolley Museum."

Two key clicks later I learned that the Seashore Trolley Museum was located in Kennebunkport, Maine. One minute later I grabbed my coat and drove to Glooscap's auto-body shop in Victor's car. For some reason I felt compelled to tell Glooscap I'd be going to Maine.

I sat on a folding chair in Glooscap's office and watched as he tamped tobacco into his pipe. He struck a match, lit the wad, and sucked until the bowl glowed orange. He then exhaled a lungful. A hazy plume shot from his lips and gathered in a cloud above his head, a smoke signal indicating he was ready to talk.

"So, you are going to Kennebunkport," he said.

"I am." On the drive over I had called Glooscap and told him about Northampton Station, now mothballed in a trolley museum. I told him that Northampton Station had once been a refuge for Paul Herz. I also told him about my conversation with Lucius Bethune, Herz's former neighbor. According to Bethune, the elevated train stop was the only place Herz felt safe. "It's a long shot, but I think Herz is up there."

"Hmm," Glooscap droned. It was as close as he came to uttering a contraction. "Are you going alone?"

"Yes," I said. "Odds are he's not there, but I had a strong reaction when I saw the photo, and I want to follow through on it."

"Perhaps Harraseeket Kid could accompany you."

"I'll be fine. I just wanted to let you know where I'd be. You have my number."

"And you have mine."

• • •

I pulled into Kennebunkport at three p.m. and located the trolley museum on Log Cabin Road. The air was cold and the grounds were bare. The museum gate was locked against vehicles, but it was simple enough to step around it on foot. I shifted the Plymouth Acclaim into park and looked around. I saw nobody on the museum property, so I drove back to town.

A midwinter hush deadened downtown Kennebunkport, and the impending twilight snowballed with frozen inertia. I drove along, the only car on the road, and saw an inn on Route 9 with its lights on. I pulled into the lot and went to see about a room. The desk clerk, a youngster with a mop of blond hair, checked me in and handed me a key.

"Any bags?" he asked. "I'm the bellboy, too."

"No bags, but maybe you can help me on something else." I showed him a photo of Paul Herz. "Have you seen this man around town?"

"Let me see it." He took the picture and studied it. "The face looks familiar, but I can't help you beyond that."

I walked up to my second-floor room, which was small and neat with a large bay window that faced Route 9. I cracked it an inch to let in the ocean air and contemplated my next move. Tired, I decided to lie down instead, and the pillow could not have been fluffier. I must have been more worn out than I realized, because I fell asleep and didn't awaken until a chambermaid knocked on the door in the morning. I went to the lobby and found the same desk clerk on duty. He handed me a receipt to sign. I filled it in and slid it back to him.

"I remember now," he said.

"Excuse me?"

"The picture you showed me last night, I remember where I saw the face before. It was on the front page of the *Boston Globe*, the serial killer Paul Herz."

I thanked him and left the inn.

• • •

It snowed the night before, and the Kennebunkport cleanup crew had already plowed and sanded the sidewalks and streets. I walked among the shops in Dock Square and tried to formulate a plan, except a plan wasn't formulating. At a donut shop, I got a bagel and coffee and read the local paper. I went back to my car and drove to Biddeford Pool and watched as the waves crash on the rocks, hoping for inspiration. Nothing inspiring came. I drove to Old Orchard Beach and stood on the end of the town pier, awaiting enlightenment. Lightning didn't strike. I drove back to Kennebunkport.

I went to Allison's Restaurant and ate a hamburger platter and apple pie. After the meal, I sat at the bar and drank coffee. No beer and whiskey, I wanted to stay sharp. The afternoon ticked by, the sun waned low, the bartenders changed shifts. I left Allison's and went to the car and drove to the Seashore Trolley Museum on my theoretical whim, which no doubt was a waste of my time.

I parked in front of the museum on Log Cabin Road and got out of the car. According to a frost-caked sign, the museum was closed until Memorial Day. I stepped around the gate and onto a carpet of white unmarked by footprints. Herz, if he was even here, could have come in from any direction. Or he could have been here before the snow started to fall. Or he might not be here at all. I walked past car barns and trains and buses, keeping my eyes alert and my pace deliberate. My knee ached with each step. I walked past trolleys and streetcars and switch towers. The snow came up to my ankles, deep enough to muffle the footfalls.

And then I saw it, Northampton Station. It sat roughly eight feet above the ground on steel girders, just like the photo online. I listened. All I heard was wind. The horizon had swallowed the sun, and the moon was but a sliver. Except for the hoary glow of the silver flooring, the area was completely dark. I edged to the station and stood under it. The only marks in the snow came from my shoes. Herz couldn't be here. There'd be footprints if he were here. I listened again. Nothing this time, not even the wind. He wasn't here. Or maybe I just didn't want him to be here. Then I noticed something on the snow, a candy wrapper. Butter rum Life Savers, Herz purchased butter rum Life Savers at Cantabrigian Wine and Liquors across from St. Peter's.

I shinnied up an I-beam and peeked into the station, a hollow cavern that blotted what little moonlight there was, making it darker inside. I climbed over the half wall and lowered myself onto the platform. The air huffed in cadence, as if the station were alive. My eyes adjusted to the blackness.

Halfway down the platform I saw what appeared to be a sleeping bag, or maybe it was a pile of rags. Nightfall made it tough to discern things. I pulled myself along the floor like a combat Marine and crawled to the cloth pile. It was a sleeping bag. Next to it was a shopping bag. I opened the shopping bag, and inside the bag I found three hoods.

The hoods, the candy wrapper, Northampton Station—I had found Paul Herz's hiding spot. I shoved the hoods in my coat pocket and sat against the wall and took deep breaths. Herz had been here, but where was he now? Then I realized I had a problem. When Herz returned he'd see my trail in the snow, a trail that led from Log Cabin Road to Northampton Station. He'd see my car, too. Herz would take off as soon as he saw my tracks. He'd be in the wind again. I felt a sense of relief. If Herz took off, I wouldn't have to deal with him. I relaxed.

A shuffling noise ended my tranquility. I looked around the station but saw nothing. Probably the wind. I heard the shuffling again. It sounded like shoes shuffling. Goose bumps erupted on my skin. My spine tingled. Where was the shuffling coming from? And then I saw it. At the far end of the station a shadowy figure appeared. The figure of a man.

He must have been hidden in one of the recesses. The man stood on the edge of the platform and looked out to the museum grounds, reminding me of a sea captain on the bow of a ship. He lit a cigarette that illuminated his face. It was Paul Herz. I froze against the wall. Herz stared back into the station. He seemed to be staring right at me. He turned again and gazed at the grounds.

I crawled toward him. Herz dragged on the cigarette and flicked it into the air. The orange tip arched to its apex and slowly descended. Slithering on my belly, I was ten feet from him. Herz stuck his nose in the air and sniffed. Was I downwind? He pushed a hand into his pocket and came out holding a small object. The object reflected in the moonbeams. Cellophane on a pack of cigarettes? Should I get out of there and call the police or stay put and capture him?

My cell phone rang.

In a single motion that looked rehearsed, Herz spun and shot at me with the Taser. I rolled on the platform like a man on fire, and the electrified darts missed. I grabbed the wires leading back to the gun. Herz dropped the Taser and pulled out a pistol. I bounded to my feet and came at him low. An errant gunshot rang out. I blitzed Herz, exploded into his chest with my shoulder, and lifted him off his feet. He stumbled backward when he landed. His calves bumped the half-wall border, throwing him off balance. He swung his arms, attempting to regain his footing. It didn't work. Paul Herz fell off the platform. I ran to the edge and looked down.

It was only about an eight-foot drop, but he had landed head-first on an outcropping of Maine ledge. With a fluffy layer of snow covering it, the granite mantel could have been a pillow. The white powder surrounding his noggin blackened with blood. Paul Herz lay dead on the ground, just like his brother Roland at Gay Head Light.

I punched 911.

CHAPTER 55

Law enforcement from Maine and Massachusetts sorted out the killing of Paul Herz. It was ruled self-defense. No charges were brought against me. Back in Charlestown, things got back to normal, whatever normal means in the projects. I was glad to have my predictable, if mundane, job back. People don't die when you give them food. Harraseeket Kid and Glooscap were also back in sync, banging out dents in Andrew Square. Father Dominic gave me time off to relax, and that's exactly what I planned to do, relax. And then the doorbell rang.

I went down to answer it and saw Captain Pruitt and Detective Adam Jenner talking on the porch. I let them in and they followed me upstairs. Once inside my apartment, Pruitt extended his big black mitt to me.

"You did a hell of a job, Sparhawk." We shook hands. "I busted your balls pretty good. No hard feelings?"

"None, Captain."

"I didn't think so." Pruitt rubbed his forever-furrowed brow. "Paul Herz knew you were there at the trolley museum. When your cell phone rang, the call came from Herz. We found a disposable in his pocket. Herz called you exactly one minute before you called 911."

"He probably heard me opening the shopping bag."

"What shopping bag?" Pruitt asked.

"The shopping bag on the platform, it crinkled when I opened it. Herz must've heard it," I said. "In the bag I found some red hoods. I should have told you, but I figured you didn't need them. Herz is dead, the crime has been solved."

"We need those hoods, Sparhawk. The hoods are evidence. Give them to Detective Jenner, and he'll catalog them," Pruitt said. "I've had enough backslapping for one day. I'll be waiting outside, Jenner."

Pruitt went down the stairs.

"The hoods?" Adam asked.

"I'll get them." I retrieved them from my bedroom and handed them to Adam Jenner. "Here you go."

"Do you have a bag? It's evidence."

"Sure." I snapped open a shopping bag from the kitchen and dropped the hoods in, one at a time, saying, "Uno, dos, tres."

"Bilingual now, huh?" Adam closed the bag. "Thanks, Dermot."

And then he hugged me, just like after a football game.

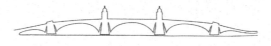

CHAPTER 56

It was a blustery Saturday in March, and I was sitting in the front row of the noontime AA meeting at Saint Jude Thaddeus with my newly appointed sponsor, Mickey Pappas. At the end of the meeting we stood for the Lord's Prayer; we folded and stacked the chairs; we swept and mopped the floors. I had two weeks of sobriety under my belt, and it felt good. At the door, I told Mickey I needed to talk to him.

"No problem, Dermot. I'm listening."

"I'm having drunk dreams. Every night I dream about drinking. I'm in the Horseshoe Tavern or Finbar's Saloon, buying rounds, drinking shots."

"There's nothing wrong with a drunk dream. We're powerless over our dreams, Dermot. You're not doing anything wrong."

"That's a relief."

"I've had many drunk dreams." He clutched my shoulder. "And I came up with a solution that I'm gonna share with you, because that's what sponsors do."

"What solution is that?"

"You're an alcoholic. Next time you have a drunk dream, enjoy it."

At home I cooked a fried egg sandwich in an iron skillet and ate it in three bites. I was about to rest on the couch when the phone rang. Buck Louis was on the other end.

"There's a lady in front of the house. She walked to the door and walked away a couple of times. She's at the door again."

I went downstairs and saw Ellen O'Dell on the steps. This

couldn't be good. Her husband had been shot dead in my down-stairs apartment, a shot issued by Buck Louis. I had pushed Ellen hard for the truth about Father Netto Barboza, maybe too hard. I opened the door and invited her in.

We went upstairs and sat at the kitchen table. I asked Ellen if she'd like anything to drink. She said that she'd like a cup of tea. I lit a burner under the kettle and put out a plate of Effie's Oatcakes while we waited for the pot to boil.

"I'm sorry about Bill," I said. "Things went too far."

"That's not why I'm here."

We sat quietly, the kettle whistled, and I poured the steaming water. We ate and drank in silence. She finished the cup of tea, placed it in the saucer, and said, "I don't think my husband killed Father Barboza."

"I respect your loyalty, Ellen, but the evidence is irrefutable."

"Please listen to me. Can you do that?"

"Yes, of course."

"Bill did some pretty stupid things and so did I. But the things Bill did, he did to save our family." She got up from the table. "The affair I had, the one that Father Barboza counseled me to end, I was seeing Detective Adam Jenner."

"Jenner?"

"It came out of nowhere. Adam and I would run into each other at the supermarket or the bank. I kept bumping into him around town. It was almost eerie."

"And the affair started."

"It was strictly for sex at first. We'd meet at a hotel lounge and get a room. Sometimes we'd go to his friend's house." Ellen's eyes glistened as she spoke. "Gradually the affair became more inti-mate. I'd talk to Adam about things."

"Did you talk to him about Father Barboza?" I asked. "Did you tell him that your husband thought you were having an affair with Father Barboza?"

"I did."

"Did you talk to him about Bill Jr. accusing Father Barboza?"

"I did."

"Adam Jenner learned all he could about your personal life."

"And I foolishly told him. He was using me for information, not sex. When I finally put it together, I felt like an ass." She sniffled. "What I'm saying today came to me in hindsight. I wasn't aware of it when it was happening." She laughed. "I thought Adam just wanted to get laid."

"I understand."

"I finally realized it wasn't by chance that Adam and I bumped into each other. Adam set it up. He stalked me. All the chance meetings weren't by chance at all."

"He's cunning."

"I asked myself, why? Why would Adam care about my family? I never came up with an answer. But an idea came to me, and the idea won't go away. It makes no sense, and I'm probably not making any sense to you."

"Tell me, Ellen."

"Okay, I will." She sat again. "My husband didn't kill Father Barboza. Detective Adam Jenner killed him."

"Yup, it makes sense." The idea of Jenner killing Father Barboza didn't stun me when she said it. "Why are you telling me?"

"I don't want my son thinking that his father was a murderer if he wasn't. If Bill *was* guilty of killing Father Barboza, then fine, we'll live with it. We're already living with it. But if Bill didn't kill him, I want Bill Jr. to know that his father was not a murderer."

"Why not go to the police?"

"Are you kidding? If Adam Jenner *did* kill Netto Barboza, he'll kill me next. And then Billy would have no one."

Everything Ellen O'Dell said made sense. I was afraid to ask the next question, because I was pretty sure I knew the answer, but, of course, I asked it anyway.

"What do you want from me, Ellen?"

"I want you to find the truth," she said. "I want you to find out whether my husband is innocent or guilty of killing Father Netto Barboza."

"You're putting me in the middle."

"You put me in the middle when you opened this thing in the first place." She walked to the door. "Are you going to do the right thing or not?"

I found DA Francis Ennis standing in the lobby of the Suffolk County Courthouse between sessions. The place was a hubbub of activity. Criminals and lawyers huddled in discussions. Cops and court personnel stepped in and out of trial rooms.

"Francis," I said.

"Welcome to Philistine City, Sparhawk, home to every criminal imbecile in Suffolk County. What's up?"

"I have a hypothetical for you."

"Oh, boy."

"What if I told you *hypothetically* that Adam Jenner is a dirty cop? What if I told you that Jenner killed Father Barboza and framed Bill O'Dell for the fall?"

"Hypothetically, do you have any evidence?"

"Not really."

"Hypothetically speaking, even if you had evidence, I'm on the outs with Boston Homicide because of CPAC. You know how it works with the blue wall of silence. Cops never investigate other cops, not vigorously anyway. And even if they did, there is no way I'm going there. I'm afraid you're on your own, Sparhawk."

"I was afraid you'd say that."

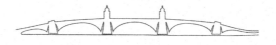

CHAPTER 57

I called Boston Police criminalist Kiera McKenzie to talk to her about the murder of Father Netto Barboza, and I must have called her cell phone.

"It's Sunday, Dermot."

"I forgot it was Sunday." I'd lost track of the days. "I'll call you back tomorrow if that's okay."

"The Barboza case is closed."

"I don't think it should be closed. A cop manipulated the evidence."

"We established that already. The cop was Bill O'Dell. Let it go, Dermot."

"I think I can prove that Bill O'Dell didn't kill Father Barboza."

"How?"

"By exposing the real killer," I said. "If you don't want to get involved, I'll understand. We're talking about taking down a cop, and you work with the cops."

Silence lingered on the line.

"Okay," Kiera said. "Tell me your theory."

"Here's what I think happened, and here's what I'd like you to do."

I laid it out for her.

"You're asking me to put my career on the line."

"I know I am," I said.

"Let me think about it." She hung up.

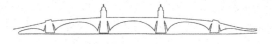

CHAPTER 58

Two days later I received a phone call from Superintendent Dennis Hanson of the Boston Police Department, a man I had never met. Hanson told me to come to his office immediately, to discuss an urgent matter. It sounded like an order, but I said yes anyway. He told me he was at police headquarters, One Schroeder Place in Roxbury. I told him I knew where it was.

"I'll get there as soon as I can, but it might take a while. I don't have a car today."

"No need for a car, Sparhawk. There's a police cruiser in front of your house. Officer Partridge will drive you here."

"That's what I call super service."

Standing on the sidewalk with his hands clasped behind his back was Officer Partridge, a tall, white man with dark blond hair. Without a word, he reached out his long arm and opened the rear door of the cruiser to let me in. He hopped into the driver's seat and drove south on the expressway to Melnea Cass Boulevard. Three minutes later he pulled into police headquarters, jumped out, and opened my door. I fought an urge to tip him. Partridge then escorted me to Superintendent Dennis Hanson's office.

I waited in the hallway, but not for long. Hanson's door opened.

He was a fit man with steely hair and resolute eyes. His cool demeanor said "Don't even think about bullshitting me." He was decked out in a dark-blue uniform, pressed to a crease. The dimple in his Windsor knot complemented the cleft in his solid chin. His face flushed with the healthy pinkness of a baby. He probably shaved hourly to keep it that way. Hanson was a picture of police perfection.

"Come in," he said.

Hanson stood at attention behind his large spartan desk and waited. I wondered if he was waiting for me to salute. Getting antsy, I broke the silence.

"Nice office."

He continued to say nothing. On the wall behind his desk hung a diploma from the College of the Holy Cross, summa cum laude, which topped my summa cum sump pump from BC. Hanging next to it was another sheepskin from Suffolk Law School.

"I called you here for a meeting, Sparhawk," Hanson finally said. "The meeting will commence in the crime lab in precisely twelve minutes."

"I left my stopwatch at home."

"You're a hoot, you know that?" He remained at attention. "I called you here early so I could size you up. This meeting will be tough."

"And you want to make sure I'm up to the task."

"Precisely."

"Am I passing muster?"

"I don't like comedians. In fact, I despise them. I've got no time for clowns, Sparhawk." He checked his brass and copper. "I only deal with serious people, so save the wisecracks for your drinking buddies in the barroom."

"Maybe I ought to leave."

"You can't leave. You are far too important to these proceedings to leave."

Proceedings?

"Let's cut the bullshit, Superintendent. Tell me why I'm here, and if *I* deem the reason important enough, I'll stick around. Otherwise, I'm gone."

"Okay, Sparhawk." A quick smile appeared on Hanson's face and disappeared just as quickly. "Let's go to the meeting. You'll find out the reason."

"Fine, let's go."

"Just so you know, I'm in charge of both Homicide and Physical Evidence."

"Congratulations."

"You just don't get it." Hanson pressed a button on his desk phone. Officer Partridge came in. "Please take Mr. Sparhawk to the crime lab. I'll be there shortly."

Officer Partridge took me to the crime lab, where Captain Pruitt and Detective Adam Jenner were waiting. My good graces with Pruitt had apparently worn off.

"What the hell's going on here, Sparhawk?"

"I'm not sure."

A minute later criminalist Kiera McKenzie came in with a folder and an evidence bag. Her strawberry-blonde hair looked extra wavy today. Affixed to the evidence bag was a red seal with a case number on it. The seal was broken. Superintendent Hanson entered the lab with two plainclothesmen. Hanson spoke first.

"You have the floor, Mr. Sparhawk." He waited a second and said. "Criminalist McKenzie briefed me on your theory regarding the murder of Father Netto Barboza. That's why we called you in today. We want to hear what you think about the Barboza murder."

Hanson caught me flatfooted. My mind raced for a place to begin.

"I'll start by giving my conclusion first, and then I'll show how I arrived at the conclusion." I looked at Kiera McKenzie, who stared past me. *Had they gotten to her?* I pointed at Jenner. "Detective Adam Jenner murdered Father Netto Barboza."

The two plainclothesmen looked at me for the first time. Captain Pruitt's eyes blinked, not an easy reaction to elicit from him.

"What is this?" Jenner said.

"What are you talking about, Sparhawk?" Pruitt seconded.

"Captain Pruitt, Detective Jenner, you'll have your chance to speak." Superintendent Hanson opened his palm toward me. "Continue, Mr. Sparhawk."

"It is important to keep in mind the timetable of events, especially the handling of evidence, the chain of custody if you will." I stepped to the middle so everyone could see me. "The sticking point for me was the red hoods. The copycat killer had to have access to a red Resnick hood, a unique brand that only the killer and the police knew about, a brand that only the killer and the police had access to."

Detective Jenner spoke. "Bill O'Dell had access to the red hoods. He knew about the brand, too. And O'Dell had motive. Father Barboza molested his kid."

"Bill O'Dell did *not* have access to a red Resnick hood. And Father Barboza never touched Bill O'Dell's kid," I said. "Father Barboza was framed for the pedophilia by Bill O'Dell himself."

Detective Jenner shook his head in a dismissive manner. "And O'Dell killed Father Barboza after he set him up? And then O'Dell went to your house to kill you, to shut you up? Think, Dermot! O'Dell shot up your place."

"You're half right, Adam. Bill O'Dell came to my house to shut me up. But he came to my house because I boxed him into a corner. He didn't know what else to do. He was off his rocker."

Detective Adam Jenner nodded as if I was finally making sense. "Fine, he was off his rocker. He was probably off his rocker when he killed Father Barboza, too."

"But why would he kill Father Barboza?" I asked. "Bill O'Dell knew Father Barboza didn't molest his son. He knew this because he coerced his son into falsely accusing Father Barboza in the first place. So why kill Barboza?"

"I'll tell you why," Jenner said. "Father Barboza was sleeping with O'Dell's wife."

"No he wasn't, but I'll circle back to that later." I reorganized my thoughts. "If we set aside Bill O'Dell's family problems, it still comes down to the red hoods. Whoever killed Father Barboza had to have access to a red Resnick hood. And to get ahold of a Resnick hood, Detective Adam Jenner manipulated the evidence."

Captain Pruitt barked, "Manipulated what evidence?"

I looked to Kiera McKenzie for help.

"I found two DNA sources on Father Barboza's hood," Kiera said. "I'm referring to the hood filed into evidence. One source belonged to Father Barboza. The other belonged to Father Axholm, the first victim in the serial murders."

Captain Pruitt asked, "The evidence was contaminated?"

"The evidence wasn't contaminated," I said. "The evidence was manipulated. At the time of Father Axholm's murder, there was only one hood in evidence. Detective Jenner took the Axholm hood after Forensics processed it, and he used that hood when he killed Father Barboza. He tied it around Father's head after he murdered him."

Captain Pruitt probed further, "Why didn't the two DNAs show up sooner? Why are we finding out about it now?"

Kiera answered, "The data-entry people fell behind, because we had a backlog of evidence. The evidence from Father Axholm's case hadn't been entered into CODIS by the time Father Barboza was killed. We knew there was a second DNA source on Father Barboza's hood, but the source didn't match anything in CODIS. It didn't match because Father Axholm's DNA hadn't been entered yet."

Captain Pruitt said, "Maybe it was O'Dell, not Jenner, who stole the hood from Axholm's evidence box."

Pruitt's loyalty was laudable if misplaced.

"Bill O'Dell could not have stolen it," I said. "A police officer out on medical leave cannot access evidence in an ongoing investigation."

"That is correct," said Hanson.

"Bill O'Dell went out on medical while Forensics was still analyzing Father Axholm's hood. When Forensics finished with the hood, the crime lab *then* filed it away, but it was still being processed when O'Dell went out on leave. In courtroom lingo, O'Dell had no opportunity to steal the hood."

"Wait a second." Detective Jenner countered. "Anybody with a crime-lab card could have stolen the red hood, anybody on any shift."

Captain Pruitt weighed in. "The serial killer himself could have splashed Father Axholm's blood on a second hood when he killed him." Everyone in the lab looked at each other. It was an excellent argument. "It's possible that neither Jenner nor O'Dell killed Father Barboza. Paul Herz could've spattered Axholm's blood on another hood."

Superintendent Hanson nodded. "Excellent point, Captain. Keep going, Mr. Sparhawk."

"Detective Jenner finally discovered his mistake." I paced a few steps. "Because Bill O'Dell was out on medical leave, he didn't have access to the evidence room. When Jenner realized this, he must have panicked. But then he got lucky."

Superintendent Hanson asked, "Got lucky how?"

"He got lucky when Father Del Rio was murdered at the monument," I said. "And it was all hands on deck to find the serial killer. Father Barboza blended in with the other murder victims." I wanted to get this next point right. "Here was the risky part for Detective Jenner. Initially, he *wanted* Forensics to closely examine Father Barboza's hood. He *wanted* Forensics to find two DNAs on the hood."

"This is absurd," said Jenner. "Why would I want that?"

"Because the discovery of Father Axholm's DNA on Father Barboza's hood would point to Bill O'Dell for the murder, that's why."

"That's why?" Superintendent Hanson looked skeptical. "I'm not persuaded, Mr. Sparhawk."

"Think about it," I said. "Because of Ellen O'Dell's sham affair with Father Barboza, and because of the sham pedophilia charges against Father Barboza, everyone would assume that Bill O'Dell killed him. Everything pointed to O'Dell. And then Jenner got lucky again when O'Dell got killed in my house." I turned to Hanson. "By the way, Superintendent, Ellen O'Dell told me that she had an affair, but it wasn't with Father Barboza. It was with Detective Adam Jenner. She will testify to this fact."

Captain Pruitt stepped away from Jenner. Superintendent Hanson maintained his unreadable face.

I continued, "Let's go back to the restrictions placed on Bill O'Dell when he was out on stress leave," I said. "With the help of Kiera McKenzie, we established that the hood on Father Barboza's head was first on Father Axholm's head, and that the hood was removed from Axholm's evidence box after the evidence was processed."

Detective Jenner said, "This is total bullshit. There's a red hood in Father Axholm's evidence box."

"There is a red hood in Father Axholm's evidence box," I said. "And it *is* a Resnick hood, but it is not the hood that was on Father Axholm's head when he was murdered." I paused. "Last week I gave three red hoods to Detective Jenner. When I hunted down Paul Herz in Maine, I found three hoods in his bag. I turned them over to Jenner."

"Not true." Detective Jenner put his hands on his hips. "You only gave me two hoods, Dermot. I filed them into evidence. You can check the paperwork."

"I gave you three hoods. Two you filed into evidence, the other you put in Father Axholm's case box, and I can prove it."

"Hey, guys." Detective Jenner looked for help, turning to Hanson. "Are you going to listen to this joker over one of your own, Superintendent?"

Superintendent Hanson said, "Continue, Mister Sparhawk."

"The DNA proves that Adam is the killer. Criminalist McKenzie analyzed the hood in Father Axholm's box for DNA."

"Come on." Detective Jenner fought on. "What DNA? Maybe I touched the hood after it was processed. That can happen. And it doesn't prove a thing."

"She didn't test for your DNA, Adam. She tested for mine."

"I tested for Mister Sparhawk's DNA," Kiera said, and then she delivered the knockout punch. "I reanalyzed the hood in Father

Axholm's evidence box. Nothing we found matched the evidence from the first test, and we immediately concluded it was a different hood. Then we tested the hood for Dermot's DNA."

Superintendent Hanson asked, "And what did you find, Ms. McKenzie?"

"We found Dermot Sparhawk's DNA on the hood."

"My DNA convicts you, Adam," I said. "It proves it was one of the hoods I handed you."

Superintendent Dennis Hanson looked at the two plainclothesmen and said to Adam Jenner, "Internal Affairs wants to have a talk with you, Detective."

They took Jenner's badge and gun and escorted him out of the lab.

Hanson turned to Kiera. "Ms. McKenzie, call my administrator and schedule a meeting with me. I believe you have a bright future with the BPD."

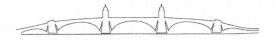

CHAPTER 59

I sat on a folding chair at an AA meeting in Somerville. The coffee urn percolated in the kitchen, men and women rushed in from the cold, the group secretary sorted through the announcements. I thought about the serial killings, and the toll they took, and the truths they exposed.

Dead Bill O'Dell was cleared of the murder of Father Netto Barboza. When I told his wife, Ellen, that he had been exonerated, she said it was small consolation, but at least her son wouldn't grow up thinking his father was a murderer. I told her that Detective Adam Jenner had been officially charged with the murder. She said nothing in reply.

I met with Blackie Barboza and told him what happened to his brother. When I finished, Blackie nodded once and wrote *Thank you* on an index card and handed it to me. That's as good as it gets in the projects. I keep the card in my top drawer.

I sent a letter to Mister Gomes in Fall River, telling him that Detective Bill O'Dell was the man that hired his son Lopo to threaten me off the Barboza case. I said that O'Dell had been killed inside my house, depriving Gomes of his revenge. I told him how badly I felt about the whole thing with Lopo. In an effort to win Vasco some points, I informed Mister Gomes that Vasco had provided information that proved vital in finding the truth about his son's death, an exaggeration perhaps, but not much of one.

Victor Cepeda said he'd had enough of the cold Boston winters and moved south. He left his apartment in the projects for the beaches of Puerto Rico. He also left his car. Before Victor vamoosed to the Caribbean, he handed me the keys to the Plymouth

Acclaim. Whether it was a parting shot or a parting gift, I'm still not sure. I decided to accept it as a gift. The gas tank was full and the inspection sticker was valid.

Astrid Bordeaux sold her house in Billerica and moved away, leaving no forwarding address, vanishing with no overtures. Losing Astrid was by far my biggest regret. The relationship was finished, and I had no choice but to accept it. If I ever saw her again, it wouldn't matter because whatever we had once would be gone. An odd sensation came over me when I pondered the defeat. I knew what William S. Burroughs must have felt like after he blew his wife's head off in their William Tell reenactment.

And then I thought about Paul Herz. The police, working with the staff at Saint John's Seminary, identified two more priests and one more seminarian that had been murdered over the decades. Each victim was found with a red Resnick hood on his head. But the victims lived in three different New England states, and the red hoods in evidence remained isolated within those states. The police also analyzed the time gaps between the killings and found that they corresponded to Paul Herz's hospital stays.

The AA meeting started with a moment of silence. Mickey Pappas hurried in and sat next to me. We listened to the preamble, which stated that the only requirement for AA membership is a desire to stop drinking. The qualifying speaker gave his talk, emphasizing the importance of gratitude. When he finished, we went around the room and identified ourselves.

When it came to me, I said, "I'm Dermot. I'm an alcoholic."